The First Ghost

Marguerite Butler

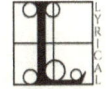

LYRICAL PRESS
Kensington Publishing Corp.
www.kensingtonbooks.com

Lyrical Press books are published by
Kensington Publishing Corp. 119 West 40th Street New York, NY 10018

All Kensington titles, imprints, and distributed lines are available at special quantity discounts for bulk purchases for sales promotion, premiums, fund-raising, and educational or institutional use.

Special book excerpts or customized printings can also be created to fit specific needs. For details, write or phone the office of the Kensington Special Sales Manager:
Kensington Publishing Corp.
119 West 40th Street
New York, NY 10018
Attn. Special Sales Department. Phone: 1-800-221-2647.

Kensington and the K logo Reg. U.S. Pat. & TM Off.
Lyrical Press and the L logo are trademarks of Kensington Publishing Corp.

First Electronic Edition: February 2011
eISBN-13: 978-1-61650-232-4
eISBN-10: 1-61650-232-0

First Print Edition: February 2011
ISBN-13: 978-1-61650-858-6
ISBN-10: 1-61650-858-2

Printed in the United States of America

This book is dedicated to my writing group, the Fangsters. Thanks for the endless encouragement, advice and cups of virtual coffee. No one could ask for a better group of friends.

Acknowledgements

I couldn't have done this without my writing group, the Fangsters: Grace, Andy, Alan, Celina, Kim, Sophie, Steve, Beth, Lori and Marla. Special thanks go to Celina, Alice and Grace for beta reading endless versions of this manuscript. Thanks to my editor, Christy Phillippe, for catching my foolish errors and making me look better than I am.

The dead have no respect for anyone trying to have a life.

Portia Mahaffey always liked that she was the only woman in her family without a psychic 'gift'. But a concussion awakens her latent ability to see ghosts. And one of those ghosts is prepared to haunt her until Portia agrees to convince the police her death was no accident.

With no choice but to help Corinne, Portia reluctantly uses her new gift and some good old-fashioned detection to track down the truth.

Seeing the dead is just the beginning. Portia's world becomes filled with hungry demons, mercenary shadow beings, vengeful poltergeists…and one very alive murderer willing rank her among the dead.

Who knew hanging with the dead could be so hazardous to the living?

Books by Marguerite Butler

The First Ghost

Published by Kensington Publishing Corporation

Chapter 1

Almost there. I could see my train and rummaged in my pocket for my pass, confident I would make it--until the whistle sounded. "No!" Hot coffee sloshed out of my commuter mug, soaking my glove. I said a few naughty words, hoisted my tote bag and ran for the train. If I missed this one, I would be at least fifteen minutes late, and like they say, failure was not an option. My boss had zero sense of humor about tardiness and I was not crawling back to the family business.

This was about more than pride. We're not talking about plumbing or insurance or even running a store. My family owns and operates Mahaffey-Ringold Funeral Home, proudly tending to your corpses since 1942. But not me. No way, no how. I was the family freak and I liked it that way.

All the Mahaffey women were clairvoyant. My mother saw spirits. My cousin Eleanor relived the last moments of death from personal objects. Her sister communed with the dead in Europe. My aunt saw visions of the past and occasionally even the future. I was the only woman without some sort of "gift." No dead people or spooky visions for me. Nope. Just a nice apartment and a decent day job, which I was about to lose if I didn't get on that train.

I focused on finding my rail pass without dropping my coffee or tote bag and trying to run in heels. I didn't pay attention to where I was going.

Wham! Headfirst.

I laid there on the ground for a moment, stunned. "Ow." I sat up and rubbed my temple.

"You okay?" somebody called.

I waved them off. "Fine. Only thing hurt is my pride." Which wasn't strictly true. Both my knees and my head hurt. I'd wiped out hard. My pants weren't torn, but the fabric on the knees was damaged. I located my steel mug, which had leaked most of its precious coffee into a brown pool on the concrete.

Staggering to my feet, I stepped right into a slushy puddle. My heel caught in a crack in the pavement. Now both my gloved hand and my foot were freezing. I swore a little more and tugged at my foot, trying to free my stiletto from the crevice.

The train whistle sounded again. I looked up in panic. The last whistle meant I had two minutes to board that train. At the moment that seemed vitally important.

Then everything in my life changed.

The air became electric, super-charged the way it does just before a storm hits, even though there were no hurricanes bearing down on Dallas. The hair on my arms stood on end, and not from the cold. A current hummed through me. My vision sharpened. Things looked different, like the world had suddenly snapped into focus. It was as if I'd put on a pair of new glasses.

A tiny, older gentleman with a head of wild, white hair like Einstein stood on the tracks in front of the train. He worried and twisted a hat as he stared up at the yellow engine.

How the heck had he gotten down there? Did he jump the railing? Was he confused? Other tardy commuters ran for the train in a mad scramble, ignoring the man on the tracks.

I tugged again on my shoe.

"Hey! Get off the track!" I yelled at him. "That train's about to move!" It was about to move without me on it.

The man ignored me. The whistle blasted a third time and the train rolled forward. I dropped my tote and my mug, which rolled down into a gutter. "Hey!" I waved my arms in desperation. "Get off the track! Hey! You! Old guy!" The little man turned to look at me, but he didn't move, just kept twisting that hat. What the hell was wrong with him? "Move!" I screamed.

The train picked up speed. "Somebody! Stop! Stop!" People looked now, but not at the man on the tracks. They edged away, giving me sideways looks. "Can't you see him? He's going to get run over! He's--"

I turned away with a sharp cry, unwilling to look. I don't know what I expected, but I expected *something* to happen. I thought there would be screaming and horror as people realized what had just happened. I thought the brakes would screech. I even thought I might hear the train hit him, but instead it slowly rumbled out of the station.

I stepped out of the stiletto still trapped in the puddled crevice and scanned the tracks for carnage.

Nothing.

Unless of course you considered the people staring at me. I locked eyes with a man, but he averted his and moved away.

"Pardon me, miss. Have you seen my mother?" I turned to the voice that came from right next to my ear. The same little man from the tracks, apparently unharmed, stood at my elbow.

I reached out to grab his coat and swiped my hand right through him. "What the--" I took a startled step back with the foot still wearing a stiletto, overbalanced and fell. My head made contact with the concrete for a second time that morning and everything went black.

* * * *

I hurt all over, especially my head.

I didn't want to open my eyes, but I had to look around. Bright. I blinked to clear the fuzziness. All I saw was industrial white and green. Curtains. Machines. Beds. Someone lay in the next bed, but her face was turned the other way.

The woman sitting on the edge of my roommate's bed had to be at least a hundred years old. She had wrinkles on her wrinkles and a huge mound of teased and sprayed hair colored an improbable shade of blue. She wore the official senior uniform of a hot pink velour tracksuit and a bored expression. She looked around like she was waiting for something.

"Where am I?" I knew I was in a hospital. What I meant was: *What hospital am I in and how did I get here?* But I could only manage a few words.

The woman looked right at me, but she didn't answer.

How rude.

I tried again. "What hospital is this?"

She looked more intently at me. "Can you see me?"

"Of course," I replied.

She patted her fluffy hair helmet. "Well, la-de-da. I thought I was in invisible mode. Must have been the blow to your head."

Which explained my headache, but not the harpy. She looked down at the lump of bedclothes. "Wait here," she said to the motionless figure. "I'll be back."

I blinked because she suddenly stood right next to me and I hadn't seen her move.

"Ow!" I cried out. "You pinched me."

"You really can see me. And feel me, too."

"Who are you?"

"Not yet, doll. First you tell me your name."

My head hurt too much to argue. "Portia. Portia Mahaffey."

"Ohhh." Her voice trailed off into a coughing fit. "That explains it. You're one of *those* Mahaffeys, aren't you? You must be Imogene's daughter."

"Do I know you?"

She laughed again. "No, doll, but I know your mother real well. We talk all the time." She patted my arm. "Your mother said you didn't have the gift, but it looks like she was wrong."

I stared at her. Mother never talked about the family gifts. Ever. "How do you know about that?"

"I know lots of stuff, honey. I'm Death. But you can call me Hephzibah. Pleased to meet you."

I closed my eyes, hoping she would be gone when I opened them.

This was a bad dream. I'd suffered a blow to the head. I was obviously hallucinating. With my eyes closed, the throbbing in my head worsened. I opened them gingerly.

"Boo."

Hephzibah was real.

"We're gonna be good friends," she said. "I can tell. I should have known you were Imogene's kid. You look like her. Red hair and all them freckles. Don't you ever get any sun? That skin could use a little color to it. So when did you first start seeing spirits?"

"Is that what you are? A spirit?"

"More or less. I'm Death. Sort of an escort for the dead, a guide if you will, to the other side. I cross people over. So when did your gift finally arrive?"

I squinted at the clock hanging on the opposite wall. "Ten minutes ago? Maybe fifteen? I think. I'm not really sure." My hands shook and I fought the urge to bury my head under the covers. I was too old. The Mahaffey gift always arrived with the first agonies of puberty. This couldn't be happening.

Hephzibah whistled. "Brand spanking new, huh? Better get ready. Hospitals are chock-full of spirits."

"So far you're all I've seen. Maybe I won't really see ghosts."

"You will."

"Maybe not."

"If you see me, you'll see ghosts. Trust me on this one, doll. So are you single? Married?"

"Single. Why are you here?"

"Oh, I'm just waiting. Business call, so to speak." She tilted her head in the direction of the neighboring bed. "I got here a little early. Sometimes it's hard to pinpoint the time."

"He's dying?"

"She. Any minute now."

It was a sobering thought. "That's so sad."

"Yeah, it's a real kick in the pants."

"How did she...I mean will she...I mean...what..."

"Her? Murder. Sad, really. She's pretty young. Younger than you even."

"Isn't her family here? Shouldn't they be with her?"

"She ain't got any family, unless you count an aunt in Omaha."

"What about friends? She shouldn't die alone."

Hephzibah shook her head. "Just you and me, kid. She ain't got nobody else."

The machine that had been softly beeping next to the woman's bed screeched. My headache flared like someone had stabbed me behind the eyes with an ice pick.

"There we go," Hephzibah said. "About damn time." She popped a stick of gum in her mouth.

The room exploded into activity as nurses and doctors swarmed the room, trying to revive my roommate. I could have told them the outcome.

Someone closed the curtain separating our beds. Hephzibah continued staring, like she could see through it.

Of course my mother picked this moment to walk into the room. When she spied Hephzibah standing by my bed, she dropped the cheerful vase of flowers, which landed with a crash.

"No! No! My baby," she wailed and collapsed in a crumpled heap.

"I'm okay, Mother."

"Imogene? Portia's okay, honey." My stepfather, Walter, helped Mother struggle to her feet. "See? It's just a bump on the head."

"Hiya, Imogene. Sorry to scare you like that," Hephzibah said with a grin. "I'm not here for your girl. We was just having a nice chat. Oops, gotta go. It's been real." And just like that she walked through the curtain and out of sight.

Mother gave me a shrewd look and ordered Walter down to the gift shop to buy more flowers, drowning out his protests. "Because, darling, Portia needs flowers to brighten up the room. Don't you, Portia? See? Off you go."

Mother is so fanatical about keeping the family's psychic gifts private that she's never revealed it to Walter, not in twenty-three years of marriage. Even my brother doesn't know about the women in the family. It's *that* kind of secret.

One of the nurses trying in vain to save my neighbor attempted to steer Mother out of the room, but she was seeing her daughter and no one was stopping her. The frantic beeping turned into a long wail and finally silence.

"Time of death, ten fifteen," someone said. I could hear the snaps of gloves being pulled off and the shuffle of paper boots. I wanted to console them and tell them it was inevitable, that it was her time, but I couldn't find the words. Besides, I had my mother to deal with.

Mother held up an overnight case. "I brought you pajamas and a change of clothes, your toiletries and…"

"I doubt I'll be here much longer." Oh, how I hoped that was true. This was happening too quickly. I had just had a conversation with Death.

"But I want you to have your things. I can cancel my appointments tomorrow."

"I'll be fine, Mother. You don't need to stay. Honest."

She put her hand on her hip and studied me a moment. "So how long has this been going on?"

"You mean Hephzibah? About fifteen, maybe twenty minutes? Since I woke up here." That was it! Maybe it was just the *here*. Maybe it was just the hospital. Maybe all I had to do was stay out of hospitals. I could do that.

"Then you *were* talking to her. Oh, honey, I'm so proud. It finally came."

"Ease up, Mother. I'm not a little girl getting her first period. I don't know that I've actually gotten *anything*. I saw Hephzibah. I haven't seen any dead people or anything else spooky or weird. Please don't make a big deal of it." At the moment I said it, I meant it, but then I remembered the little man on the tracks. I closed my eyes. "Oh, crap," I whispered, fighting my rising panic.

"Don't make a big deal? Portia, this is big news. I have to call your Aunt Bella and cousin Eleanor and--"

"No."

"What do you mean, no? It's a big deal in this family when someone's gift arrives. I had honestly given up on you, but--"

"I'm not sure it's forever. I've probably got a concussion. I'm hoping Hephzibah disappears with the rest of...the symptoms."

"Do you think so?" Her eyes were worried. "I hadn't thought of that."

"I don't feel quite right. I think for now you shouldn't tell anyone. Until we know it's permanent and all."

She wrung her hands. "If you think so, dear."

"I do. Oh, look. Here's Walter."

He stood smiling in the doorway, holding a huge pink bouquet with a vase shaped like a pink cloud that read "*It's a Girl*."

"Do you like them?" he asked. "It's the best I could do."

* * * *

Waking up in a hospital room is disorienting enough on its own, but try doing it with a sad-faced stranger staring at you from close range.

She looked like someone who had lost her puppy. "Can you see me? You look like you can see me," she said. She had long, honey-blond hair and a chubby but pretty face.

I knew where this was going. "I can see you." I sighed. "Are you a ghost?"

"I'm Corinne," she said as though this explained why she was sad and sitting on my hospital bed. Yes, she had to be a ghost.

"What can I do for you, Corinne?"

"I think I died here today," she said uncertainly.

"Oh." That explained a lot. My dead roommate. "Shouldn't you be gone? I'm mean didn't she...you know...take you wherever...you go?" I finished lamely, not sure how to frame the question. I'm not in the habit of talking to dead people. "Didn't Death come by to pick you up?"

"She wouldn't go." I jumped at Hephzibah's voice so near my elbow.

"Don't do that."

"Sorry, doll."

"I have questions," Corinne said. "I'm not ready to die yet."

"I hear that all the time. No one is ever ready. Trust me," Hephzibah said soothingly. "Come with me and everything will be clear as day."

"I want my answers first. Where am I going? Did someone tell my Aunt Susie? Who did this to me? Why? What's going to happen to Billy?"

"Slow down. Slow down. I told you. Just come with me and we'll get you some answers. As for the worldly things, it's best to forget them. They don't matter to you anymore."

Corinne crossed her arms. "I'm staying here."

Hephzibah gave me a look. "A little help here?"

"Me? Don't look at me," I said. "I am not my mother. I don't meddle in the affairs of the dead. Unh-unh. No way, Jose. Not gonna happen." I desperately wished to be anywhere else. Anywhere. Even the dentist's office.

I'm not a curmudgeon, I swear. But I've seen what the dead can do to the living, how much they can demand. It's a slippery slope, and I had no intention of setting a single foot on it. I liked my life and really, why should I spend it fixing things for people who are gone? Life is for the living. Dead people should cross over to whatever comes next and leave the living in peace.

"At least promise the girl you'll call Aunt Susie in Omaha."

Corinne's face brightened. "Would you? That would help a lot."

"Of course she will. Won't you, Portia? Her name is Portia," Hephzibah whispered to Corinne. "She sees dead people."

"But only for a little while. I'll be myself soon. Then all this talking-to-the-dead stuff is over. I'll call the aunt. But that's it." The way I figured it, calling the girl's aunt was helping the living. I could do that. It seemed reasonable.

"What about Billy? Who'll take care of my Billy?" Corinne's voice rose. Hephzibah shot me another *help me* look.

"Who's Billy?" I prayed she didn't have a child she wanted me to adopt and raise. It would be hard to turn down a dead mother.

"Billy is my dog. My roommate hates him." She sniffled. Her blue eyes were sad, but dry. "Please take care of my Billy."

"A dog? No way. I'll call your aunt, even though I'm sure the people at the hospital have already done it, but if it makes you feel better, then fine. A phone call? Yes. A dog? No."

"It's a little dog," Hephzibah said. "I've seen it. A little bitty dog. Man's best friend."

"No. I'll get evicted. I can't have pets in my building." Honestly, what would I do with a dog?

"At least find the doggy a good home."

I glared at Hephzibah. "This is your gig. Not mine. Why are you dragging me into this?"

"I'm afraid Corinne is sort of fixated on you." Hephzibah shrugged. "It happens."

"I'm haunting you," Corinne said cheerfully.

"Sometimes they're a little reluctant to let go of this life. You can help them along their way. It's your destiny, Portia."

"You're a Mahaffey," Corinne said. "Death told me."

"Hephzibah, doll. Call me Hephzibah. Yeah, I told her a little. I figure it'll smooth things along."

"I promised the phone call, but that is it. I don't do dogs. Sorry." I hardened my heart. See, that's what happens. You promise one thing and suddenly they need more. It's never enough with the dead. And if I helped one ghost, more were sure to follow with their requests.

Corinne started weeping dry tears again. "You're not at all like Death said you would be. You're mean. I am so out of here."

"Good girl," Hephzibah said. "Let's go."

"Stay away from me." Corinne pointed an accusatory finger at her. "I'm not going anywhere with you until I'm good and ready."

And then she vanished. I blinked a time or two to make sure.

"Well, that's good," I said. "She's gone."

"She'll be back," Hephzibah said. "I told you. She's fixated on you. This is really important. She needs to come with me and separate herself from this world. She can't stay here. Do you want to have conversations with her ten years from now? That's what could happen if... Just help her out. Call the aunt. Find a home for the doggy."

I closed my eyes. "Fine. I'll try." If it would make it stop. "Only this one time. Don't send any more ghosts my way."

She patted my arm. "I knew you would help. You're a good girl, Portia. You're a Mahaffey."

Chapter 2

I kept my eyes closed and mentally whined. Why did I have to be born a Mahaffey? Why a bump on the head today of all days? Why did my first encounter with a ghost have to be with an overwrought dog lover? Why? I was hoping to slip off into sleep, but I heard soft sounds in my room.

When I opened my eyes to see a gorgeous man with dark hair, blue eyes and a killer smile standing at the foot of my bed, I had two thoughts. The first was: *I hope this isn't a dream.* The second, which unfortunately I said aloud, was: "Please tell me you aren't another ghost."

He smiled as if I had said something witty. "Sorry I disturbed you." He had a lovely voice, warm and baritone.

I smiled back at him. If he was a ghost, he was a nice change from Corinne. I wouldn't mind being haunted by those eyes.

"I'm Portia." It's hard to flirt when you're lying in a hospital bed.

"I know." He tapped the chart he was holding and something clicked in my addled brain. Oh. White coat. Reading chart. "Are you my doctor?"

"I was the attending physician when they brought you into the ER. I wanted to see how you were doing."

Drat. "I guess I'm going to be fine."

"I can see that." He smiled again and my heart did a little flip that had nothing to do with my health. His smile lit the sterile room. "Do you mind?" He moved closer with his penlight and peered into my eyes. "Don't blink."

I tried to not blink and to look beautiful at the same time. It isn't possible. I blinked like a nervous owl until he finally had to hold my eyelid open with a gentle finger. He had wonderful hands.

"Sorry about that," I said.

"Not at all. You're the perfect patient." He sat on the edge of my bed.

Oh, be still my heart. There was that smile again. "Do you visit all your patients?"

"Only the beautiful ones."

Holy crap. He *was* flirting. I did a little giddy dance inside, but for some reason I was tongue-tied. I searched frantically for something witty to say, but what popped out instead was, "Were you her doctor, too?"

He pulled back slightly with a puzzled look. "Her?"

"Her. That girl." I motioned toward Corinne's now empty bed. "The one who died."

"Oh, that girl. Yes, I was the attending when she was brought in, too. Very sad. She was so young."

"She didn't have any family or anyone except her aunt."

He sat up straighter. "Did you know her?"

"No, I...um..." I'm a dreadful liar. My mind searched for something plausible. "I overheard somebody talking."

"The nurses?" He frowned. "Hospital personnel shouldn't be gossiping like that."

I didn't mean to get anyone in trouble. "I don't think it was a nurse. I...I'm not sure who it was." I put a hand dramatically to my forehead and felt the bandage there. "I'm not quite myself today. Maybe I misunderstood. I hoped that her aunt knew. That's all."

"It's sweet to be so concerned about a stranger." The warm smile was back. He was either the most compassionate doctor I'd ever met or he was totally digging me. Somehow I wasn't sure whether to be creeped out or flattered.

"I sort of feel responsible for her." As I said it, I realized it was true and I knew I was going to help Corinne. Just this one time. Just this one ghost. "No one should die all alone. Did they get in touch with her aunt?"

"I don't know. I just did the ER intake. I can check."

"Would you? It would really set my mind at ease. I'm not sure how long I'm going to be here."

"I imagine they'll let you go home tomorrow afternoon. We only admitted you because you were unconscious for so long. That's not normal given the severity of your injury."

"I thought it was just a bump."

"It was. I meant the injury *wasn't* that severe. You shouldn't have been out of it for so long. But your eyes rolled up and you were muttering about a man on the train tracks and...well...it was a little spooky," he admitted, not looking at all stalker-ish. "When I heard you were okay, I wanted to see for myself."

"I know I fell, but I don't remember much after that."

"That part is normal for a head injury. At least you didn't damage anything permanently. You should probably stay at home for a couple of days to heal up. You...uh...do live around here, right?"

He was so cute and transparent. "I'm local," I said with a smile. "I wish I could stay at home, but my boss is a real Cruella de Vil. It's back to work for me. She would fire me for any old reason."

"Even with a doctor's note?"

I considered the offer. "Not then, but she'd make my life hell. It's better that I go in. How early will they let me out of here?"

"Not too early. You have to be cleared by the specialist first and you definitely aren't going to work tomorrow. Maybe the day after that. If you wanted to give me your number, I could call you." He made a note on the clipboard. "About the aunt," he added.

My smile grew. "You can call me for any old reason." I gave him my number.

* * * *

Dr. Wonderful was absolutely right about the timeliness of my release. I spent the better part of the next day being poked and prodded and annoyed by a rainbow of lab techs and nurses and doctors wearing colorful scrubs.

By two o'clock that afternoon I was pissed off and ready to check out of the hospital. I sat in my wheelchair like an invalid in the U-shaped drive-through waiting to be picked up like luggage, watching cars cycle through and wondering where the heck my brother was. Harry is rarely on time, but you'd think he could manage to pick up his only sister from the hospital after he had promised me faithfully that he would. I wrapped the hospital blanket tighter around me. Much more of this and I would have to go back inside. My toes already felt numb even though I'd put my boots and wooly socks back on.

"Are you sure someone's coming to pick you up?"

I recognized the morose voice without turning my head. "I wondered when you'd be back, Corinne."

"I was so depressed, I needed to find chocolate."

"You can eat?" That was interesting.

"No." Corinne sounded even sadder.

"All the more reason to cross over."

"No."

I sighed and glanced around to make sure no one was measuring me for a straitjacket. Thank God that in the wireless age people can seem to be talking to the thin air. No one was paying me any mind.

"I've been thinking, Corinne. I'll call your aunt for you and give her whatever message you want, even if the hospital already did. And I'll check on the dog. I'll make sure he's got a good home. How's that?"

"Really? You'll do that?"

"Miss?" An orderly gave me a puzzled look. I looked at him like he was daft and tapped my ear like I had an earpiece in it. He nodded and wandered off. I was going to have to buy a wireless set for real and wear it before I got carted off to the funny farm.

"Yes, I'll do it. But you have to promise to let Hephzibah take you across, okay? Deal?" She was silent for long enough to make me look over at her. "Hello? Earth to Corinne?"

"What are you doing?" Harry stood there holding open the door to a gray Honda Civic.

"I didn't recognize the car. Where's your Chevy?"

"It's a rental. The Nova's getting a new suspension and Mother has the van. Are you getting in?"

I scowled back. "Took you long enough to get here. I'm frigging cold."

"So get in the car."

A gentleman would have offered to help me, but this was no gentleman. This was my twin brother. I had to schlep my belongings into the car myself. "Thanks for the lift."

"Yeah, Mother said I had to. How's your head?"

"It hurts. How's Jennifer?"

"We broke up." He pulled forward slowly, trying to avoid the wheelchair orderlies, but as soon as he cleared the patient-zoned horseshoe he stomped the gas. The rental lingered for a moment and then leapt forward, mashing me back against the seat. I closed my eyes. Harry's driving is enough to scare anyone half to death and if I looked up and saw Hephzibah riding shotgun with us, I'd probably start screaming.

"Sorry about Jennifer."

"Why? You hated her."

I winced at the squealing of brakes. Honking and swearing told me we were merging onto the turnpike.

"She was silly and shallow," I said. "You can do better."

"She had big boobs."

"On second thought, maybe you two deserved one another."

He swore and the car swerved to the left. I braced myself against the dash, still refusing to open my eyes.

"I'm not exactly a hot commodity on the dating circuit, Portia."

"I was just kidding, Harry. You're a catch."

More swerving and swearing. "Yeah, right. I live at home."

"And whose fault is that? Move out, deadbeat. You've got a job."

"I work at a funeral home. Women think it's creepy."

I think it's creepy and I grew up with the business, but I wasn't in the mood for a Harry pity party. "Listen to you, Mr. Negative. You make your own luck."

The sudden squeal of tires and smell of smoke caused my eyes to fly open and I squeaked at the sight of how close we had come to actually loading ourselves into the open back of a broken-down eighteen-wheeler. Harry swore and jerked the wheel hard to the right without checking his mirrors. I gripped the door handle and closed my eyes again.

"In case you haven't noticed," Harry said, continuing as if he hadn't almost killed us both, "I bear a passing resemblance to Howdy Doody."

"In case you haven't noticed, we're almost identical."

"It's totally different for you. Red hair and freckles are cute on a woman. On guys, not so much. And women aren't tall and skinny. They're willowy. Guys think it's hot." I rolled my eyes. Harry was always dating some idiotic lingerie model or something and then lamenting how shallow she was.

"Six feet isn't willowy, bonehead. It's freakishly tall. What do you think that does to my dating options?"

"You could date shorter men."

"You could date ugly women."

That cracked us both up, and after he screeched across three lanes of traffic and shot down the off-ramp at double the legal speed, he turned left to Italiano Soda Fountain instead of right toward my apartment. Good thing, because I had a serious craving.

It was way too cold for the chocolate malted shakes, but Harry cranked up the car's heater. We were giggly and silly from the sugar rush when he dropped me off at my apartment.

Hephzibah hadn't made an appearance, but Corinne sulked in the backseat for a while and then vanished. I'm not sure exactly when. Since I spent a lot of the time with my eyes shut, I didn't see her go.

As I turned the key into my apartment and opened the door, *poof*, there Corinne was, looking royally pissed. So much for no ghosts outside of the hospital. Ignoring her, I threw my plastic bag of clothes down on my chair and carefully set down my *It's a Girl* bouquet.

I adore my little apartment. It's just an efficiency, but the design is modern and open. The living area blends right into the kitchen. Only the bathroom and bedroom are self-contained.

The lush, beige carpet is lovely because I like being barefoot. I have an elegant leather sofa and a fireplace with a stone hearth. Not that I've ever lit a fire in it, but I could if I wanted to.

Best of all, in the morning the sun comes in the kitchen window and the room glows with the warm light. Have I mentioned that I adore the place?

And there Corinne was, sitting on my lovely leather couch, glaring at me when I'd done nothing to the girl. It wasn't my fault she died. I had a bad day, too. Okay, hers was worse, but still. This was exactly why I wanted nothing to do with ghosts.

"I am so not in the mood right now," I said.

"Really? You were yucking it up a minute ago with your friend."

"Brother."

"Whatever. You haven't done anything that you promised."

"I just got out of the freaking hospital. Give me a break, okay?"

"At least go get Billy."

"I said I would help you. Don't push it. I will call your aunt in..."

"Omaha. Aunt Susie."

"Right. I'll call her. And I'll check on your dog, but it's going to have to wait. I need a shower." I touched the bandage on my head. Blood crusted my hairline.

"But she's going to be worried."

I sighed and sat on the couch. Corinne was wearing me down. Was it really only yesterday she had died? This psychic stuff was exactly as I had feared. You can't get away from a ghost. I counted to ten. Get rid of the ghost and get my life back. I could do this.

"I'm sure they've told her already," I said. "That's what hospitals do. She knows." I put my hand up to stop her protest. "I said I would call her and I will. But you have to give me a little time. This is all new to me."

"What about Billy? You don't know my roommate. Ruth hates dogs."

"Nothing is going to happen in two days. Nobody is that heartless. I'm sure she's got Aunt Susie on her way to pick up Billy or something like that. Maybe she's given him to one of your friends."

Corinne sniffled. "I don't have any friends."

Cripes, but the girl was pathetic. "Tomorrow," I said wearily. "First thing in the morning I'll go to your apartment and confront..."

"Ruth."

"Right. Ruth. But you have to let me sleep now. I feel like crap and I have to work tomorrow."

She sniffled some more, but finally agreed and vanished.

After removing the bandage, I took a long, hot shower. My head was tender and the dried blood required a second shampooing. It wasn't until after the shower that I peeked at myself in the mirror. How could Dr. Yum possibly flirt with me? I was way paler than normal, and the dark circles under my eyes were disgusting.

On my right temple was a huge knot. I peered closer. I didn't have stitches. They had used something called Dermabond to glue the gash shut. I was promised it would heal with minimal scarring, and I had to admit it was hard to see where the gash had been. The lump was about the size of a quarter and looked grossly squishy. But when I touched it--OW!--it was actually quite firm.

I wrapped myself in a blue chenille bathrobe that I liberated from a spa trip two years ago and padded into the kitchen to make a cup of cinnamon tea.

I removed the blue willow teacup from its hook and turned. The cup slipped from my fingers at the sight of four men seated around my kitchen table.

The men were vague, flickering images, playing cards. They ignored me. One of them leapt to his feet and went for the other one's throat. Two men tried to pull him off his victim, who flailed around wildly. The image jumped like an old TV picture and they were seated, peacefully playing cards.

The scene repeated again.

And again.

By the third repetition, my heart rate had returned to normal, but I no longer wanted tea. After satisfying myself that the cup didn't appear damaged, I padded back into my living room.

"It's just a residual." Hephzibah made herself comfortable on my couch.

"Please tell me this type of thing won't happen to me all the time."

"It's okay, doll," Hephzibah said. "It's just a residual of an event. They aren't really ghosts. In fact, most psychics can't even see them. Your gift must be pretty strong."

"Lucky me."

"Don't worry. They won't always be there. Residuals tend to come and go. Betcha they fade away soon."

"I appreciate the info," I said. "Don't take this the wrong way..."

"I know, it's late. But we need to talk, doll."

I was heartily sick of spooks and spirits, but how do you tell Death no? I dropped onto my sofa with a sigh and pulled my robe tighter. "So that residual. Does that mean someone died in my kitchen?"

"No, it's more like an impression from a strong event. It doesn't mean it happened exactly in that spot. Residuals can drift. It happened somewhere around here. Probably a long time ago. Eventually they fade away. We need to talk about Corinne. She's still refusing to cross over."

"Tomorrow. I'll work on it tomorrow. What is it with everyone? The girl is dead. Why such a rush?"

Hephzibah hesitated. "There are consequences for too much delay. Corinne needs to cross over soon. It ain't good for her to stay here. The dead and the living need to be kept separate."

That was something I agreed with wholeheartedly. "I promise. First thing tomorrow, I'll call the aunt and check on the dog. Then she can cross over."

"It's not going to be that simple."

"Why not? She said she would go if--"

"She says that now, but Corinne is an unsolved murder. If you can't get them to cross over immediately, they have a hard time letting go."

"So I'm wasting my time? Then why am I doing this? She can't stay here. I don't like being haunted."

"You're right there, doll. She can't follow you around forever. What I'm trying to say is that you're going to have to do a little more than make a phone call and check on a dog in order to get her to turn loose of this world."

I punched a pillow in frustration. "Like what?"

"Like finding out who killed her."

"What? You can't possibly be serious."

"Serious as a heart attack." She laughed at her own joke, which turned into a hacking coughing fit. "I need a cig."

I stared at her in disbelief. "Not in my apartment you don't."

Hephzibah sighed. "You young people never enjoy the good stuff anymore. I miss the sixties. Now that was a time."

"Back to today. Hephzibah, I'm a secretary, not a detective. I have no idea how to solve a murder. Even if I wanted to, which I don't."

"You don't have to really solve the thing. Maybe ask a few questions. Talk to the police for her. Just, you know, assure Corinne it's being taken seriously, that she hasn't been forgotten. I think I can get her to cross over then. That's a good girl."

"What makes you think I'll do it?"

"You're a Mahaffey."

Chapter 3

Why on earth had I set my alarm so early? I hit the snooze button and wiped my bleary eyes.

"Oh no, you don't," said Corinne. "You promised me. *First thing in the morning*, you said. Remember?"

I rolled over. She'd learned a new trick and now hovered directly over my bed. "Get out of my bedroom."

"No. Get up. We're going to my apartment to see what Ruth has done with Billy. Get up, lazy bones."

I groaned. I had promised to visit Corinne's apartment on the way in to work. I'd called my boss to see if I could get another day off, but her attitude was that if I was well enough to be released from the hospital, I needed to come in to work. She didn't outright threaten me, but she hinted darkly about the amount of work piling up on my desk.

Fortunately, Corinne's apartment was reasonably close to mine in Canterbury Park, just north of Dallas. It would mean a detour of several blocks in the freezing cold, but it would be worth it to rid myself of being screeched awake by a cranky ghost. The thought of living with Corinne for the next forty years brought me upright.

"I'm up. Now leave so I can shower and dress. I'm not doing it with you hanging around."

"Fine. I'll wait in the kitchen."

"Good. Play some cards while you're at it. And make a pot of coffee."

She started to sniffle. "You're just mean. I loved coffee." And with that she floated through my wall, presumably to sit, or hover, in my kitchen.

* * * *

True to my promise, an hour later I stood, bundled and freezing, on the landing to Corinne's former apartment. Having mastered the art of hovering, she no longer walked. At first I found it disconcerting, but it's extraordinary how quickly you can adjust to things. Like ghostly roommates. And Death popping in and out.

"I hope Billy isn't too sad. Do you think he'll be able to see me?"

I looked over at her. She had floated up to eye level with me. I'm not used to seeing other women outside my family eye-to-eye. "Why haven't you checked on him yet by yourself?"

"I can't. I don't seem to have free rein. I'm sort of tethered to you." She stuck her lower lip out.

I knocked on the door. "Don't pout at me. It wasn't my idea for you to stalk me."

"I'm not stalking you. I'm haunting you."

"Like there's a difference." I knocked again. "Maybe she's gone." I shivered and pulled my woolen hat tighter as a gust caught me.

"She's here. Her car is in the lot."

The door opened a fraction. The security chain was still latched.

"Ruth?" I said. "Ruth Yeshu?"

The door opened a little wider, but the chain remained intact. A pointy nose and beady eyes were visible through the crack. "Who are you?"

"My name is Portia Mahaffey. I was a friend of Corinne's."

"She's dead."

Duh. "Yes, I know. I'm here about the dog."

"What dog?" Ruth said.

"Corinne's dog. I'm supposed to check on Billy."

The door closed slightly as Ruth removed the chain and then it opened wider. "I don't know what you mean."

"That bitch," Corinne breathed. "If she's done something to Billy..."

"Cut the games, Ruth," I said loudly enough to drown out Corinne in my ear.

Corinne floated into the apartment hunting for her dog. "Billy? Come to Mommy." She made smoochy noises.

"I'm not here to take Billy," I said. "You can keep him if you want. I...I promised Corinne that if anything ever happened to her, I would make sure Billy was taken care of."

Ruth finally stepped back and let me inside. She pulled her sweater tighter. It was much too big for her and it swallowed her skinny frame. "It's too cold to do this at the door," she said.

"He's not here," Corinne said.

"You're too late," Ruth said to me. "I got rid of the dog."

"Already? Don't you think that was a bit hasty? What if her aunt wants him?"

"Not my problem." Her ferret face was hard and mean.

It was hard to concentrate over Corinne's wailing. "My sweater. She's wearing my sweater. She took my dog and my sweater."

I loomed over Ruth. "I'm making it your problem. I want Billy and I want all of Corinne's stuff packed up for her Aunt Susie. Someone will pick it up."

Ruth's beady eyes narrowed further. "How do I know you were really her friend and not some scammer? You don't have any legal right to tell me what to do."

"You're wearing Corinne's sweater," I said.

"Maybe it's my sweater."

"Lying bitch!" Corinne screeched, making me wince at the volume. "It's mine. Mine!"

"It's Corinne's sweater, all right. I know that for a fact."

"So what if you saw Corinne with it?" Ruth crossed her arms over her skinny chest. "We wore each other's clothes all the time." Yeah, right. Corinne wore double digits and Ruth couldn't be any bigger than a six.

"I was with Corinne when she bought it." Hey, I was getting the hang of lying.

"Marshall's. Just last week," Corinne said.

"...at Marshall's last week," I added.

Ruth's mouth dropped open, but she closed it quickly. "How come I've never seen you before? Corinne didn't have friends."

"That she told you about."

"I never even wore the sweater," Corinne lamented.

"I don't think she ever wore the sweater," I said.

"It still had the tag on it." Corinne peered closely at the sweater.

"I'll bet you pulled the tag off and took it," I said. "What else have you helped yourself to? Maybe I should call her Aunt Susie. Maybe I should call the police. I'll bet that's theft. Stealing a dead girl's stuff. That's low."

Ruth wrenched open the door. "Get out."

There were bright spots of color on both her cheeks. This was kind of fun.

"I'm not leaving until you tell me what you did with the dog. Where's Billy?"

Ruth started to look frightened. "I told you. I don't have the dog. I took him to the pound over on Lexington."

Corinne burst into noisy sobs.

Ruth gave me a shove. I stumbled backward and she slammed the door. "Go away!"

"You'd better hope he's okay." I lowered my voice to a whisper. "Come on, Corinne, it's okay. We'll get him. They keep animals for three days, I think." That sounded right. I had heard that somewhere. Corinne cried harder. I looked around to see if people were staring, but it was too cold. Everyone had heads down rushing along. "Let's go back to the DART station. After work, I'll get Billy."

On a map, Dallas Area Rapid Transit, or DART, looks like an octopus with the main body of the beast being in the city proper. Several legs run up through the park cities and farther north, up the technological corridor, all the way to Plano and Carrollton. I can get almost every place I need by train or bus.

"But it's Wednesday and I died on Monday. We have to go now, before it's too late."

I gritted my teeth and called Cruella de Vil. Of course, my boss is really named Ginger Deville of Smithson, Parker, and Deville, but Cruella suits her. I'm sure she would club puppies if it helped her relieve stress. I trudged toward the station with cellphone at ear, prepared for the groveling.

Joy of joys, Cruella's voice mail picked up, and I tried to spit it all out before a live human could pick up. "Hi, it's me. Portia. Listen, I have to take care of something really, really super important this morning. I am coming back to work today, and I'll work through lunch and stay late until my desk is clear, but I have to do this and I appreciate your understanding so--"

"Portia?" I winced as Ginger's crisp voice answered. Should have hung up quicker. "I thought you said you were coming back today."

"I did. I am. I just have to take care of something." Or be stalked for eternity.

"What could be more important than your job?"

"I...uh..." Here I had thought my lying skills were improving. "I have to see the doctor one more time. And pick up some...medicine. Yes, I need to pick something up. That's exactly what I'm doing." That part wasn't a lie. I was picking up a dog, and getting rid of my ghostly roommate would be the best medicine ever.

"You said the doctor had cleared you to work. I need you here, Portia. I can't run around short-staffed. Where is the demand letter for the Butcher case? And my schedule? It hasn't been updated in days. I hardly know where I'm supposed to be when. If I miss a court setting because I wasn't properly notified..." She let the implied threat hang there.

"I'll get everything caught up. I'll have the letter on your desk by lunch, and I'll get all your things typed and the schedule updated before I leave today. Promise."

She sighed heavily, implying the huge sacrifice on her part for having a slothful secretary who had managed to get hurt. "Get here as quickly as possible." *Click.*

That was it. Not even a *How's your head?* Four years ought to warrant a card at the least.

* * * *

To get to Lexington, I rode the red leg into the hub and switched to the blue one. It was inconvenient and time-consuming, but the distance was much too far to walk.

I tried to ignore Corinne on the train. She hovered close by, but there was no way I would talk to her and get myself hauled off by security.

The train jostled to a stop at the terminal nearest the Lexington address I had gotten from information. As soon as I departed the train, Corinne was yammering again. I ignored her until I reached the pound. Then I realized that I had no idea what Billy looked like.

"So what kind of dog am I looking for?"

"Billy's a pug."

"Those are little dogs, right?"

"Oh yes, he's a big dog in a little body. He's got the most expressive eyes and a beautiful smile." I rolled *my* eyes to express disgust at anyone who described her dog's smile.

The smell inside the ugly concrete structure was two parts antiseptic and one part nervous animal. A woman in a green shirt that said *Animal Control* looked up.

"Help you?"

"I'm looking for a dog."

Her expression brightened. "Any special type of dog? We have lots of animals here for adoption. Oh. Or did you lose a dog?"

I thought for a moment. "I have a friend who lost a dog."

"He would have to claim it himself."

"That could be a problem. Does it cost money?"

"There is a fee and of course the boarding costs since we've housed the animal for him. And if he can't provide proof of vaccination, he'll have to pay for those, too, before we release the animal."

She looked at me shrewdly. "If you were interested in adopting a dog, you could adopt one for as little as fifty dollars."

Crap, that was expensive. Still, I got what she was saying. It's cheaper to adopt back your own dog than bail him out. "That's very reasonable."

She smiled broadly. "Let me show you the dogs. We have so many animals here in need."

"I'm looking for a little dog. One that could live in an apartment."

I followed her back through heavy doors that made me think of a jail. "The dogs are this way. We house the cats separately."

"I'm sure they appreciate that."

As she led me back into the kennels, the nervous animal smell grew stronger. I tried not to wrinkle my nose. And the noise. Dear heaven, the *noise* when she opened the door. Dogs of all shapes and sizes barked and yelped. Their howls echoed off the walls of the concrete bunker.

Once inside, I could see it really was a jail, a doggy jail. The inmates all rushed the bars, clamoring to be taken out. I've never seen so many dogs in one place. Corinne floated off past me, flitting anxiously about. "Billy? Mommy's here. Billy?"

"Take a look around," said the animal control gal loudly over the din. "See if anyone takes your fancy. We've got an adoption room, where you can spend a little time with any dog you might be interested in."

"I don't see him," Corinne said.

"Are there any more dogs?"

The woman looked at me like I was crazy. How could anyone want more dogs than this? "Maybe in the infirmary. But those dogs aren't available. We don't adopt out sick animals."

"I really want a small dog."

"You and everybody else." She walked past cages of large, shaggy creatures, down to the end of the row. "We've got a couple of dachshunds. And a little schnauzer. He's old, but very sweet. He'd make a perfect apartment dog."

"My sister has a pug," I lied. "I'm very partial to pugs."

She looked at me curiously. "There is a pug. But we took him to the infirmary."

"My Billy!"

I ignored Corinne, which was hard because she was doing somersaults in the air. Lovely. Add another skill to her floating repertoire. "Is he sick? What's wrong with him?"

"Actually he seems depressed. He won't eat."

Looking around the doggy jail, it wasn't too hard to figure. "Could I see him? Maybe he just doesn't like it here."

I followed her back out of the hellish bunker. The moment the heavy door clanged shut behind me was a blessed relief on my eardrums. Pure bliss.

The infirmary turned out to be a separate building. It was much quieter and less jail-like. More like a vet's office. In the back of one of the cages, was a fawn-colored lump.

"Does it have a name?"

"No. Someone left him here in a box. No note or anything."

"Billy," Corinne shouted, somersaulting again. "Billy!"

The lump stirred and lifted his head.

"Hi, dog. Um. Billy?" He cocked his head and wagged a curly little pigtail uncertainly.

"I think he likes you," the woman said. "Talk to him."

"Hi, Billy," I said, feeling stupid talking to a dog. "Come on over and see me." He looked at me. His tail wagged hesitantly. "Can I take him out?" I asked the woman.

Billy spotted Corinne's ghost. He could indeed see her. I know this because he suddenly leapt to his feet and barked.

"I'll take him," I said.

In retrospect, I should have tried to adopt an orphan from Africa. It would have been far simpler. Who knew there was so much paperwork involved in picking out a dog? A *dog*, for crying out loud.

I practically had to sign my life away. They wanted references and background info and my own freaking pedigree. You'd think they would be glad to unload an animal, but it was worse than wedding vows. I promised to feed him and water him and walk him and vaccinate him until death do us part. Sheesh.

A whole hour's worth of paperwork and interrogation later, I was the proud owner of one pug. I'd had to purchase a leash and collar there since I hadn't had the foresight to bring my own, which had shocked the woman. I couldn't explain that I'd had no idea when I left the house this morning such things would be necessary.

Billy trotted along on the leash, inspecting every pant cuff and curb we passed, lifting a leg to water the ones he found appealing. He had a square body and a massive, comical head. His smushed-up face was black with the biggest, popped-out eyes I'd ever seen on something that wasn't a squeeze toy. His ears were little velvety flaps.

I gave him a pat. I admit that the ears were quite soft. Maybe a dog wasn't so bad. He licked my hand frantically. His oversized tongue barely fit into his mouth; mostly it lolled out the side. I wiped my hand on my pants.

Billy seemed thrilled to be on the leash and kept looking up at me like *now what?* Truthfully, I had no idea. How would I get him home? He was too big to hide in my purse like a Hollywood Chihuahua, and I couldn't just tuck him under my arm like the old ladies in furs shopping down Hillman Street. He was small enough to be no protection from rapists and muggers, but too big to sneak onto the train. I gave up and called Harry, who grumped and complained and then snickered in disbelief at the idea of me with a dog.

"Just come get me," I snapped.

It was bitter cold outside the terminal, but I couldn't go inside anywhere with Billy. Dogs are extremely inconvenient. As I waited, Billy sat there happily blinking. Corinne cooed and baby-talked him. Blech. I would never do such a thing. His curly pigtail wagged in appreciation.

I realized that I had no food and no place to keep a dog that didn't have thick, soft carpeting just begging to be peed on. I was shivering and pissed by the time Harry finally pulled up in a long white hearse.

"You're going to ride in that?" Corinne's eyes were wide.

"Welcome to the family business." I scooped Billy up. He was surprisingly heavy. "This dog needs a diet," I said, climbing into the passenger seat.

"No, he doesn't. He's perfect," Corinne said.

"Looks like a ham hock with legs," Harry said. "What possessed you to get a dog? Shouldn't you be at work?"

"Don't ask," I said. "Just drive. I've got to stash this...I mean, I need to take my new darling home. Unless...I'll bet you've always wanted a doggy."

"Fat chance. I don't know why you got the damn thing, but I sure don't want it. I can't keep a plant alive. And it'll cramp my dating style." He put the car in gear and jolted forward into traffic with barely a glance. Indignant horns sounded behind us.

"I thought you were so lonely and unloved."

"Met a girl last night at a club." He winked. "Turns out her roommate is even cuter. They think I'm adorable."

"Lucky you." I met a bunch of old ghosts playing cards and killing each other. Then I promised Death to try and help solve a murder.

Billy made little snorking noises with his nose, and he drooled on my leg. He stood with his paws braced on the window. I was glad someone enjoyed the ride. I closed my eyes as the hearse weaved in and out of traffic like Harry was playing Grand Theft Auto.

* * * *

I'm not allowed pets at my apartment, but a furtive look around assured me that the place was deserted. I carried Billy in and deposited him on the floor. He immediately ran the perimeter, sniffing everything and making horrible snuffling and wheezing noises. *Snork!*

"Does he always sound like that?" I asked.

"It's something pugs do," Corinne said. "Isn't it cute? Aunt Susie breeds pugs, you know. She gave me Billy when I moved here so I wouldn't be too lonely for home."

I found the pug's phlegmy noises less than charming, but I was in too deep now. Billy seemed excessively interested in my sofa.

"Oh no, you don't!" I nabbed him just as he started to hike his leg. Everywhere I looked in my apartment, I saw lovely things waiting to be destroyed.

Over Corinne's objections, I put Billy in the bathroom and sacrificed a pillow for him to lie on. "Don't pee on it," I instructed him. "It's your bed."

Afraid to check my watch, I trudged back down to the DART station for the second time that day, wondering if I still had a job. Being a secretary at a successful law firm pays well, and I have gotten very accustomed to my creature comforts. The other secretaries aren't bad to work with and we go out once a week, sort of a ladies night out, but in a more genteel, fine wine-and-dine sort of way than Harry's wild nights. My apartment isn't cheap, either. It's centrally located near good shopping and restaurants.

But my boss. Ginger "Cruella" Deville is the most self-absorbed, impossibly bitchy boss I've ever had. I had the stomach flu last year and missed two days. She called me eight times.

My head was down, braced against the cold. As I withdrew my DART pass, I saw it: something large hunched next to the ticket scanner. It had to be eight feet tall and hairless. The amorphous shape reminded me of a slug. Its head raised, sniffing the air. It turned and looked at me. Its malevolent red eyes caused my heart to race. I knew I was looking on pure evil.

Its lips drew back in a snarl, and it unleashed a frightful howl, then flew right at me. I wanted to run, but I froze. My eyes closed, and my purse slid from my numb fingers. I felt the thing pass me like a cold chill stinking of wet dogs and rotten eggs.

An older gentleman handed me my purse off the ground. "You okay?" he asked.

I nodded. My hands shook so violently it took me three tries to swipe my pass through the scanner.

"You sure you're okay, miss?" The kind old man was still behind me.

"Yes," I whispered. "I'm having a bad day."

I was so distracted as I sat in the nearly empty car, I almost missed the ghost.

He sat politely across from me with his hat in his hands. I took a moment to register the faint blurring around the edges that marked him as not quite corporeal. I had seen him before. It was the man from the tracks.

"Do you know my mother?" It was a child's question, but he had to be at least sixty.

"No," I said softly.

"Excuse me?" The older gentleman had gotten on the car with me.

"Nothing," I said. "Sorry. Talking to myself."

When I looked back, the seat across from me was empty.

Chapter 4

I tried to sneak into the office. It was lunchtime, and I figured Cruella would be power-lunching somewhere or getting her nails manicured.

Melissa sat at her desk. She has these enormous dark eyes that always look startled, which normally makes her hard to read, but today her expression was pure annoyance. "Finally," she whispered. "Where have you been?"

"The hospital," I whispered back. "Thanks for visiting."

She blinked like the idea had never occurred to her. I had a dim idea there might be flowers or balloons or even a card waiting for me on my desk, but instead there was a terse note. *See me. Ginger.*

Fabulous.

Melissa leaned closer. "Cruella has been on a real tear. She missed an appointment yesterday."

I groaned. "Was it an important client?"

"Worse. Her hairdresser. Now Mr. Illyvich says he can't work her in for another whole week. She's terrified he's going to butcher her color in revenge for being stood up."

Cruella and her stylist have some sort of weird love-hate thing going on. If Mr. Illyvich was pissed at her, she would take it out on me. Never mind that she was a grown woman who should be expected to keep up with her own appointments for a couple of frigging days. The Mr. Illyvich appointment had been on her calendar for two months.

I took a deep breath. Either Cruella wanted to rant and spew and load me up with work or she wanted to fire me. Either way it was going to be unpleasant.

I tried to skulk past Cruella's door, but her head poked out. "There you are. In my office. Now." I don't enjoy being talked to like a wayward child, but I gritted my teeth. Better to get it over with.

"Have a seat." Ginger swept her hand toward the chenille love seat and settled herself in her leather chair. She steepled her fingers and looked over them at me. "We have a problem, Portia."

"And what sort of problem would that be, Ginger?" My tone was a little more aggressive than I'd intended.

She raised one overly tweezed eyebrow. "I'm talking about dereliction of duty."

What the fuck? I'm in the army now? I kept my tone measured and calm. "Ginger, I was hurt."

"Team players play hurt."

I was careful not to roll my eyes. Cruella's father had been a football coach, and she was prone to inappropriate football metaphors. "I was in the hospital."

"Do you see my hair? Do you?" It looked the same as always. For all the money she spent on it, no one had hair that shade of red. Burgundy is a wine, not a hair color. "I heard about Illyvich," I said soothingly.

"Gregor Illyvich is considering dropping me from his client list. Do you know what that means? Honestly, Portia! I never thought you would be so irresponsible. It isn't just the hair. You've really put this office behind. We have interrogatories due, and Mr. Butcher keeps calling about his demand letter. I can't do anything on his case until Skeevick turns down his offer."

"I had a *head* injury, Ginger. It's not like I went to the Bahamas."

She shifted uncomfortably in her seat. "I'm going to have to let you go."

"What? You can't do that." I was sure when she'd started the lecture that she was choosing shame over termination. What was the point of both? "You can't fire me for being hurt!"

"Don't shout at me." She leaned backward in her chair. I realized I was halfway across her desk. "I've already buzzed security." Her eyes bugged, reminding me of Billy.

I allowed myself a little smile. "You can't fire someone for being hurt." I leaned in closer and lowered my voice. "I'll sue."

She fumbled under the desk, looking for her panic button. It was on the floor. She needed to stomp on it, not press it, but I wasn't about to tell her. "I don't think so," she said. "Where were you this morning? You weren't in the hospital then."

She was right, but I had the trump card and we both knew it. "I returned to work over doctor's advice based on a conversation with you. I want a month's pay."

"A month? You're crazy. Go ahead and sue. You'll never win."

"It isn't about winning in court. That isn't where cases are won and lost. Isn't that what you always say?"

"You'll embarrass yourself." She tossed her head, which was hard to do since she was leaning back in her chair as I loomed over her. Sometimes it's good to be tall.

"I don't think I'll be the one embarrassed, Ginger. Your colleagues will love to hear what I have to say."

She knew it was true. She had gossiped indiscriminately in front of me. Even worse, I knew everything about her: from her true hair color to which parts of her body got waxed. I made all her appointments.

She pursed her lips. "One month's pay."

"And a good reference for my next job."

"I can't believe it," she said. "After all I've done for you."

* * * *

By the time I made it to the DART station, my victorious feeling had faded. I had a check for a month's wages and a box with the contents of my desk. I also had a ghost and her dog crashing at my place. I took a deep breath. I could do this. I got myself this job, and I could find another. I would get the ghost to cross over, find some place for the dog to live, get myself another job, and reclaim a normal life, one without dead people and their problems.

It's weird how creepy an empty train is when you're used to the crush of rush hour. There were a few important-looking business types with briefcases and one or two retirees, but the station was largely deserted. I thought I would have the car all to myself, but an old man with hound-dog eyes and a newspaper tucked under his arm followed me in.

An entirely empty car and he had to sit right next to me. Even worse, he reached in a back pocket and pulled out a pack of cigarettes. I looked pointedly at the *No Smoking* sign. He gave a little smile and took one out, but he didn't light it.

I got up and moved. If he was a mugger, this was his unlucky day. He looked small and weak. I was tall and pissed. I tried to ignore him, but he half-turned and leaned back, looking at me mournfully as the train lurched forward.

"What is your problem?" I snapped.

"We've got to talk, doll," he said in Hephzibah's voice.

"Yow!" I jumped to my feet and toppled over. I scrambled back up into the seat.

"It's just me," Hephzibah said. "Don't freak."

"But...but..."

"Mind if I light this?" She held the cigarette up.

"Yes, I do."

"I can commandeer bodies when I need to. Sometimes it's easier to talk to someone in public that way. Anyone looks in, they'll just see you having a conversation with an old man, not talking to the air. Pretty nifty, huh?"

"Yeah. Nifty." I took a deep breath. "Actually, it's weird. But I'm okay now." I wasn't okay. I was far from okay. Mother never mentioned anything about Death commandeering bodies.

"Listen up, doll. I can't keep this up forever, and the clock is ticking. Corinne is in danger."

I held up my hand to stop her. "Really quick. I saw this...this...thing. Big and fleshy and stinky."

"I was afraid of that. We've got too many unclaimed souls wandering around. That was a demon." Hephzibah made a face. "Nasty things."

"A demon? Mother never mentioned demons." Mother and I were going to have a long talk.

"Your mother doesn't see them, doll. Few do. For someone so late to the game, you've got a wicked strong gift."

"Lucky me. So what was this demon doing in the train station?"

"It was hunting."

"Hunting what?"

"Unclaimed souls. It's dangerous out here for ghosts like Corinne. That's what we need to talk about."

"The demon wants Corinne."

"Among others. She's not the only one out here. I was worried about the Reclaimers. I didn't know we had a demon on the loose."

"What would the demon do with the ghosts if it catches them?"

"Eat their souls."

"Ew! That's horrible."

She shook her head. "You've got no idea. It's like this, doll. If Corinne doesn't cross over within the week, the Reclaimers will come for her."

"Reclaimers?"

"Mercenaries. They hunt unclaimed souls. Not like the demon, of course. They don't eat them. They take 'em and forcibly cross them over. It ain't pleasant."

"What happens to them when they're *reclaimed*?" I swallowed hard.

"Depends on who hired the Reclaimers. They work all the sides. Corrine's got sort of a grace period right now, but the clock is ticking. She's got four days left, and then she's at risk."

"What about the demon?"

"If it finds her, she's toast. She can outrun it for a while, but if it corners her--and they are damned good at doing that--bad things, doll. Very bad things. We got to get this gal crossed over." She looked down at the cigarette she was holding. "I wanna smoke this thing so bad I can just taste it."

"Don't you dare. That thing would kill you if you weren't already Death."

"Hey," the man said in his own voice. "Speak for yourself, girlie. You don't look so hot, either."

* * * *

I kept a sharp lookout for Corinne all the way home, or at least I tried to. It was hard with the sleet pelting me. At the moment I couldn't care less what my woolen hat did to my hair. I pulled the hat tighter until I could tuck the edge under my collar. Shoulders hunched against the precipitation, I darted along the edges of buildings, trying to seek out as much shelter as I could.

I never spotted Corinne, and by the time I squelched into my apartment I was thoroughly cranky. I looked at my pristine fireplace and promised myself that at my next trip to the market I would spring for one of those little Insta-Flame logs.

Dropping the box of my belongings inside the door, I thought about nothing more than putting the kettle on. The murderous card players occupied my kitchen table, but I was so accustomed to their presence I was thinking of naming them.

Then I heard it. Long, low and mournful.

Owwwwooooo. Owwwwoooooo.

My first thought was that Corinne had learned another new trick. This haunting thing was old already. If she started rattling chains in the attic at night, I was summoning the demon to eat her.

My second thought, and unfortunately the correct one, was that I had a very loud dog in my bathroom trying to get me evicted. "Billy!" I dove for the bathroom and wrenched the door open, prepared to scold him for howling. Instead, my jaw hung open, wobbling up and down fruitlessly with no sound coming out. It had snowed in my bathroom.

I blinked a few times and realized it was a toilet paper blizzard. Billy had found something to do other than howling. A closer inspection revealed that Billy had also entertained himself by gutting the pillow I put in there for his comfort. He'd also peed in the shower.

Mother wouldn't approve of the words I used, but the dog didn't care if I cussed him. He jumped and licked my face as I bent over to survey the damage. He'd done a nifty job of clawing the doorjamb. It would take a whole can of spackle and some paint if I wanted to keep my security deposit when I moved.

I looked down at the joyful dog wagging his curly tail. He regarded me with those enormous liquid eyes and cocked his head as if to say, *Like what I did with the place?* I sighed. It was probably my fault for leaving all those things handy for him.

"We're gonna have to reach an understanding, dog, or one of us is out of here. Got it?"

His tail wagged, and he darted past my feet.

"Hey! I was starting a lecture. Come back here." I chased him into the kitchen. The red message light of my phone blinked at me. I couldn't think of a living soul—or a dead one, for that matter—I wanted to have a conversation with. Good thing Corinne hadn't appeared yet. I'd have given her an earful about her destructive dog. Things were turning out exactly as I had feared. Three days' worth of ghosts, and already I had lost my job and had my bathroom ruined.

A sense of duty and, I confess, a niggling curiosity made me push the Play Message button.

"Hi, this is...uh...Dr. Feller. Ethan. Ethan Feller. From Our Lady of Mercy Hospital? You gave me your number?"

Why, yes, I did. This was a message I actually wanted.

"I promised to call you about that girl who died. About the aunt. She was notified and has made arrangements to take the girl's...uh...remains back to Nebraska. Anyway, I promised to call...so...I was thinking that maybe if you wanted to go out for drinks sometime or something, my number is..."

"Yes! Yes! Yes!" I did a happy dance around the room looking for something to write with. "He called. He called. He really called."

Billy thought dancing was a fine idea and pranced around under my feet, doing his best to trip me. He wheezed and snuffled in his excitement. He started to run a circle around the table, then paused and cocked his head to look at the card players.

"Do you see them, too?" I asked.

"Well, isn't this cozy?" Corinne hovered over the table, arms crossed. She didn't seem to notice the man choking his fellow player right under her. Hephzibah was right. Others didn't see what I did. I envied them. "Looks like someone had a good day."

"Actually my day sucked," I said with a grin. "I got fired, your little pooch here has trashed my bathroom, and by now I'm sure the neighbors have figured out I'm hiding a dog."

Corinne made a sound like sucking air. "Sorry about that. I didn't mean to get you canned. Why the dance of joy then?"

"Because the hottest doctor in the whole world called me," I said smugly. "Okay, the hottest doctor at Our Lady, anyway. But still, dance of joy worthy."

"A guy? Good for you."

The pouting was getting old. Granted, there would be no more hot dates for Corinne. That part of her life was done, but she needed to get over it. "Yes, good for me. In case you've been too preoccupied to notice, the last couple of days have been pretty shitty for me. I hurt my head. I lost my job. And I see dead people. In fact, I seem to have acquired a dead roommate. Oh, and a dog who's bent on destroying my bathroom. It's about time something good happened."

"He looks hungry," she said. "Have you fed him?"

I blinked. "No. What does he eat?"

"Dog food, of course. Tell me you at least put down a bowl of water." She looked around. "Don't you know anything about animals?"

"When I woke up this morning, I wasn't expecting to acquire a dog. I'll get him some food. There's one of those big chains around the corner from the Laundromat. I see people taking their dogs in there. Billy can go, too."

"Never. It's much too cold for him. Isn't it, puppy boy?"

"Hey, if I'm going out in it, he can, too."

"You're wearing a coat."

"So is he. It's not too far, and he can poop on the way. He has to poop and pee, right?"

"I'll go, too."

"I don't think that's a good idea, Corinne. It isn't safe out there for you."

"Not safe?" Her eyes narrowed. "I'm already dead. What else could happen?"

I wasn't sure how much to say, so I settled for, "I saw some weird things today." Like soul-eating demons. "I think you should stay here where it's warm and comfortable."

"Like I care about that. Remember the part about being dead? I'm coming with you. You can't stop me."

She had me there, and she knew it. She could follow me all over the world and yap in my ear until I went crazy. "Promise me that if I tell you to run, you'll do it."

* * * *

The second Billy saw the leash come out, he raced in circles, making little snork-snork noises.

I poked my head out first to make sure the coast was clear. The rain had eased up, but the sidewalks were still slick. Canterbury Park is a little more pedestrian-friendly than Dallas, and there was a fair amount of foot traffic for the wretched weather. Folks darted in and out of the shopping along the trendy square filled with boutiques and niche markets. I passed the square by and continued on to the less trendy, but heavily trafficked chain stores. They weren't pretty, but they had what I needed.

Along the way I stayed on alert for potential demons or other nasties, but I didn't see anything scarier than the guy in a dirty down jacket arguing loudly with himself as he jaywalked through traffic.

Deftly dodging the spray from vehicles swooshing through puddles, we arrived at Petland only moderately cold and wet. Billy immediately remedied his wetness with a thorough shaking, managing to do to me what the traffic hadn't.

"Gee thanks," I muttered, brushing at the muddy slush on my clothes. He took the time to shake each paw and lick his balls before agreeing to accompany me through the store.

He pin-balled down the aisles, snuffling with pleasure, hiked a leg and watered a sack of cat food. A hasty look around assured me that this had gone unnoticed.

Who knew there were so many types of dog food? Three aisles? Were they kidding?

"He likes this one." Corinne floated near the sacks. "He likes the chicken flavor. And this gravy over the top. It has vitamins for a shiny coat."

I checked the prices. "No freaking way."

"Can I help you?" A woman in a blue smock with handy pockets for treats stood at the ready. "What's your baby's name?" She bent over to Billy, who flopped over exposing his belly. She rubbed it as he snork-snorked appreciatively.

"His name is Billy. I'm looking for dog food," I said. Duh. "I don't know what kind to get."

"I just told you," Corinne said.

I ignored her. "I adopted him today, and I've never had a dog before."

I obviously said the magic words, because the clerk lit up like a kid at Christmas. "Oh, how wonderful! That is wonderful. Good for you. You saved a life today." She beamed at me. "Now this is what the vet recommends." She pointed to the same pricey bags Corinne had tried to steer me toward.

"Hah!" Corinne said.

"Why is it so expensive?"

"It's very balanced nutrition."

"What's wrong with this kind?" I pointed to a yellow bag. "I see them on TV."

The clerk gave me a pitying look. "Nothing wrong with it, if you don't mind feeding your dog corn and fillers."

"Corn is bad?"

"It's a common allergen. It adds bulk to the food, but it isn't digestible. So you know what that means." She looked meaningfully at Billy's rear. "What goes in must come out."

"Gotcha. So this expensive stuff makes less poop."

"Exactly." She gave me a huge smile. She had me, and she knew it. I looked at the prices and shook my head again. For that price, Billy had better shit gold bricks.

I had thought I would buy a little sack of food for a few days and maybe a water dish, because he wasn't drinking out of my good china. Turns out, my arms couldn't carry everything I ended up with. Billy needed food and the gravy for his coat—if the food was so balanced, why did he need supplements—a dog bed that was guaranteed to be rip-tear proof, chewy treats and toys to keep him from destroying my apartment, pooper-scooper supplies. Ugh.

I balked when it came to buying animal parts for him to gnaw on. I said no to pig's ears and cow hooves. Billy was thrilled with the bins of bones and bits. His smashed-up little nose was going crazy whuffling and snorking.

"What's that?" I pointed to a long, slender thing that looked an oddly shaped rawhide chew. "A bull stick?"

Andrea blushed and whispered in my ear.

"Ew! Who buys things like that?" Dog lovers had a lot to answer for in my book.

I left with my arms laden with packages and my bank account considerably lighter.

Corinne was insufferable all the way home. Where's a demon when you need one?

Chapter 5

I woke the next morning with two thoughts. First: I had no place to go. No one was expecting me to show up anywhere. I could lie in bed all day long and no one would care or would even miss me, which was both liberating and depressing. Second: The whining at the door was a dog, and if I didn't take him outside immediately, he would do something vile to my carpet, assuming he hadn't already.

So much for lying in bed. I pulled on some ugly sweats, jammed a wooly striped hat on my head and grabbed a leash. Billy danced at the door, snuffling with either joy or desperation. It all looks the same on a pug.

A quick peek outside showed me the coast was again clear. I opened the door wider and Billy darted out, half-dragging me through the parking lot. He stopped abruptly, sniffed and watered the tires of the closest SUV. Then he started to squat.

I panicked and dragged him over to the row of scraggly evergreens that passes for landscaping. I should have scooped the poop and taken the evidence away, but I'd left the supplies inside, and quite frankly the prospect was too horrible to face first thing in the morning.

I glanced at the steaming pile. There were little bits of blue in it that resembled the color of my towels. I thought I had left a washcloth in the bathroom yesterday.

This was the dog that needed forty-dollar dog food? So far he had eaten toilet paper, a pillow and a washcloth with no evidence of gastric upset.

"Keep this up and you're getting the crap with corn in it." We beat a hasty retreat inside before anyone saw us.

I put the kettle on. Corinne had yet to make an appearance. She was staying away longer and longer. I had no idea where she went, but I was determined to get her crossed over, find a job and a new home for Billy and bag myself a doctor. Hopefully today. It's good to have ambition.

But in order to call Aunt Susie, I needed Corinne. The card players had vanished during the night, and I could once more enjoy my kitchen table. I warmed my hands, wishing the sun would come out and bathe the room in golden light. Billy seemed impervious to the gloom and happily polished off his balanced meal. Then he entertained himself by savaging a terry-cloth wiener dog Corinne had insisted I buy for him. At least he was enjoying it.

I hate waiting. "Corinne?" I said sharply. "Where the hell are you?"

"Where do you think I am?"

She floated over my head. "Come down where I can see you without breaking my neck, please. We need to talk." She drifted down, wafting from side to side like a feather settling. She seemed more ephemeral every time I saw her. "Do you still want me to call your Aunt Susie?"

"Yes, please. I need to know that she's going to be okay."

That actually sounded reasonable. "So when is a good time?"

Corinne glanced at the faux antique clock on my mantel. "She's at work right now."

"That might not be the best place. How about tonight? Will she be home?"

"How should I know?"

Corinne wasn't going to make this easy. "Does she do anything on Thursday nights? Bowling league? Ladies' Auxiliary? Gun club?"

"Of course not. She goes to bed pretty early."

"Okay, then. Tonight, say six or seven o'clock, we'll give Aunt Susie a call. Then you can cross over in peace."

"Tonight?"

"Tonight," I said firmly. "You promised. Billy is taken care of, and after Aunt Susie there's no reason to hang around here anymore."

Corinne's lower lip trembled. Hephzibah had been right. Here it came. She was going to ask me to solve her murder.

"What's going to happen to me?"

"I don't know. I'm sure it's something good. You seem like a good person."

"Do you believe in heaven?"

"I guess so. I never looked at it that carefully." In fact, I had spent my entire life running from the issue. I was afraid to look. You would think with a family in the death business I would be at peace with the issue of dying, but I wasn't. Oh, I knew there was something more. I had always known there was more, but once people crossed over, I really had no idea. "My mother thinks so, and she's been clairvoyant her whole life, so she should know."

Corinne nodded. "I always went to church and I was pretty sure until... well...I'm sort of nervous."

Where was Hephzibah now? I had no idea how to deal with these issues. This was why I hated working in the funeral home. "Perfectly understandable," I said. "But I think it's time to find out. Tonight."

Corinne nodded. I could tell she was crying even though no tears streamed down her cheeks and she didn't make a sound. "It's just...never mind," she mumbled.

"Tell me."

"Somebody killed me. And now he's going to get away with it." Her shoulders shook, and she ducked her head, letting her honey-colored hair hide her face.

No, no, no. Not this conversation. "Do you have any idea who killed you?"

The hair curtain swayed as she shook her head. "I don't know who. I don't even know why."

"Maybe it wasn't murder. Maybe it was an accident." I couldn't imagine anyone wanting to kill Corinne.

"That isn't possible."

"Maybe the police have solved it."

She lifted her head. "Could you find out? Please? That would mean a lot. I don't want him to get away with it."

Against my better judgment I said, "I'll see what I can do."

What else could I say?

* * * *

The day stretched ahead of me, long and empty. I had made a promise to Corinne, and I really had no idea how to fulfill it. I had made promises to myself, but the prospect of job-hunting filled me with terror. I'd rather face another demon.

So I did the only thing I could think of. I called Harry.

An hour later, Harry picked me up in a blue Mahaffey-Ringold van. I hoped it didn't have a body in it. The big hearses are mostly for funerals. The van does the bulk of pickup and delivery.

He frowned when I climbed in. "Did you have to bring the dog?"

"I didn't want to leave him alone all day." I was afraid of further damage to my bathroom door or unabashed howling.

"You've gotten weird on me. Don't you think it's time you got another car?" He shifted gears.

"That might be hard."

"Oh?" He stomped on the accelerator with such ferocity I had to close my eyes. If Harry on the freeway was a scary prospect, Harry dodging pedestrians and city traffic was truly a near-death experience.

I gave him the CliffsNotes version of losing my job. He made appropriate brotherly noises and then asked the dreaded question. "Is that why you wanted me to pick you up? You're coming back to work for Mother and Walter?"

"No, absolutely not." I was so horrified I made the mistake of opening my eyes. A large semi bore down on us at a terrifying speed. Harry wrenched the van back onto our side of the street just in time. The truck driver laid on his horn indignantly. Harry beeped back at him and careened around a corner.

I had one arm holding Billy in my lap and another gripping the armrest. Billy stood with his front paws on the dash, snorking happily.

"I need to talk some things over with Mother. Mother-daughter stuff."

"Yeah, yeah, I know. Drop you off and disappear. Don't worry. I need to take Mrs. Hazelthorne to the crematorium anyway." He jerked his chin toward the back of the van.

* * * *

Harry let me off at the side door and peeled out as though it was a dire emergency to deliver Mrs. Hazelthorne within the next thirty seconds. Good thing most of Harry's passengers were already dead.

The bell tinkled as I went in the employee entrance. Mother was entertaining a "client" in her office.

"Oh hello, dear," she said. "Mrs. Hazelthorne, this is my daughter, Portia."

Mrs. Hazelthorne was plump, but in a shapely way, with gray hair fluffed about her head like a huge cotton ball. "Two of you? Dear me, this is my lucky day. So very nice to meet you, Portia."

Mrs. Hazelthorne sat in a chair poring over the pages that Mother turned for her. She didn't appear to have mastered the art of floating yet.

"Mrs. Hazelthorne is newly deceased," Mother offered. "We're finalizing her funeral plan before her husband arrives."

"Definitely the pewter urn," Mrs. Hazelthorne said. "The living room is very nautical, and pewter would fit right in with all the blue tones."

"Now about the hymns," Mother said.

"Let me see." Mrs. Hazelthorne tapped her chin. "I always liked *Jesus, Savior, Pilot Me*, and *Rescue the Perishing*. Those would be nice, don't you think?"

"Oh yes," Mother said. "I've always been partial to Fanny Crosby. May I suggest *Blessed Assurance*?"

"That sounds nice. What do you think?" Mrs. Hazelthorne looked brightly at me. "What a cute little doggy," she exclaimed, spying Billy for the first time. The pug was sitting there with his head cocked and a bemused expression on his face.

Mother's mouth hung open. "You did get a dog. I thought Harry was making it up."

"I'll explain later," I said. The front doorbell tinkled.

Mother stood. "That will be Mr. Hazelthorne."

"I'll get him," I offered. I unclipped Billy's leash and he trotted at my heels. I hoped he didn't think he was my dog now. He'd probably transfer his loyalty to anyone who fed him.

Mr. Hazelthorne was a phlegmatic, red-eyed man. He had obviously been crying, but was otherwise stoic. I introduced myself and took him back to see Mother.

"Nice dog," he said. "Betty Lou always fancied little dogs."

I assumed Betty Lou was Mrs. Hazelthorne. When she saw her red-eyed husband, she grew weepy herself. I had to leave the room. I'm so not cut out for this kind of work. I wandered off to the chapel where services are sometimes held.

The chapel is very traditional, bordering on old-fashioned. It's what people expect. Burgundy carpeting and dark wood. Seating on both sides with a wide center aisle. The benches look like standard pews, but the pieces come apart. The size can be adjusted. It's supposed to be easy, and taking the things apart really is, but Harry and Walter need about an hour with a rubber mallet to put them back together. Up front is a platform with machinery hidden by drapery. Coffins come in on rollers and then are raised into position. The sound system is new, too. Mother sank a bunch of money into the place before the economy tanked. Now everyone wanted funerals on the cheap. She swore they were doing okay, but I worried.

Hephzibah sat at the organ, flipping through the hymnals. "Boy, them Lutherans are a serious bunch. Give me something with a beat any day. Is Betty Lou about ready?"

"I have no idea." I sat next to her on the bench. "Mother is doing the service arrangements with the husband right now."

"Good. Betty Lou wanted to see her Clarence one more time."

"Speaking of, I'm calling Corinne's aunt tonight. I think she's almost ready to cross over."

Hephzibah gave me a look. "Did she you hit you up about solving her murder?"

"I promised to make sure it was being handled. That's as far as I go."

"Unh-huh. Sure it is, doll."

"I don't think Corinne expects me to solve her murder. She'll go with you."

"If you say so. Hey, you haven't seen an old guy hanging around the dang train station, have you?"

"What kind of old guy?"

"A dead one. Sometimes they get away from me. Lester Jacobsen had a heart attack, and he was supposed to make it to the hospital, but he didn't. I heard a rumor that he's wandering the rails."

I was pretty sure I had seen him twice. "Any idea what he looks like?"

"Little guy. Bushy mustache. Lots of white hair."

"I saw him. He asked me about his mother, which I thought was weird."

"Sometimes people don't know they're dead and they get confused. If you see Lester, try to hang on to him. I'm afraid he's gonna be demon chow if I can't locate him soon."

"...and this is where we hold services, unless you have another location in mind," Mother said, leading Clarence Hazelthorne into the chapel.

He looked around. "This will be fine. Betty Lou would like it here."

"Oh, I do, Clarence. I do." Mrs. Hazelthorne clasped her hands together.

"I'm not sure about the urn," he said. "I think the brass might be nice and shiny over the mantle."

"Trust me," Mother said firmly. "Pewter is the only way to go. May I make some hymn suggestions?"

I stayed out of the way until Mother had safely guided Mr. Hazelthorne through the arrangements Mrs. Hazelthorne had chosen. He shuffled out the door.

After a few sniffles and some hand-wringing, Mrs. Hazelthorne went meekly with Hephzibah. They simply joined hands, took a step, and vanished. A little puff of air blew past my face. I'm not sure what I expected. Maybe smoke and a flash of light? Angels singing? Maybe a little drama? It was so mundane. Hands. Step. Gone.

Goodbye, Betty Lou.

Mother beamed at me. "We have so much to discuss," she said. "I'll make the French vanilla coffee."

I followed her down to the little kitchenette in the employee section. It was very quiet, with Harry and Walter both gone. When the place is slammed, Mother brings in more part-time planners, including my Aunt Bella. There are two people who specialize in "preparing the deceased." They're sisters, and behind their backs Harry and I call them the weird sisters. They're a little strange, but loyal to Mahaffey-Ringold. I know they worked for my grandparents, but they look old enough to have worked for my great-grandparents.

As the coffee percolated, Mother and I sat at one of the blue card tables that passes for an employee lunchroom. None of the renovation money had gone into improvements here. The linoleum was worn dull, and the metal chairs groaned with every shift in weight. I opened my mouth to speak, but an unseen visitor cleared his throat.

Billy growled softly.

"Show yourself, please," Mother said. "It's rude to listen in on other people's conversations."

"Rude, am I?" A young man appeared. He had slicked-back hair and a pencil-thin mustache. His eyes were so dark they looked black. His clothing was old-fashioned. Twenties? Thirties? I'm not good at that sort of thing. He checked a golden watch on a chain. "Isn't it a wee bit tardy to be drinking coffee, what?" He smirked.

Mother sighed. "Portia, this is Boris. Boris..."

"Oh, I know who she is. Can she finally see me? How marvelous."

So this was the infamous Boris. I knew he resided here and that he was in the habit of popping in and annoying Mother. Sometimes he played the organ.

"I see you," I said.

"Smashing dog! Is he yours?"

"For now."

"Hullo, poochie." Boris hovered over Billy, who growled. "Well, aren't you the cranky one? Hah! He'll fit in just fine around these uptight killjoys."

"Did you need something?" Mother asked.

"Just being social." Boris raised an eyebrow. "I take it I'm impinging on some sort of hen party."

"You are," Mother said.

"Fine," he sniffed. "TTFN." He snapped his fingers and vanished.

Mother waited a moment. "I know you're still here."

"All right. All right. I'm going this time."

Silence.

"I mean it, Boris."

"Damn it," he said.

She waited a moment longer. "He's gone now. I've been around him so long that I'm sensitive to his presence. That happens when you're around one ghost for years and years."

I shuddered at the thought. Then a question occurred to me. "What about Reclaimers? I thought they came for people who didn't cross over? And what about demons? Are there other things I need to look out for?"

The coffee was done. Mother got up to pour us each a cup. The strains of *Roll Out the Barrel* being played on the organ drifted down the hall from the chapel.

"Reclaimers? You've been talking to Hephzibah. Reclaimers have only been around the last forty years or so. Things were getting cluttered with too many ghosts. In the sixties it became popular to linger and haunt members of the establishment. Too much war and too many drug overdoses. So the Reclaimers were drafted. They hunt unclaimed souls for a bounty, but older ghosts, like Boris, are pre-reclaimer. They can't be touched."

"But demons?"

"Demons are a real risk for ghosts. They aren't picky. They'll eat anyone they can catch. Mahaffey-Ringold is on sacred ground. Demons can't come here, so it's a popular place for some of the older spirits to hang out."

"I know about Boris and that snooty old lady, whatshername. Lady Hildegard? How many of them live here?"

Mother studied me curiously. "How did you know about demons, anyway? Have you actually seen one?"

"Ugly and smelly."

She set down her cup. "Honey, I'm impressed. I've been hoping to see one for years. Only a few days and your gift is so strong."

"I'm being haunted," I blurted out.

"Already?"

"Remember the girl who died in my hospital room? She was murdered, and now she won't cross over. I promised to look after her dog." I gestured to Billy, who had stretched out under the table, all four legs spread-eagled, snoring softly.

"Ah," Mother said. "That explains the dog."

"I've promised to call her family, but..."

"It's difficult," Mother said. "Some are reluctant, but persuading them to cross over is a skill that comes with time. I'm sure you can reason with her. Good Lord! What is that smell?"

I glanced under the table at Billy. "He's been a little gassy today."

"What are you feeding him?"

"Money. He eats money."

"You should try something for sensitive tummies."

"I didn't realize you were a dog expert. Maybe you should--"

"Don't even think about it. This was your charitable impulse. Speaking of, I suppose you need a temporary job."

"You haven't gone precognitive on me, have you, Mother?"

"Don't I wish." She took a sip of her coffee. "You're here in the middle of the day."

"I could have the day off."

She smiled at me over her cup. "Cruella let you off? I doubt that. We could find you a permanent position here."

"I'll find a new job soon. I'm not cut out for the funeral business."

"If you insist," Mother said. "But I think your new skills would be handy. Be here tomorrow by noon to clean the chapel. We have an afternoon viewing. Don't worry. She's already crossed over. Just make sure things run smoothly." The chorus to *Ain't We Got Fun* drifted down the hall. "And keep Boris off the organ."

"Anyway, about the girl haunting me. Her murder is unsolved."

Mother put down her coffee. "No. Absolutely not. Do *not* get involved in that sort of thing. It's a dreadful idea. You'll end up like Eleanor." She said my cousin's name with great distaste.

"I know you don't approve, but is what Ellie does so bad?"

"Bad things can happen. Do you want to be labeled as a witch or treated like some fruitcake? Do you want to be another Elizabeth? Do you?"

"It doesn't seem to have hurt Ellie."

Her face darkened. "Ellie isn't even very good at what she does. So she can read things from objects. Big deal."

"But she works with the police. She's helped solve murders and kidnappings."

"She's provided tiny bits of info on cases they probably would have solved anyway. Really! The dog-and-pony show she puts on."

When I was younger, I didn't get Mother's obsession with secrecy. I realized that the women in my family were different. On my tenth birthday, I learned just how different. Mother said we were special, but I knew it wasn't all roses and accolades. Mahaffey women had been hunted as witches, burned as heretics and locked up as insane. Even with the current acceptance, fad even, of all things ghostly, she fears the repercussions of public exposure.

My cousin Eleanor has broken this taboo in a very public way. She has her own TV show, *PI: Psychic Investigators*.

"The way Ellie carries on you'd think she could cure cancer. That stuff on TV is nothing but trouble. She gets people so stirred up." Mother was gearing up into a full-blown Anti-Eleanor rant. I couldn't very well tell her I meant to go ask Eleanor for help with Corinne's murder. Mother didn't understand my predicament.

How could she understand when her experience with the dead was little old ladies picking out pewter urns and mauve coffin linings? She didn't see demons or residuals. God only knows what other horrors were waiting for me out there. But I did need one thing from her.

"Mother, can I borrow the hearse?"

Chapter 6

Walter had the formal white hearse and Harry the van, but I was happy to have the black hearse for transportation. Driving a hearse isn't as bad as it sounds. The gas mileage sucks, but people are afraid to cut you off and the police never stop you.

The funeral home was already on the edges of Canterbury Park, but Billy and I headed even deeper into the wilds of suburbia to reach Eleanor's split-level, ranch-style house with its concrete walkway. All the houses were uniformly tidy with brown brick facades and hedges stretched across the front yards like green mustaches. Suburban paradise. I'd rather die than live here. Give me the anonymity of the city over the forced chumminess of the 'burbs any day.

I parked at the curb and mentally girded my loins. At least at this time of day Ellie's perfect hubby and perfect daughters would be gone. The front window curtains fluttered. I had been spotted.

I trotted up to the door, which opened before I could knock.

Eleanor's hair hung in a smooth red pageboy. I could probably blow-dry mine out the same way if I spent a small fortune on curl-relaxers and round brushes and an ionic dryer. Probably.

"This is quite a surprise." Her expression smoothed when she saw Billy at my heels. "What a precious little dog!" She squatted down. "Hello, baby." Billy wagged all over and flopped, presenting his belly for rubbing. "Aren't you the cutest? Come in, Portia, and I'll get a treat for this little angel. It's much too cold for him. Why doesn't he have a sweater on?"

"Everyone's a dog expert today."

She didn't seem to be expecting anybody, and yet Eleanor had a pot of coffee and a coffee cake on the ready. That's how they do things in the 'burbs. We sat at the blond oak table with a tasteful winter arrangement featuring plastic berries and a cardinal so realistic I wondered if Eleanor had added taxidermy to her list of accomplishments.

"I assume this isn't purely a social visit?" She sipped her coffee, swirling the hazelnut creamer until her coffee was an even beige. "What is it you want?"

"It could be a social visit. I'm not looking for money or anything like that."

She arched an eyebrow. "You never visit. Don't think I'm being rude, but the girls will be home from school soon. Julia and Trinity have violin, and Mackenzie has ballet. The dance studio is completely across town from the music studio, of course. I simply divined a need for guidance." She took a little sip and primly set the cup on a coaster depicting an idyllic snowy scene. "So spill."

I gave her a carefully edited version of my week, starting with the bump on my head. "And when I woke up, I saw dead people." I heard a sharp intake of breath.

"I can't believe you didn't call me right away."

"It was...it was the bump on my head. I wasn't thinking clearly." I didn't mention the extent of my ability. It would only antagonize her and I needed her help.

"Can you hear the dead? Do they speak to you?" She leaned forward.

"Hah! Try getting them to shut up." I omitted Hephzibah and the demons and Reclaimers. I did tell her about Corinne's murder and her reluctance to cross over.

To her credit, Eleanor listened intently, only stopping me occasionally with a question. "And you need my help solving this girl's murder?"

"I don't actually intend to try and play Nancy Drew. I just want to talk to the detective and...I don't know...assure Corinne it's being taken seriously. I don't even know how to approach the police about this."

Ellie sipped her coffee with great satisfaction. "So you naturally thought of my police connections."

"That's it exactly. I was hoping you had an in, that you could give me a name."

"I'll go to the station with you."

I shifted on the seat cushions with little bows wound decoratively around the chair back. "That isn't necessary."

"Nonsense. You need my help. I loathe phone conversations. I always deal with the police in person. You simply can't pick up any sort of vibe over the phone."

This wasn't a battle I could win. I agreed to meet her tomorrow afternoon for a trip to find the detective on Corinne's case.

Ellie's glance strayed to the window and the hearse parked at her curb. "I'll drive," she said. "You'll also need my talents, of course."

"I'm not looking to solve the crime myself, Ellie."

"It's no trouble. It's what I do. Do you have anything that belongs to her?"

Another battle I couldn't win. She was determined to show me what she could do. The production she creates of picking up impressions from objects makes me queasy. "I don't think so." Billy stirred under my feet. It was too warm in the kitchen, and he leaned against my leg panting. "Nothing but the dog."

"Can you get something? Something personal?"

"Sure, but Corinne doesn't know who killed her."

"That's all right. I still might be able to get an accurate picture of the last moments of her life."

"I'm supposed to call her aunt in Omaha tonight. I'll try to get some things. I can tell her I want some personal mementos."

"What are you going to do with the dog? He sure is a sweetie pie. Aren't you, baby," she cooed, rubbing his soft ears.

I perked up. "You want him? He needs a home."

"Are you serious?" She looked truly delighted. "The kids have all been after me for a dog. I was researching Cavalier King Charles Spaniels, but I'm afraid they might shed. Julia wants a Bichon Frise, but Trinity is thinking poodle. Neither one of those shed, you know. Mackenzie wants a Chihuahua like Paris Hilton, but I refuse, simply refuse, to give in to a trend."

I promised to hand over the dog as soon as Corinne crossed over. I was feeling positively giddy, but as I looked out the window, I noticed a woman standing by the hearse. She was blond from a bottle with cheap clothes and a hard-bitten, been-there-done-that expression. She didn't scan with the neighborhood.

I blinked and she was gone, but my uneasiness remained.

Eleanor babbled away. I turned back and tried to concentrate. "We really should be working as a team. If we put our talents together..."

I pictured Mother's face. "No publicity. I don't want to hear my name in any interviews."

"Honestly, Portia, you're as bad as Agnes." Eleanor's sister Agnes is a Sister, Sister Mary Esperanza to be exact, but I was hardly as reclusive as a nun who converses with the dead in the ruins of a Romanian nunnery.

I rolled my eyes. "I don't shun the world, El. I'm just not prepared for life in the public eye."

I looked out the window and for a moment I thought I saw a figure sitting inside the hearse. It could have been a trick of shadow and light. When I looked more carefully, the seat was empty.

* * * *

The feeling of impending closure buoyed me to the evening. "You know what to say?" Corinne asked for the zillionth time.

"I'm sure you'll remind me if I forget." I dialed the number off my notepad.

Billy sacked out by the fireplace, snoring and farting happily. How any creature so small could make so much noise was beyond me.

The phone rang several times. "I don't think she's there," I said.

"Hello?"

"Is this Susie Simpson?"

"Of course it is. It's her," said Corinne, floating near my cellphone.

I put a finger to my lips.

"Why yes, it is. Do I know you?"

"No, you don't. I am...I mean, I *was* a friend of Corinne's. I promised her--"Deep breath time. "I promised that if anything ever happened I would take care of Billy and make sure you were doing okay and stuff." That sounded weak.

"Cori's friend? She never mentioned you. Did you work at the lab with her?"

"No, we...uh...met at a bar." I winced. That sounded like I had picked her niece up. "Through friends," I added hastily. "We knew some of the same people."

"That's so nice to hear. I thought she was struggling there in the city. She never mentioned friends."

Here was the hard part. "Corinne talked about you a lot, how much she loved and admired you. I thought you should know. In case she never told you. I know she meant to."

"I'm so sorry," Corinne whispered. "I should have called her more."

"She says...she always said she should call more."

Aunt Susie made a strangled little noise. "Thank you. I know how it is. Young, single girls in the city are too busy for silly things like phone calls. But it's sweet of you. I'm glad Cori had a friend."

I felt like a heel lying to this nice woman. "I want you to know, if you need anything, anything at all, you can call me. I promised Corinne."

Susie was quiet a moment. "That's a very unusual thing. Most people your age wouldn't make plans for dying. I didn't know that Cori thought about such things. Maybe with her parents dying when she was so young..."

"That must have been it."

"So you have Billy? How is he?"

"He's good. He's sleeping, actually."

"There is one thing," she said.

"Of course." I had offered, hadn't I? "Anything."

"Cori's roommate, Ruth. I've called her several times about getting Cori's things, but she...she keeps putting me off. I don't know what to think."

"You shouldn't trust her. Ruth is not a nice person."

"But she was Cori's roommate."

"Ruth took Billy to the pound. She left him there in a box."

Aunt Susie gasped. "I had no idea."

"So if you need anything, you call me. I'll help you get Cori's things back." And I meant it. It would be a pleasure to confound ferret face. I gave Susie my number. With her help, I would have my hands around some personal items for Eleanor in no time.

Corinne floated out of the kitchen. I turned to sit at the table, but the card players had appeared and were silently dealing. I followed Corinne into the living room. Her head hung down, and her shoulders slumped.

"She sounded okay. I thought that was what you wanted?"

"It is," she said.

"Billy is safe. I'll help Aunt Susie get your stuff. And I'll make sure that the police are working on your case. It's time for me to call Hephzibah."

"No."

"What do you mean *no*? You promised."

"I'm not ready."

I gritted my teeth. "It isn't a matter of being ready. Ready has nothing to do with dead. Death happens. Time to accept it." I knew it. I knew nothing good could come of this. The problems of the dead are their problems, and taking them on leads to nothing but heartache for the living.

"I'm going with you."

"With me where?"

"To the police. I'm going with you to the police station."

Yikes. "That's a terrible idea. It's dangerous out there, and there is no reason for you to go."

"I could help," she insisted.

"How? What could you possibly do?"

"Information. Who else knows more about my life and what happened on my last day? I could give them clues."

"Oh, for crying out loud. You're just delaying. What clues? You said you didn't have any idea who would do this." I crossed my arms. "I don't even know how you died."

"I think I was poisoned."

"Poisoned? How?"

She floated higher, until I had to crane my neck to see her.

"Come down from there," I said. "And fill me in so I don't sound stupid when I talk to the police."

She sullenly drifted down to right above eye level. I still had to raise my chin, but I could see her easily enough.

"The last thing I remember is being at work."

"Where did you work?"

"Wollencroft Agricultural Research."

"You were a scientist?" I was impressed. Aunt Susie mentioned something about a lab.

"I was a secretary, same as you. Anyway, I was at work and it was my break and I was hungry. I went to the break room to eat and..." She looked embarrassed. "I was out of quarters and I was hungry."

"Go on."

"There was this burrito. In the fridge."

"What do you mean *in the fridge*? What fridge?"

"The break room fridge. Oh, jeez."

"Whose burrito was this?"

Corinne fidgeted. "I don't know."

"You ate someone else's food out of the fridge."

"I stole a burrito, okay? Happy now? I'm a burrito thief. And that's when I started to feel weird and I tried to go back to my desk, but I felt so hot. Hot all over. And my heart was racing and I felt all shaky and like I couldn't catch my breath."

"Then what?"

"Then I was in the hospital room and I was dead. So that's what happened."

My jaw hung open. "So no one was even trying to kill you, were they? You ate someone else's poisoned burrito."

She hung her head and sniffled. "It's true."

"Do you think the police know this? Because that's very relevant."

"See? I should go. I can help."

I sighed. She was right. She would have to go. Oh God, the police were never going to solve this. She had been accidentally killed. My heart sank.

I had one more phone call to make, and it was a testament to how distracting my new life was that I had put it off this long.

I had a cute doctor to call.

Chapter 7

I was nervous.

Dr. Ethan Feller thought I was cute a few days ago, but maybe he asked out all his patients. He was probably some type of weirdo who got off on sick and injured women. He was probably at home waiting for one of the thirty-odd patients he'd propositioned to call him back so he could take advantage of her. Or him. He was probably bi.

"Ethan? This is Portia Mahaffey. I don't know if you remember me..."

"Portia!" His warm baritone started a pleasant tingle down below. "Of course I remember you. I'm glad you called me."

And just like that, I had a date with a potentially stalkerish, but extremely cute doctor.

When I finally went to bed, Billy woke and staggered into the bedroom. I contemplated putting him in the bathroom, but it seemed like too much trouble. I naively thought he would curl up and go to sleep.

Billy wanted up with me and he made himself annoying enough that I finally deposited him at the foot of the bed. "There. Happy now?"

He started up to the head of the bed.

"No, Billy. Stay there. Stay."

He deflated and sank onto his belly with beseeching eyes.

"Don't push it, dog."

I closed my eyes. The bed stirred. When I opened them, Billy was lying just as he had been, except he was a few inches closer.

"I mean it. I'll banish you to the bathroom."

We both knew I was lying. He would howl like a banshee in an echo chamber. Billy turned three times and then he seemed resigned, so I closed my eyes again. The bed jiggled.

I wasn't going to win this battle. I rolled over and pulled the covers up tight. Billy settled in against the small of my back like a warm cushion. It was actually kind of nice, and I began to drift off to sleep.

Snork!

My eyes popped open. Billy sighed once, a long hissing sigh, as if someone had let all the air out of the dog. Then he was asleep.

And he began snoring.

I'm a pretty heavy sleeper. I can sleep through a lot. But this was no ordinary snoring. This wasn't cute little baby snoring. This was full-blown truck driver with pesky adenoids snoring. Pillows over my head did only so much to drown it out.

I nudged him a time or two. Maybe if he rolled over he wouldn't snore. It worked with my ex-boyfriend. Billy shifted, farted twice, burped once and settled back down to snoring. I settled for sleeping with my pillow on my head.

* * * *

Getting the chapel ready for the service wasn't difficult. I ran the vacuum over the plush burgundy carpet and gave everything a quick polish, including Mr. McKlusky's cherry wood casket. The flower arrangements had been delivered and set out earlier. I put out the programs and a picture of Mr. McKlusky circa WWII. I couldn't blame the family. He had spent his last years in a nursing home. I'd rather be remembered when I had all my teeth, too.

As I started out of the chapel, Boris swung into a rendition of *The Old Gray Mare*. I turned, applauding slowly. "Very nice, Boris. Knock it off please. The family will be arriving soon."

"A serenade for the lovely lady."

The Old Gray Mare morphed into *Lady of Spain*. He winked rakishly. I knew from conversations with Mother that antagonizing Boris was a poor idea. He went from genial ghost to pissy poltergeist in no time flat.

"Thank you, Boris. I do appreciate the sentiment. Let's not scare the McKlusky clan, though. I understand Mrs. McKlusky has a bad ticker."

"Hah! More business for your family, what?"

"I should have known who was responsible for the vulgarity here. No self-respecting pianist would perpetrate such common tripe." A very large woman, dripping with furs and jewels, floated imperiously down the center aisle.

Just what I needed, dueling ghosts. "You must be Lady Hildegard Brenwith," I said, plastering a smile on my face.

"Just call her Hilde and be done with it. If Hilde's a lady then I'm Prince Albert. Hah!"

"You must be Imogene's daughter." Lady Hildegard sniffed. "You may call me Lady Hildegard. Ignore the cretin."

The cretin launched into a breathtakingly bad rendition of *O Danny Boy*, pounding the keys and singing in a reedy tenor.

"I'm so pleased, your ladyship. I was explaining to Boris here that we are expecting a family any minute for a service."

"Rest assured I would never disturb the solemn grief of the living. Unlike some," she said darkly. "I'll leave you to deal with the cretin."

"I prefer Neanderthal. Or maybe Johnny-Jump-Up. Hah!" Boris was quite pleased at her rapid exit. "Snooty old witch. Always dragging some wretched opera piece half to death. Hah! How about we cut the rug to a little Porter? Eh?" He played the intro to *I Get No Kick from Champagne*.

"Boris," I said.

"Blast!" He banged the keys and zipped upward. "I never get that section right." He floated down gently until he was at eye level with me, but his feet were still a good three inches off the ground. "Never mind, love. I can think of better things to occupy our time. It's been a month of Sundays since I had a chickadee to coo over. How about I show you my real talents?"

"So this is why you left Billy in the bathroom? To flirt with this, this..."

"Hullo." Boris flitted to Corinne's side. "A female ghost under the age of fifty. Charmed, I'm sure." He took her chubby hand in his and kissed it. "Allow me to introduce myself."

"Oh no, you don't," I said. "She can't stay. Corinne is crossing over tonight."

"Or the next day." She twirled a strand of hair.

"Tonight," I said firmly. "She can't stick around, Boris, and it's no good sweet-talking her."

"Jealous, my dear Portia? Tut-tut. It doesn't become you."

"I thought we agreed you would stay home," I said to Corinne, pointedly ignoring Boris. "You shouldn't be out roaming around. It isn't safe outside."

"I never agreed." She turned her nose up in the air. "Besides, I'm going to the police with you."

"The police," Boris exclaimed. "Why on earth would you want to spend time with those boors?"

"I was murdered." Corinne ducked her head.

"Murdered? You poor darling. I can sympathize. Tell Boris all about it." He took her hand again and they both vanished.

"Boris!" I yelled into the empty room. "You bring her back! I mean it, Boris! She can't stay here."

I turned to catch a glimpse of the hard-bitten blonde from yesterday disappearing around the corner. I sprinted down the aisle and came blowing out of the chapel, almost bowling over poor Mrs. McKlusky, who clutched her chest. "Did you see a blond woman come this way?" I asked. Mrs. McKlusky and her son assured me that the only person who had exited the chapel had been myself.

"You gave Mother quite a fright." Junior McKlusky glared at me. I apologized and went about getting them ready for Mr. McKlusky's service. Walter arrived to conduct the service. He's ordained and delivers an uplifting, if dull, service.

A quick glance at my watch assured me I had time to grab a cup of coffee before playing greeter. Good. I needed a boost. I found Boris moping alone in the break room. "I take it Corinne was able to resist your charms?"

"She left me to go look after some pooch. Would it be the cunning little dog from yesterday?"

"The same. The McKlusky family is here for the funeral."

Boris rolled his eyes. "On my best behavior. I've heard enough of your stepfather's sermons to last me a lifetime. They're deadly boring. Hah! Get it?"

"Then why do you stay? Why not cross over now?"

"I can't. I've been here too long." He sank lower. "I can't leave either. I'm tethered to this place. It started as habit and now...I can't. Thank you for the depression." He sighed heavily and vanished.

I started the coffee. The guestbook was in Mother's office. I could run it out to the front in case a few eager beavers showed up early, rush back here for coffee and make it back to the chapel in time to look appropriately sober when greeting mourners.

I ran to Mother's office and located Mr. McKlusky's guestbook and two of the good pens. A quick look around the chapel assured me that Walter, Mrs. McKlusky and her son were the only ones here. Walter gave me a weak smile and looked like he would rather be somewhere else than taking the doddering old woman and her cranky son around. I gave him a thumbs-up back, but didn't go in to rescue him. He needed to finalize the service with the family and that could be done without my help. I have no knack for dealing with the bereaved. I'm guaranteed to say something insensitive and stupid.

I raced back for my caffeine infusion, but I smelled something like... smoking? Was someone smoking? Surely not. This was a terrible place to be smoking. It's an old building filled with wood and chemicals. I rushed into the break room to chastise the scofflaw, only to find Hephzibah seated there in a purple nylon wind suit, happily puffing away.

"You?" I said in disbelief. "I thought you were joking. You really do smoke?"

She gave her hoarse laugh, trailing off into a coughing fit. "Coffin nails? I love 'em. Job security, doll. Guns, too. I could hardly wait for Mr. Winchester to die so I could give him a great, big smoochy kiss." She laughed again at her own joke.

"Nice," I said. "You must love twenty-first-century warfare."

"Naw, I hate bombs. Too much work. They make me feel like a damn tour guide. *Everybody this way. This way to cross over into the light. No pushing. Enough room for everyone.* Bah."

"You can't smoke in here. It's dangerous."

"Young people these days got no respect for their elders," she grumbled, but put out her light.

"Speaking of crossing over, I have questions."

"I'll answer if I can."

"Where do you take people when they die?"

"Across."

"To what?"

"To get to the other side. Sorry, doll. Some secrets have to wait."

Frustrated, I poured a cup of coffee. "So are you really Death? *The* Death, I mean? Are there more of you? I mean, how could you be everywhere? Do you always look the same? Like that?"

She held up the hand with the extinguished cigarette. "That's a lot of questions. I know this is new, but you sure are Imogene's kid. You think too damn much. I'm not the one Death, but I am Death. It's all you need to know."

"But I always thought...I mean, why look like..."

"Like I've got one foot in the grave?" She snorted at her own joke. "I crack myself up. Sorry, doll. You were expecting Brad Pitt perhaps? Ah, Hollywood. Nobody likes my true form. Not anymore. So now I look like everyone's grandma. It's what people want." She glanced up at the wall. "It's about time for me to go."

Uh-oh. "Why are you here?"

"Business, doll. I'm not stalking you. It's business." She paused. "You ain't seen Lester Jacobsen, have you? The old guy on the train?"

"No, I...business?"

From down the hall I could hear Junior McKlusky's wail. "Mother! Help!"

"Portia!" Walter yelled. "Call for an ambulance! Mrs. McKlusky's having a heart attack!"

"Gotta go," Hephzibah said. "It's been real and it's been fun, but it ain't been real fun. Later, doll."

I called 911, even though I was sure they wouldn't be able to revive Mrs. McKlusky.

* * * *

The funeral was postponed since it looked like a double ceremony, so I called Eleanor to pick me up. She arrived with every hair in place in a shiny new SUV. The leather seats were as soft as Billy's ears.

"I thought you had a funeral, Portia."

"Plans change." I was thinking of making that my new motto. Everything changes. "Where do we go?"

"Into the city."

From the grim set of her mouth, you'd have thought she was piloting a tank into combat. Her sober focus became more reasonable as we drew closer to the police department. I had thought we would go to the downtown municipal building, which is quite nice. We didn't. Ellie turned the SUV south.

Canterbury Park is mostly upscale, a more moderate clone of Highland Park. But where the southern edges kissed Dallas, the area changed. Every town has its slum, I guess, and it makes sense to put a police station where the crime is. We were entering a war zone.

I've been fortunate enough to never need the police services, and the closest I've come to a run-in with the law was a ticket for double parking before I wrecked my car two years ago.

You could feel the economic slide from upscale commercial to low-rent lease and all the way down to abandoned buildings. The few storefronts still open were barricaded: a check-cashing window, a liquor store, a pawnshop. Men with dirty coats and gray skin wandered the streets, not yet ghosts but no longer participants in the land of the living. Even the pavement seemed defeated and had surrendered to the cracks and potholes gouging its surface. What little traffic there was rolled slowly along.

We circled the parking lot twice before a space opened up. Actually, the space on the end was technically available, but it was occupied by broken beer bottles and a snoozing wino using the curb as a pillow. Neither Ellie nor I was brave enough to roll him out of the spot, so we circled a few more times.

Finally, a teenager sauntered out with his pants riding below the equator and his hat turned sideways. I couldn't guess if he was a suspect, witness or victim. I was just glad that he backed his tattered ragtop out of a spot close to the front door.

Ellie beat two other cars that all dove for the opening at the same time. One drove away to continue trolling. The other cussed us and gestured out the window. Ellie ignored him, but I flipped him the bird on her behalf. It was the least I could do.

I repeatedly checked around me for signs of Corinne, but in spite of her protestations, she seemed to have deserted me now that I was actually at the police station. The whole point of her not crossing yet was so that she could help.

Inside was chaos. Aimless souls wandered about, shuffling papers. Above it all hovered an extremely large black man. When I say hovered,

I do mean up around the fluorescent light fixtures. It shouldn't have surprised me, but the Canterbury Park Police Department was haunted.

I lowered my eyes, but he noticed me staring at him and swooped in for a better look.

"Looky here what the cat drug in." He had a soft Southern accent. "I do believe Ms. Eleanor got a real live ghost hunter with her."

I could hardly carry on a conversation surrounded by people, so I gave him a little smile and a wink. It would be rude to ignore him. Meanwhile, Ellie marched up to the desk and announced our presence to a bored woman in a PSO uniform. She smirked at the sight of Ellie and picked up the phone.

I made a lame excuse about washing my hands.

"I usually do that when I leave," Ellie called after my retreating back.

There wasn't anyone around the narrow hallway. I cautiously opened the door into the dimly lit ladies' room. The smell convinced me I didn't want to wash my hands here. I most certainly wasn't desperate enough to use the restroom. I had come for a conversation.

"Hee hee!" The ghost rubbed his hands together. "I surely shouldn't be in here, but don't mind if I do. I'm half-starved for a little conversation. The name is Lincoln, as in the president who freed the slaves, and Brown, as in the color of my skin."

"Portia Mahaffey."

"Mahaffey? You must be related to Ms. Eleanor back there. Y'all do have a passing resemblance what with the hair and being so tall."

"Cousins," I said. "Is this your regular haunt?"

"Oh yes, ma'am. Here I died and here I stays."

"How awful. Police brutality? Another prisoner?"

He had a huge booming laugh and a mouthful of white teeth, surprising on someone who must predate modern dentistry. "Nothing so violent as that. I'm afraid it was a run o' the mill heart attack, Ms. Portia. But I was in such an angry state I just couldn't move on."

"And now you can't."

"It's all right. As locations go, this one is pretty lively. I like to cause a little mischief now and then. And they always blame the prisoners." He winked and boomed out another laugh.

"Portia?" Ellie knocked on the door. "Are you okay in there?"

"Uh...yeah. Making a phone call. Be right there." I lowered my voice to a whisper. "I gotta go, but it was nice to meet you, Lincoln Brown."

"Likewise. Stop by anytime."

I paused and looked up at him. "I bet you see and hear everything that goes on."

"Enough."

I had an idea tickling the back of my mind that a friendly ghost might be a dandy informant. "Good to know."

Ellie was at the counter engaged in conversation with a huge bear of a man. He had to be a detective. He wore a jacket that was not so much fabric as upholstery. He also wore a *why-me* expression.

"Portia, this is Detective Arthur Fierro. I was telling him about your friend's murder."

Fierro had strong features, a square superhero sort of chin and a nose that would have been tragic on a woman, but worked for him. His dark eyes were surprisingly soft in such a hard face. "And I was telling your cousin here that there isn't a murder. Pleased to meet you, though."

"At least hear us out," Ellie said. "Lieutenant Horton promised me that."

"I know. My desk is this way."

He led us through a maze of badly dressed men and cluttered desks to a little cubicle in the far corner. His desk was by far the messiest I had ever seen. The secretary in me ached to attack the towers of paper listing dangerously to one side.

I saw Lincoln out of the corner of my eye. He had followed at a distance and was hovering with apparent interest. This was good.

Detective Fierro glanced around for spare chairs, finally stealing them from the nearest cubicle. He flopped down in his seat and leaned back as the chair groaned. Ellie perched on her seat. I sat in mine and almost tipped forward. Someone liked their chair tilted downhill.

Fierro popped peanuts in his mouth from a little plastic bag. "Lunch," he explained. "So Corinne Simpson was a friend of yours."

"That's right."

"So how come your name hasn't surfaced until now?"

"Maybe you haven't been talking to the right people."

He rubbed his jaw. "I was given to understand she didn't have many friends, just acquaintances."

Snowing a seasoned detective was going to be a lot harder than intimidating Ruth. "That's true. Corinne didn't socialize a lot. But we had a lot in common."

"Such as?"

"Well, we were both secretaries. And...dogs. We were both dog lovers. Especially pugs."

"Dogs, huh?"

"Yes, and..." I glanced around, but Corinne was nowhere to be seen. She had been right. I needed her. Where the heck was she? "Mostly the dogs. We talked about our families, about her Aunt Susie in Omaha and... we were both single girls in the city. You know how it is."

"Why is it you believe Corinne was murdered?"

"Why do you think it was an accident? She was poisoned."

"You seem very sure."

"I am sure."

"Detective," Ellie interrupted. "You should know I've gotten very clear signals from the girl's belongings." She slid her eyes over to me. *Thank you, Ellie.* She was craftier than I had given her credit for. "Tell him, Portia."

I took a deep breath and plunged in. "Ellie felt a strong sense that Corinne was killed, but that the poison was intended for someone else. She was an innocent victim."

Fierro leaned forward, the corner of his mouth twitching. "Go on. How was this poison administered?"

"A burrito."

"A poison burrito?"

"Yes, a poison burrito. Only it wasn't Corinne's burrito. She was hungry and ate someone else's burrito out of the fridge, and then she felt sort of dizzy and lightheaded and she...she died."

He was looking at me with more interest now. "Whose burrito did she eat?"

I felt my face flush. "She didn't know. Ellie, I mean. Ellie couldn't tell. But it wasn't Corinne's burrito."

His mouth twitched again. "Anything you want to add?" he said to Ellie. "Feel free to chime in here."

"Portia pretty well summed it up."

He stood. "Well, ladies, thanks for coming. I'll be sure and let you know if something turns up."

"Don't you need my number?" I said. "Don't you want to write any of this down?"

"Not really. I'm aware that Corinne Simpson's last meal was a burrito, but I'll be sure and check out the stuff you told me. We know how to reach Eleanor if it comes to that."

We were getting the brush-off. I looked at the mounds of files and spotted a familiar label. My fingers itched. What I wouldn't do to get a look at that file. I looked around until I made eye contact with Lincoln. I nudged my chin toward the file and silently hoped. I took several steps away from the desk.

Lincoln was a genius. Right as Detective Fierro turned to go, his coffee cup went flying, spraying papers, people and a wilted ficus with hot coffee.

Fierro had a rare talent for cursing. Ellie and I had both been sprayed, and as we slunk off to the bathroom, I pulled my coat tighter around the file stuffed in there.

I would have high-fived Lincoln if I could have found a way to do it.

I made it as far as the restroom, but the door was locked. "Occupado," came the muffled reply. Crud. I had no intention of removing the file from the building, just reading the contents. I was brazen, but I had no wish to experience jail life firsthand. I don't pee in public.

As soon as the door opened, I slipped inside to read the report. There was a lot of cop-speak. *I did make contact with W1, blah blah.*

Now this part was interesting. Corinne had been poisoned with a large dose of heart medicine. They were debating accidental overdose versus intentional. What's more, they had traced the source of the drug to one of the scientists. Very, very interesting. He must be the one who poisoned Corinne. Now if I could only figure out why.

Poor Corinne had died of a heart attack brought on by the drug. And she was younger than I'd thought. Twenty-four and an orphan, alone in the city, with only a dog as a friend. Plus she wasn't model-thin. Being over six feet myself, I know how cruel kids are to anyone different. Corinne probably came here to make herself over, to create a new life and identity.

"Portia?" Ellie knocked on the door. "Are you in there?"

"Be right out," I said.

"Ms. Mahaffey?" It was Detective Fierro. "I'm going to go to the break room for a minute. I hope anything that might have accidentally ended up in your possession finds its way back to my desk. Lieutenant Horton is a big fan of your cousin's, and I'd hate to piss him off by arresting her family, but there are boundaries. We have an understanding?"

"Yeah, yeah," I said. "I hear you." Mother would have a fit. Not only was I working with Ellie, but I was stealing police reports and hanging out in ladies' rooms with men. Lincoln had been reading over my shoulder the entire time.

"Poor kid," he said. "You sure she didn't kill herself?"

"Positive. She's been staying at my place. She won't cross over until her murder gets solved."

"I can understand that," he said. "Just don't let her roam the streets. It's goddamn dangerous out there."

I nodded. "There's been a demon sniffing around the train station."

Lincoln shuddered. "That's some good information. I'll pass it on to any free movers."

"Free movers?"

"Spirits that travel place to place. Not everyone is tied to a location or a person."

"I didn't know that."

"You know about Reclaimers?"

"I've heard."

"Bastards have been trying to nab me for the last twenty years."

"And here I thought you were from before that, from before the Reclaimers. You can escape them?"

"It ain't been easy. That's for damn sure. They stopped getting after me for about the last five. Not sure if they done give up on ol' Lincoln or what." He shivered. "Hope I've seen the last of them bastards."

"That's some good information," I said. Lincoln Brown was going to be a useful ghost to know.

"Your girl don't know none of that, right? They've got some funky rules about crossing over of her own free will unless taken by Reclaimers. Shit. I'da know what's the point of that, but there you are. Anyways, I'm okay out in the parking lot. I'll keep my eyes and ears open. You come by and see old Lincoln from time to time. Hear?"

"Deal. I owe you for this report." I cautiously opened the door. Lincoln slipped on ahead.

"Coast is clear," he called back.

I sneaked back and slid the folder into one of the less towering stacks of paper and slunk out to the car. Ellie was in her Suburban with the engine running and the heater cranked up high enough to melt plastic.

That wasn't the only thing hot.

"I have never been so embarrassed! What were you thinking?"

"Sorry."

"Sorry doesn't cut it!"

"So what do you want, Ellie? Money? A finger? My firstborn? You'll have to wait a while for that." Like forever.

"Warn me before you do something like that in the future. I have a reputation to maintain."

"It was sort of an impulse thing. But I learned some useful information."

She sighed. "I'm glad you want to help the girl."

"Thanks for going along with me. I appreciate your help."

She smiled faintly. "Detective Fierro isn't a believer in psychic phenomenon."

"So I gathered. At least he talked to us."

"He tolerates me because of Lieutenant Horton. I helped Horton on the case that got him promoted to lieutenant."

A sudden cold flash made me shiver. "Brr."

"I've got the heater up as far as it will go."

"Then your Suburban is drafty."

"It is not. You have coffee all over your jacket. Maybe it's the wetness making you shiver. You even have coffee on your face."

I pulled down the visor and exposed the little mirror. The blond woman in the mirror was angry and hard. Her eyes were red as though she had been crying. I shrieked and slammed the visor shut.

Ellie swerved violently. "What is wrong with you?"

Marguerite Butler

"Th-there w-was a f-face," I chattered, feeling cold down to my core. A quick look over my shoulder assured me that no one was in the car. "I s-saw a w-woman."

Ellie's face lit up. "A ghost? You saw a ghost? In my car? How exciting!"

"I've seen her before. She's haunting me, I think."

"What does she want?"

"I don't know. She hasn't made contact yet. I've seen her a couple of times."

"O spirit, please reveal yourself," Ellie intoned.

"Don't be stupid," I said. "She'll talk when she's ready. Besides--" I shivered again. "She doesn't look exactly friendly."

"How does she look?"

"Royally pissed."

I checked the mirror as Ellie drove me home, but the angry woman didn't show herself again.

Chapter 8

Ellie rolled up as close to my front door as she possibly could. My heart sank as I saw a large yellow sheet of paper stuck to the front door. Notes from the manager were never good. It was starting to rain, so I sprang for the door. As I reached it, I could hear a ghostly howl. Unfortunately, I knew that noise. It wasn't a ghost. It was an unhappy pug.

Aroooooo!

I glanced at the yellow note from the manager. I had three days to get rid of Billy or they were filing an eviction case. I had two days before the Reclaimers came looking for Corinne. She had to go. So did her dog.

I'd put everything up out of Billy's reach in the bathroom except his bed and toys, but he had shown me his displeasure by peeing in as many places as possible. He'd christened the walls and cabinets and--judging by the smell--the shower. And by howling. According the notice from the manager, he had fielded no fewer than seven complaints.

Billy wiggled all over and spun in circles, barking with joy at the sight of me, not the least bit abashed. I clipped his leash on and took him out to pee in the bushes. No sense in skulking about since everyone knew he was there. I could feel faces watching me from behind the blinds. Screw 'em. They'd already reported me for having a dog. Let them report me for allowing said dog to crap in the bushes. Billy stopped to lift his leg at a few tires. "Good boy," I muttered.

Either Billy wasn't sensitive to my dark mood, or he didn't care. He was happy as hell. Why shouldn't he be? I scoured the pee chamber with bleach, then I dumped a heaping scoop of money in his food bowl and heated some four-for-a-dollar ramen noodles for myself. He savaged his food, wet and messy.

I looked down at Billy. "Hey, dog, I've got a date. What do you think of that?" Billy snorked in reply and kept eating. The microwave dinged and I paused, looking in at the noodles.

Drinks. We had said drinks. Did drinks mean dinner?

I erred on the side of caution and ate the ramen. Better go in fully prepared. Sure, Ethan was adorable and charming, but that was no guarantee of steak.

My hair played nice and my makeup was good, and I dressed in record time.

I checked the clock. All dressed up and no prince. It was way too early. He wouldn't be here for another half hour, and speaking of, where the heck was Corinne?

"Corinne? Corinne?"

I hate waiting.

I turned on the TV and found one of those obnoxious dating reality shows. It was one slick guy I wouldn't touch on a bet and five sluts all vying for a little time and trying to swab his tonsils. Ick.

Why does time crawl when you want something? Maybe Ethan was lost. Maybe he wasn't coming. Maybe he had to work.

I sniffed. Something was burning. No. Wait. More like cigarettes.

"Hephzibah?"

"How you doing, doll? Was today useful?"

"I think I know who killed Corinne. And I think I know how. One of the scientists at her workplace poisoned her with his heart meds. I just don't know why."

"That was useful. Where is she?"

I shifted. "I don't know."

"You've lost her?"

"No. I mean, I don't think so. I don't know where she went. She followed me to the funeral home and then she got mad about something and said she had to check on Billy and I haven't seen her since. She was supposed to come with me to the police station and help, but when the time came…" I shrugged. "I don't know what to think about her."

Hephzibah nodded. "She's starting to separate herself more and more from this world. I think she's about ready to cross over."

I glanced around to make sure Corinne wasn't lurking. "I met Lincoln Brown, at the police station."

"I know him."

"Why is it that we have to keep everything secret? It seems more fair to tell the dead the rules."

She studied me. "I can't even tell you all the rules. You've got to find most of it out on your own. They shouldn't know the rules at all."

"But why? It doesn't seem fair."

"That's from the outside looking in. Trust me on this."

"Do I have a choice?"

"No, but they do. And the choice has to be freely given, not made out of fear or coercion. Otherwise it's Reclaimers. Hope you never have to see that one. Sometimes they accidentally destroy souls while they try to take them." She looked me up and down. "Don't take this the wrong way, but you look hot. Gotta date?"

I glanced at the clock. "He's late."

"Bummer. I used to hate that in a man. I'm not so picky anymore." She winked. "I'm real happy for you, doll. You've been kinda stressed and cranky. You need to get laid."

Saved by a knock on the door. She gave me a meaningful look. "Corinne is running out of time. The mark is already fading."

"Mark?"

"The mark. The one that shows her as claimed. Reclaimers can't touch her if she's claimed, but the mark only lasts so long. Once that's gone, then she's in play. Reclaimers can bag her if they find her."

On that cheery note, I answered the door. Dr. Ethan Feller was even more gorgeous than I remembered: dark wavy hair, blue eyes, strong chin. And he was short. Really short.

My dream man was perfect and handsome and a doctor and short.

Have I mentioned short?

His chin tilted upward, taking in my full six feet. "You looked a lot shorter lying down."

"I'll get my flats."

* * * *

Ethan was short, but he wasn't cheap. Drinks turned out to be the bar in Mastrioni's, a ritzy place on the north side of the city. He had his own car, too, a nice, safe Toyota. Bland, but I gave him a pass. Maybe he was environmentally conscious.

He was funny, too.

Short and funny.

The preliminaries are always awkward, but Ethan made them easy as he drove us to the restaurant. "Okay, I'm thirty-two, from Phoenix, Arizona. My parents still live there, which should make me a prime catch. Never married. Non-smoker. And...uh...five-six and a half. You?"

"Twenty-eight. I'm a local girl. My mother owns a funeral home with my stepfather. I've got a twin brother. Never married. Non-smoker. And six feet tall without the heels."

He glanced over and smiled. "I don't usually date tall women."

"I don't usually date short men."

"Or patients. That's sort of frowned on."

"I'm not your patient. I just passed through the ER."

He laughed. "That's how I rationalized it, too. I guess that was my lucky day."

"I've had better days. But I'm glad something good came of it."

"That was a nasty bump."

What could I say? Now I see dead people? And one is living in my house with her dog? A demon has been following me around? Death shows up unannounced to comment on my sex life?

I settled on, "I lost my job because of missing too much work."

"Can they do that? That has to be against the law."

"I'm a pretty good secretary. I'll find another job soon. And I've got part-time stuff to tide me over. What's it like working in an ER?"

"Nothing like TV. Mostly a lot of car crashes and a few gunshot wounds. Lots of sick street people."

"So it's not all fast and furious?"

"Sometimes," he said thoughtfully. "It's either crazy busy or boring, but I like helping people and I can't imagine working in an office. I like the crazy hours and the busy times. It suits me."

"I can see that."

Mastrioni's was quiet and dim. A perfect date location. As we walked in, I was conscious of people staring. Even in flats I was a head taller than Ethan. Once we were safely perched on bar stools, the difference was far less noticeable. He ordered a martini, and I had a cosmopolitan, safe choices for us both.

First dates are always tricky. Do you do the petite salad and water thing or go straight for steak? If I can't stand my date and know I never want to see him again, I go right to the bottom of the menu for the surf and turf. Ethan was a nice guy, and I wasn't sure what ER doctors made. Still, with the height difference and all, I wasn't sure enough about longevity to pretend I ate healthy rabbit food all the time.

I went for a safe grilled chicken and pasta. Slightly healthy if you ignored the alfredo sauce and in the middle of the price range. Plus there weren't any green bits to get stuck in my teeth. I suspected he might be too polite to tell me and I didn't want to walk around that way. I wouldn't mind ending with a little kissing. He had a gorgeous smile.

Things were going well. He was smiling at my stories and laughing in the right places. I touched his hand lightly, and he turned it over for palm to palm contact. Subtle, yet enticing.

He was everything I had hoped. Well, everything but tall. But I was reevaluating my position on height. The activities I had in mind didn't need to occur standing up, although they can if you're a little creative.

Then I smelled it, the fetid, goatish scent of a demon.

Startled, I looked around the room. I didn't see it, but I did see the hard blonde glaring at me. Her eyes widened when she realized she had been spotted and she vanished. The demon smell was stronger. Where was it?

"Are you okay?" Ethan looked at me strangely. "Were you looking for something?"

"Did you see the restrooms?"

"To the left."

"Thanks. Be right back."

I took my clutch and walked slowly, taking the opportunity to look around the busy bar. The booth where the blonde had been was empty, but the demon smell was stronger.

I reached the door to the ladies' room and almost vomited. That's how strong the smell was. As I grasped the restroom door, something brushed my hair. I whirled around and there it was, right on top of me. It loomed over me, breathing its horrible stench into my face. I wanted to faint or panic or run, but I couldn't move. I tried to lean back, but I was up against the door. Then it spoke to me.

Not being fluent in demon, I couldn't understand a word, but the menace in its deep, guttural voice was clear. I was being warned off. It sounded like an old record being played back slowly in reverse, something Harry and I did as little kids. It gave a gravelly chuckle, and then, in a sudden whoosh of hot air, it was gone.

My hands shook as I went into the restroom. I sat in the stall for a moment to compose myself before deciding that cold water would do the trick. I opened the stall door and stared in the mirror over the sink. I let out a strangled shriek. The face in the mirror wasn't mine.

Anger flooded in, overtaking and drowning the terror.

"Who the hell are you and what do you want?"

The blonde stared back sullenly. She was older than I had thought, on the far side of fifty. Life hadn't been kind. She had a world-weary, beaten-down face. Two smears of blue over her eyes passed for eyeshadow, and her pink, frosted lipstick was crooked.

"She said you would help me."

Finally, a voice from my stalker. "Corinne? You've been talking to Corinne?"

"She said you could see me, that you could help me. I've been waiting." Her voice was as harsh as her face. "My name is Starla Mueller. I got murdered. And I want you to make the sonofabitch pay."

Chapter 9

"I don't know what Corinne has told you, but I'm no detective. I don't solve murders. All I've done is get some information for Corinne," I said.

"I don't need a detective. I know who killed me. I need you to make sure the bastard doesn't get away with it."

"Whoa. Whoa." I put my hands up. "You totally have the wrong person here."

"I don't think so. You got into that police station. You could make the detective listen. My no-good, two-timing, loser, rat-bastard husband killed me, and he's gonna get away with it. Nobody gives a shit. The police don't know nothing about what happened. And Joby's gonna marry that piece of crap Wanda." Her thin lips trembled. "That's just wrong."

I was going to get sucked in. I could feel it. "You can't stay here. There's a..." Lincoln Brown's warning about too much information rang in my ears. "It's not safe here. Can you find where I live?"

She sniffed. "I can follow you."

Having Starla along for my date was not what I had in mind. "But I'm staying here for a while and you can't. You just can't. It's dangerous. If you smell something really, um, smelly...in a backed-up sewer kind of way, run. Get out as fast as you can, okay? And stay in here. I'll come back."

She put her hand on her hip. "You want me to wait in the bathroom for you? You're kidding, right? Honey, I was a cocktail waitress. I belong at the bar. I'll sit there."

"Fine. Do what you want. Just remember what I said about the smell. And no eavesdropping. Got it?"

"Whatever."

I poked my head out, but the coast looked and smelled clear. I also didn't see Starla, but I knew she was near. "Don't stand so close," I muttered. The cold chill near my left hand moved farther away. Mother was partly right. I was starting to feel it when ghosts were near, but it hadn't taken me years.

"Are you okay?" Ethan's forehead wrinkled with concern.

"I needed the ladies' room."

"You ran out of here so suddenly."

"It was sort of an emergency. How's your food?"

We stayed longer than I intended because the conversation was so easy. The car ride home was freezing. I had no doubt that Starla was along for the ride. I couldn't help but feel inhibited knowing that she was listening in. It's hard to flirt with a dead cocktail waitress in the car.

I invited Ethan in for a cup of tea. I wasn't letting go of him without a good-night kiss. When I opened my apartment door, a fawn-colored bullet streaked past.

"Billy!" I dove for him, but he was too fast.

Ethan took a startled step backward and lost his balance. He landed with his butt in the narrow strip of grass along the curb.

"Oh, I'm so sorry!" I helped him up. "Tell me you aren't muddy."

"I don't think so." He brushed his cute ass, giving me an excuse to stare. "What was that?"

"My dog. I am so sorry. He must have needed to potty." I cupped my hands to my mouth. "Billy! Get back here now. Billy!"

"Did he run away?"

"No." I trotted over to the bushes and squatted down. "He's probably in here somewhere."

The smell hit my nose, and a sudden fear seized me. Did demons eat little dogs?

"Ar-ar-ar-ar-ar-ar." Billy sounded like a car with a bad starter. I found him around the corner with all four legs squarely planted, barking for all he was worth at a slobbering demon. The demon ignored him, slouching away. With a sudden *whoosh* it was gone, leaving its rank odor behind.

"Come here, silly boy." He bounded over to my side, slobbering on me in excitement. "Foolish dog." I scooped him up. "I've got him," I called to Ethan. "He was probably chasing a cat." Or a demon. "Foolish, brave doggie."

I carried Billy, muddy paws and all, back to my apartment. He ran around leaving little smudges on my gorgeous carpet, but it didn't matter. I was going to be evicted anyway and when they got a look at the doorjamb in the bathroom, my deposit was toast.

"So this is Billy." Ethan bent at the waist. "Cute little guy."

Billy wriggled happily at his name and raced off to find his favorite toy.

The murderous card game was underway in my kitchen, so after I put the kettle on we moved into the living room. Sitting beside Ethan on the couch made me feel like a giant woman. I leaned back against the cushions.

I had a question in mind to ask, but I quickly forgot.

I'm not sure who moved in for the kiss first. It was a mutual meeting of lips, and as first kisses go, it was pretty darn good. Soft at the beginning. Hesitant. Questioning. Then firmer, more insistent as the answer came. And just when I was wanting more, just when I was ready to slip my arms around his waist and slide my hands down his full length to cup that enticing, slightly muddy ass, just when I was ready to lose myself completely in a moment of feeling and forget ghosts and dogs and apartments and jobs, Ethan pulled away.

He didn't go far, just disengaged his mouth. "I've had a wonderful time tonight," he murmured, close to my ear, his breath tickling me.

"Ummm," I said, or something equally witty.

"But I have to be at work tonight and if I don't stop now..." He gave a shaky laugh.

"You work tonight?"

"I have to go on duty in a couple of hours."

I pulled back. "Do you still want tea?"

"Rain check?"

Damn. Damndamndamn. "Sure." I smiled. "No problem." Damn it all.

He gave me a sweet peck at the door, and he was gone. Billy lay by the fireplace, mauling his toy and growling at it. Perhaps in his imagination he was exacting revenge on the demon.

"That's so nice," Corinne said sourly. "My murder goes unsolved, and you're playing doctor. How cozy."

"Ease up, honey," Starla said. "She went to the police today. I saw her. I saw everything." She smirked. "He's a hottie, but waaaay too short. I hope his equipment ain't the same."

"Starla!" Corinne put her hands to her cheeks. "You shouldn't watch people like that."

"Why the hell not? It ain't like I'm going to be getting any. Might as well watch."

"No one is getting any around here," I said. "This place is too damn crowded." The more ghosts that moved in, the better being evicted sounded. Maybe they wouldn't follow me when I left.

"Tell me about the police." Corinne drifted close to me. "Have they solved my murder? Do they have a suspect?"

I sighed. "They thought maybe you killed yourself or it was some kind of accidental poisoning."

"What?" She zoomed upward.

"Come back. There's more. I told them it was murder. Detective Fierro is going to look into it. You were poisoned with a heart medicine called Rymeced. You do know who takes Rymeced, right? I think Dr. Seleman poisoned you."

She stared at me in horror. "Jon Seleman? He's my boss. He's got a bad heart. He keeps medicine in his office."

"Corinne, don't take this the wrong way, but were you in the habit of eating other people's food?"

Her pudgy face convulsed with anger. "How dare you?"

"If someone knew you hadn't eaten and that you would eat the burrito, you might have been the intended target all along. Would Dr. Seleman have a reason to kill you? You weren't having an affair with him or anything like that, were you?"

"Of course not! Dr. Seleman wouldn't do something like that to me. He isn't like most of the researchers there. He's nice to the staff. Someone must have taken his medicine." She seemed truly distressed, but if I believed her, there went my one and only theory. I wasn't very good at the detective thing.

"If it isn't Dr. Seleman, it has to be one of your co-workers. I can't imagine anyone else having access to the medicine and to the burrito."

"But now he knows, right? The detective is going to treat it like a homicide?"

I hesitated. "He said he would look into it."

Starla snorted. "He ain't gonna do shit. Don't nobody care about people like us, Corinne."

I glared at Starla, but she was studying her nails, which had been painted hot pink roughly three or four weeks ago, judging by the chipped polish.

"That's not true. I wouldn't have gotten involved if I didn't care." And if you weren't both haunting me. "I do care."

"Yeah, but you're one of us," Starla said. "Just a working nobody."

"I beg your pardon, but I've got skills. I type seventy words a minute and I'm proficient in spreadsheets and accounting software."

"Hah. You're a secretary. They care more about your legs than taking a letter."

"My last boss was a woman."

"That don't mean she wasn't looking at your ass." Starla snapped her fingers.

"Don't snap at me," I said.

"I'll snap if I want to." She snapped again.

"One of my co-workers," Corinne said. Starla and I turned to look at her. "You need a job."

"Yes," I said slowly.

Corinne's smile grew. "I know a secretarial job that's vacant. I'll bet you're qualified. I'll bet you could give answers that would knock my boss's socks off, especially if you had inside information."

My eyes widened. "I am not taking a job at your office to play detective. No way. No how."

"Don't worry," she said happily. "I'll coach you."

* * * *

By morning, I was eager to get rid of Starla. I wasn't so eager to make the phone call she wanted.

"I don't think Detective Fierro wants to hear from me. We didn't part on the best terms."

"A phone call is perfect. That way he knows you ain't stealing any files. Just tell him that Joby killed me and buried my body. But if this don't work out, you can go down there and, you know, do whatever you gotta. I could tell you where Joby is. I'll bet he's shacking up with Wanda right now. He's lucky I can't get at him."

"I told you. I'll pass the info along, but that's it. I am not the enforcer. Got that?"

"Yeah, yeah."

Detective Fierro was less than enthusiastic about my call. "I told you I would look into the Corinne Simpson case."

"That's not why I'm calling. I need to talk to you about a different woman. Ellie has gotten some vibes." Good thing I knew so much about the spirit world, because Ellie was going to kill me.

"Really. Ellie."

"Yes, about a woman named Starla Mueller." I spelled it for him.

"Be right back."

He was gone for a long time.

She hovered by my ear. "What did he say?"

"Patience, Starla. He's getting the file."

"I wanna listen in."

"I don't have a speakerphone. Just get close."

She was practically on top of me.

"Took me a while," Fierro said. "I was looking in homicide, but there isn't one. What I've got is a missing persons report on a Starla Kaye Mueller."

"Missing persons?"

"Filed by her boss when she didn't show up for work."

"Good ol' Dean," Starla said.

"What about her husband?"

Papers rustled. "He claims she left him for a guy named Willerby."

"What?" Starla was outraged. "That's Dean's cousin. That's crazy."

"That's not possible," I said. "That's her boss's cousin. Wouldn't the boss know if she ran off with his cousin?"

Fierro paused. "That's right," he said. "Willerby is his cousin. What did you say your interest in this was?"

"Starla isn't missing," I said. "I...Ellie says she's dead."

"Really. Dead. What else does Ellie say?"

I glanced over at Starla. "Starla was murdered by her husband, Joby. She's sure of it."

"Show me some evidence. Joby Mueller says Starla she left him, and she's certainly entitled to do so."

"He would say that. He killed her."

"He choked me." Starla's eyes were red and angry again, the crooked pink line set grimly. "Bastard," she muttered.

"She...um...Ellie says the husband strangled her and he..." I looked at the notes I had written on the back of an envelope. "He killed her in a car and then put her in the trunk. He drove north on Thirty-Five up to the campgrounds and buried her behind his family's cabin on Lake Texoma. She's under the firewood."

"You're sure of this?"

"Ellie was very specific."

"I'll say. We'll talk to the husband again."

"You'll look under the woodpile? You'll get Starla's body? She should be buried with her family."

He sighed. "Do you have any evidence? Anything other than vibes?"

"What do you mean, evidence? Go dig up her body. What other evidence do you need?"

"We can't go tromping around someone's property digging holes. We have to have a good reason."

"I just gave you one. A dead body isn't a good reason?"

"We don't know it's up there."

"I'm telling you it is."

"I'm talking about a warrant, Ms. Mahaffey. We need a search warrant to do what you're suggesting. No offense, but there isn't a judge alive who would give us a warrant based on this. Texoma isn't in my jurisdiction, you know. I can't call up some agency and ask a detective to get a warrant based on a phone call from a psychic."

Starla zoomed up to the ceiling and careened around, cursing like a drunken sailor.

"So what do you need?"

"Real evidence. Something more than a vibe. You bring me something we can take to a judge that gives us a reason to think the husband killed her and buried her up there and I can get that warrant."

It wasn't satisfying, but it was an answer. Corinne sulked in the kitchen because I wasn't interested in her former job, and Starla was still zooming and cussing. I now had two pissed-off ghosts living with me.

"Things ain't going so well. Are they, doll?"

I flopped on the couch next to Hephzibah. "Gee, what makes you say that?"

"The mark on Starla is almost gone. Same for Corinne. We're about out of time," she said very softly.

My shoulders slumped in defeat. "You want me to go to Corinne's office?"

"You have a better idea?"

I didn't. I was fresh out of ideas other than shopping, which sounded nice, but my bank account was dwindling and I was going to be evicted. Ever try to sign a lease without a steady job? I did the only thing I could think of.

I called Harry and told him I needed a ride.

* * * *

I dressed in my most professional clothes and tamed my hair into a neat chignon. It takes a lot of spray to hold it there and a few stray curls escaped, but it was the best I could do.

I was armed with my résumé and loads of information from Corinne. I suspected some of Corinne's excitement had to do with the idea of seeing former co-workers. Her job paid surprisingly well. If the people were okay, I might even stay.

I took the red train north so I would be much closer for Harry to pick up. I was a little nervous having Corinne with me, but I didn't see or smell the demon. For a moment, I thought I caught sight of a hat and a bushy mustache, but I blinked and then wasn't sure if it was wishful thinking. Was Lester Jacobsen still riding the rails or had he become demon food?

After a breathtaking Harry-ride out past the suburbs--where I mostly had my eyes closed and prayed not to die-- my brother dropped me off at a gleaming white building near the edge of a commercial area. The exterior gave no clue to what happened inside. It could be anything from meat processing to accounting.

Inside were more gleaming white and security cameras. A guard at a console had his eyes trained on a nine-inch black and white. As I drew closer I could see it wasn't a security feed that had captured his attention, but a soap opera.

"Help you?" he said without his eyes leaving the screen.

"I'm here to apply for a job."

He glanced up. "The agency sent you? I thought they were done interviewing."

"It's for the secretarial position," I said.

"Oh. Okay. I'll let Duncan know you're here." He made a call and then frowned. "Duncan doesn't know anything about you. You sure you've got the right place?"

"Yes," I said firmly. "I'm here about the opening in the secretarial pool. My understanding is it hasn't been filled. I'm here to apply." I waved my résumé. Corinne whispered in my ear. "Are you Carl?"

He blinked. "That's right."

"I was told to ask for you. I'm supposed to report to Duncan Werner. Stephanie sent me."

It was like saying open sesame. "She must have forgot to call. Go on up. I'll tell Duncan you're coming." He waved me over to an elevator bank. "You know where to go?"

"Sure," I said.

Once inside the elevator, I relaxed. The security wasn't that tight. He'd never bothered to ask for ID. "You want to take the fourth floor and turn right," Corinne whispered.

"You don't need to whisper," I whispered back. "I'm the only one who can hear you."

Duncan Werner was exactly as Corinne had described him, a fussy man dressed in a trendy, plum-colored suit with a bald head and neat goatee. He eyed me head to toe.

"I can't believe Stephanie didn't call. I hope you're more suitable than the last candidate. This way." With the flick of his wrist, he indicated I should follow him. He led me to yet another sterile room. The whole place was so clean, I felt grimy in comparison.

He spent a moment eyeing my résumé. "We do happen to have an opening for someone with your skills." He tapped the page. "Tell me about your credentials." Thanks to Corinne's coaching, I knew all his favorite buzzwords and was able to sell Duncan on my "dedication to teamwork and a proactive approach to people-oriented problem-solving." He nodded along, quite pleased with my answers. I walked out with a job starting in two days.

* * * *

Walter picked me up in the blue and maize Mahaffey-Ringold van, but the transportation came with a price: dinner at my mother's house.

He was appropriately pleased I had a job. Then he started with the stepfatherly concern, which I guess after twenty-three years he's entitled to. "So how's life in the city? Any new friends?"

I had lots of new dead friends, but that probably wasn't what he was looking for. "Actually, I have met someone."

"Really?" He perked up. "You met a man? That's wonderful. What does he do?" In Walter's eyes this is the measure of a man. He jerked the wheel to miss a pothole.

"He's a doctor. I met him when I bumped my head."

Walter nearly drove off the road. He was like a little kid bursting at the seams. As soon as we walked in the door he announced, "Imogene! Imogene, guess what. Our girl is dating a doctor. A doctor, Imogene."

Mother appeared in the doorway, wiping her hands on an apron she'd picked up at last year's Christmas bazaar that said *Kiss me, I'm Catholic*. "A doctor? Oh, honey!" She clasped her hands.

I dropped my coat on the couch. "I don't know I'd say we're dating. Walter asked if I'd met someone."

"You aren't going out?" Mother's face fell.

"We have gone out, but only once."

"Then you *are* dating. Kissed him yet?"

"Mother!"

Harry was in the background, already seated at the table. "Good for you. You can buy a house in the 'burbs near Ellie and procreate."

"It's a little soon to pick out the china pattern."

"Can we meet him?" Walter asked.

"How about I get to know him first, okay? Then you guys can scare him off."

It was hard to blame them. My last couple of boyfriends weren't exactly husband material: a bartender, a telemarketer, and a drummer. I think the drummer scared them the most, but he was the most fun. Too bad the concept of faithfulness was lost on him.

Harry wasn't in a chatty mood. He pouted at the table, knife and fork in hand. Mother frowned his direction as she set the serving platter down. Harry was in the doghouse for something.

Mother isn't much of a cook. Tonight's menu was dry pot roast, watery mashed potatoes and mushy veggies. But there was cheesecake and it was fabulous. Walter and I had picked it up from Perulli's on the way home.

Walter carved generous slabs of roast for everyone, which meant fewer leftovers for him to choke down.

"So," Mother said brightly, "other than dating a *doctor...*" She looked over at Harry, who blushed up the back of his neck and hunkered down over his plate. "...how is everything?

Some hint of twin solidarity made me blurt out, "I'm being evicted. Pass the potatoes."

Harry made a snorking sound suspiciously like Billy's. Walter paused, mouth open, his fork in midair.

"You're moving home?" Mother asked.

"No, I'll find a new place."

"But why?" Mother asked. "You love your little place. Aren't you paying your bills?"

"Hah! I bet it's the dog," Harry said. "I don't know why you got the darn thing."

Mother and I made eye contact. "I have to keep the dog for now. Then Ellie wants him for her kids."

Mother put her fork down. "You've been to see Ellie?" I hadn't meant to go there. I kept my head down and stuffed my face with creamed corn still tinny from a can.

"It's no big deal. It was about the dog."

I shot Mother a glare, daring her to have the conversation in front of Harry and Walter. She stabbed her roast. "We can talk about Ellie later."

Harry looked much more cheerful now that I had been knocked off my perfect-child pedestal. As soon as the meal was over, he announced that he was taking me home, which was cool with me. I needed to take Billy out to piddle, assuming he hadn't already peed all over the bathroom, and if I stayed, Mother was sure to rake me over the coals about Ellie.

I felt a headache coming on and wasn't in the mood to confess my plan to Mother, but I wasn't crazy about the idea of lying to her about my involvement with Ellie, either. Avoidance really was the best solution.

Harry slammed the door to his Chevy Nova and rocketed down the drive, barely tapping his brakes at the stop sign before careening toward the outlet for the cul-de-sac. "I'm ready to move out," he announced.

"Since when?" I gripped the armrest and closed my eyes.

"Since now."

"I thought you liked having Mother cook and clean for you. It's like your own personal maid service, but it's free."

"So why don't you still live at home?"

"Because it's pathetic to still live at home."

"Then that's why I want to move out, too."

I grinned. "You're in the doghouse."

"I want to do what I want, when I want, and have whomever I want over."

"Hah! Mother caught you with a girl, didn't she?"

Harry scowled and merged onto the freeway at ninety miles an hour, swerving across three lanes of traffic, oblivious to indignant horns and fingers. "I don't want to talk about it."

"I knew it. She busted you with one of your little girlfriends. Were you making too much noise?"

"She and Walter were supposed to be gone, okay? They missed their movie and came back. Walter probably got the time wrong." He changed lanes on a whim, without apparent reason or logic.

"Walked in on you? Wait. You aren't saying she came into your room?" Harry's room above the garage was sacrosanct. Mother never set foot in there if she could help it.

"I said I didn't want to talk about it," he said through clenched teeth.

My eyes narrowed. "You weren't in your room, were you?" This detective stuff was fun. "You were on the couch. Please say you weren't actually boinking this girl on Mother's couch."

"Hah, hah, hah. Glad my life is so hilarious. I most certainly was boinking Angelique and having a damn good time if you must know. Geez, you would think no one ever had sex before the way she carried on. I guess it's not as fine as boinking a doctor. Are you done making fun of me?"

"For now."

"Good. 'Cause your getting evicted is perfect timing."

"Excuse me?"

"We should get a place together. Roommates. I could afford a way better place with a roommate. So could you. The problem is, most people piss you off."

"You piss me off, too."

"But we can live together. This is a proven fact."

It was a proven fact. Harry and I could live together without bloodshed. We had done so in the past. "Did you have a place in mind?"

"How about never being evicted again?"

"What do you mean?"

"We should buy a condo. They're selling these condos over in Benton. It's not far from your new gig, and I know you love the city but it's close enough. If we pooled our incomes, I'll bet we could swing it."

"I don't know." Benton is an older 'burb close to Canterbury Park. It's cute and a little trendy, but at least it's not like the McBurbs stuffed with chains and strip malls. "Benton's got a lot of older buildings." Which were probably riddled with ghosts. "Old buildings have problems."

"This is all new construction. You should see the pictures. It's a cool building and the condos look plush. We could pick the interior. They've already got the exteriors built. With the housing market the way it is, things are really cheap. It's a good time to buy, and I know you have savings. You squirrel away your pennies. There's even a little courtyard for your dog to piddle in. He's not destructive, is he?"

"Not at all," I lied. "Besides, he's going to live with Ellie soon. Okay, I'll think about it."

"I'll take you out there tomorrow and show it to you. They've got a real town square, and the condo building is right in the commercial district so you can walk places. And there's bus service, too. Plus you can borrow my car whenever."

"Enough." I held up my hands. "I'll look."

* * * *

Billy was happily stretched out on mounds of fluffy stuffing spread around the bathroom. Rip-proof dog bed, my ass.

I took him outside so he could contribute to the small colony of dog turds he had deposited under the scraggly evergreens. Someone would have a nasty surprise when the stench of summer arrived, but we would be long gone by then so I really didn't care.

I did care about the messages I had on my voice mail. Starla and Corinne both watched in stony silence as I hit play. The first message was from Ethan. "Hi, Portia. Just called to say I had a great time last night and I hope you did, too. Maybe we could get together for dinner this week. Give me a call."

Yes! Yesyesyes! I danced and hugged my phone. "He called." Ethan had perfect timing. He had waited a full day, which was appropriately eager, but not too stalker-ish. And he had lobbed the ball back into my court by asking me to call him. Oh yeah. I was gonna keep him around even if he was—

"He's too short for you," Starla said. She had apparently mastered the art of chewing gum and smoking simultaneously, neither of which I was aware that ghosts could do. But since I couldn't smell the smoke, maybe it was a ghostly illusion. "You look stupid together."

"I can't believe you're wasting time on a date while our murders go unsolved," Corinne said.

"Hey, I spent the day on you guys. I humiliated myself with a detective and got Corinne's old job. Both of you can shut the hell up."

The next message was from Susie Simpson. "I don't know if you remember me. I'm Corinne Simpson's aunt." Corinne made a strangled little noise. "I'm flying into town in two days, and I wondered if you could help me go and get Corinne's stuff. Ruth hasn't been real helpful." She left me her number.

"Goodie for both of you," Starla snarled. "Meanwhile, I'm lying dead under a woodpile and nobody gives a shit. The only person who missed me was my boss, and that was because I didn't show up for work."

Billy was thrilled with all the activity. Snorking happily, he raced off to the bedroom. A moment later he was triumphantly carrying his favorite toy, which I had nicknamed Dingo. Don't ask why.

He noisily savaged Dingo, tossing him and catching him and shaking him from side to side as violently as a dog with no neck can. I had excess energy myself, but my mode of attack was cleaning my apartment. In the bedroom, I made a disturbing discovery. It hadn't shown up on the buff carpet that was the same color as his coat, but the corner of my bed where Billy slept was covered in pug fur.

Pugs shed.

A lot.

I located a lint roller in dresser, but I was going to need a bunch of them.

Billy dragged Dingo into the room, tossing and catching him.

"How come you aren't bald?" I made a fourth pass over my crimson comforter with the lint roller.

He blinked his bug eyes and wheezed, his tongue hanging out the side.

Before bed, I had to take Billy outside again to do his business. Starla and Corinne followed me out there.

I stood by the bushes, barely paying attention, and tried to decide if the pot of boiling water in my kitchen should be used for cinnamon tea or chamomile. Maybe a nice mint tea.

At the same moment the foul odor hit my nose, Billy's hackles rose and he growled. A more menacing rumble came from another throat.

"Run," I yelled.

Corinne screeched and went one way. Starla went the other. The demon threw back its head and bayed like a hound at the moon.

"Ar-ar-ar-ar." Billy barked for all he was worth.

The demon hesitated and then pursued Corinne, who fled in the direction of my apartment. It disappeared through my front door, and I raced after it, flinging my door wide open. The demon stood in my kitchen, with its nose raised, like an animal scenting the air, methodically sniffing my cabinets.

I ran in, heedless of Billy barking madly at my heels. "Stay away from her. You aren't welcome here."

The demon paused and said something in its guttural voice.

"Did you hear me? Leave! I command you to leave!"

I swear it laughed. It raised arms equipped with glistening claws and heaved its sluglike bulk at me. I grabbed the only thing I could think of to swing at it.

The teapot shattered as it struck the demon, spraying the creature with boiling water and burning my hands. I hadn't expected the thing to be so solid. It howled in agony and then fled through my kitchen wall.

For a moment I lost Billy, but he peeked out from behind the sofa. He hadn't been underfoot when the pot had shattered.

A few minutes under cold water helped my red, painful hands, and some aloe helped a great deal. My arms had been protected by my thick coat.

I had learned two important things. First: this place wasn't safe. The demon knew it could find ghosts here. Second: demons can be hurt by boiling water. It wasn't the most practical weapon, but good to know.

When I went to hang up my coat, I made a startling discovery. In the fray, the demon had swiped my coat. Three long, parallel slices gaped on the right side of the coat, revealing the white filler material.

Demons are dangerous.

Make that three things I learned.

Chapter 10

It was my last free morning before starting back to work, and the knock on my door surprised me. I checked the peephole, expecting to see the manager with eviction papers, but it was a poorly dressed hulk.

I couldn't think of a good reason for Detective Fierro to show up at my front door. I combed my hair with my fingers. My curls are lovely when properly tamed, but look like an orange fright wig first thing in the morning. Since I slept in sweats, I was sort of dressed.

He smiled when I opened the door, but I wasn't fooled. Lots of nasty things had smiled at me lately, including a demon. "Good morning, Ms. Mahaffey."

"Miss," I said. "It's miss. Come on in." My hands were faintly pink this morning. Fierro noticed everything.

"Burn yourself?"

"I broke a teapot. But I have plenty of coffee. Want some?"

"Coffee's good."

I gestured to the kitchen table, mercifully free of the card players, and Fierro took a seat. He was a big guy, but moved with a sort of grace, the bulky outline more a function of bad clothing than a body gone to fat. His shirt stretched tighter as he leaned back in his chair. The man had muscles.

"Milk? Sugar? I've got half-and-half, too."

"Black," he said. "When you're a cop as long as I been one, you learn to drink coffee however you can get it."

I poured him a large mug of coffee and refilled my own, adding some froufrou French vanilla creamer until it was a lovely beige. "How long have you been a cop?"

"Nine years. I've spent the last four in the CAP Unit."

"The what?" I placed his cup in front of him and seated myself across the table.

"Crimes Against Persons." He sipped his coffee. "Rape, robbery, homicide. All the violent things people do to one another. This is good," he said appreciatively. "French roast?"

"Kona. Special blend that I buy at Baer's Deli."

"They make the best kolaches in the city."

"They do." I leaned back. "You know Baer's?"

"You kidding me? I'm a cop. I know every donut shop and bakery in the city."

"I'm guessing this visit has nothing to do bakeries and coffee blends."

He took a long drink of his brew. "You and your cousin have a lot in common, I think."

I was wary. "Eleanor?"

"You've got other cousins?"

"I do."

"Well, she's the only one I know, so that's how I'm referencing. You look like her."

I didn't think so, other than height and hair color, but these are such obvious identifiers that I get that a lot. "People seem to think so."

"I think maybe the resemblance goes deeper than superficial stuff like being exceptionally tall."

"I don't know what you mean."

"Corinne Simpson shared a room with you at the hospital." He leaned forward. "Isn't that interesting? Her being your bosom buddy and all? What are the odds? And then you show up on my doorstep asking all kinds of questions and making accusations about her being murdered. And full of information."

My mouth was dry. I gulped some coffee. "Quite a coincidence." The bitter brew burned its way down to my churning stomach.

"And then you call me up out of the blue about another gal, claiming she's been murdered."

"Ellie got a vibe."

"Ellie don't know nothing about this. She gets vibes off of objects. You got nothing belonging to Starla Mueller."

"What are you saying?"

"This has nothing to do with Ellie. You never met Corinne Simpson or Starla Mueller. Have you?"

"Yes, I have."

"Were they alive?"

I stared back. My mouth worked for a minute before anything came out. "No," I finally admitted. "No, they weren't."

"That's what I thought." He took a long drink from his coffee.

"So what are you going to do?"

"About what?" He raised his eyebrows.

"About me, I mean?"

"What do you want me to do? I came to you for information."

I allowed myself to breathe. "I never wanted this. I don't want anyone to know, either."

"That you're psychic?"

"Clairvoyant."

"There's a difference?"

"I prefer clairvoyant. I can't tell the future. I just...I hear things from spirits. Psychic sounds so shady, like I should have an infomercial."

"I see. And you want it to be a secret."

I sighed. "I respect what Ellie does, but I am not her. I don't want to be on TV or in the papers."

"These spirits contacted you? Is that how it works?"

"Something like that. I swear, I never meant to get involved. First it was Corinne and now Starla. I was in the hospital because I hit my head, and when I woke up, I saw ghosts. Then Starla found me and...you believe I talk to dead people? Ellie said you were a skeptic."

"I believe it's the only logical explanation."

"So yes?"

"I believe you. For now. You're sure Corinne Simpson was murdered?"

"She thinks so. What I told you at the station is her recollection. She ate someone's burrito out of the break room and started having symptoms immediately. The heart medicine was probably intended for the owner of that burrito."

"That's a good guess. She have any idea who it belonged to?"

I shook my head. "No, she was just hungry."

"So find the owner of said burrito and we might have a clue as to motive."

This was the opportunity to tell him about taking Corinne's job at Wollencroft Agricultural Research, but I didn't. I was pretty sure he wouldn't approve, and quite frankly, the money was too good to pass up. "Then again, Corinne had a tendency to graze the fridge. If someone wanted her dead, the burrito could have been a plant."

"Pretty risky move. Anyone could have eaten it."

"About Starla Mueller," I said.

"I went to see the husband, Joby."

"And?" I prompted. "What did he say? Did he lawyer up?"

"Don't watch so much TV. I went by to follow up on the missing person report, to see if he's heard from his wife."

"Which he hadn't."

"Actually, he claims he heard from Starla."

"But that's a lie!"

"He claims she called him two days ago from California."

"What about her stuff? I'll bet all her stuff was still at their apartment."

"It's all gone. Joby claims he gave it to her, that he shipped it to California, but he doesn't remember the address and he doesn't know how to contact her. She told him she's never coming back."

"Starla is dead." My face felt as red and angry as my hands.

"I believe that," he said.

"You do?"

He smiled, and I was reminded of Aunt Bella's cat whenever a bird flew into the window. It wasn't a nice smile. "Joby recently made a large donation of women's clothing to Goodwill. He insisted on a receipt for tax purposes. Oh, and he never received a call from California on his home phone, according to phone records."

"That proves it."

"That proves Joby is a terrible liar."

"But you can get a warrant now, right? You can dig Starla back up." Seeing the look on his face, I added, "That's really important to her. She wants a proper burial. And Joby's ass in a sling."

"I wish it was enough, but it isn't."

"But he lied."

"Which isn't against the law. It doesn't get us any closer to showing a judge probable cause to believe that Starla Mueller is dead and buried near her husband's cabin."

"Did you ask him about the cabin?"

"He claims he hasn't been there in months."

"This is so frustrating. What can I do?"

"I need information. Starting with, where was Starla killed?"

"In a car. Joby strangled her, put her in the trunk and drove her out there to the cabin. She's buried under the woodpile. That's all I know."

"When exactly did he kill her?"

"I don't know. I'll ask her when I see her."

"Can you call her?" He looked around the room as if he might locate her. "Is she here now?"

"It doesn't work that way. When Starla makes contact, I'll ask her. Anything else?"

"Where and when and why are a good start."

"I think I know why or at least part of it. Joby has a girlfriend. I don't remember her name."

"A lot of people seem to think murder is cheaper than divorce. Find out about the honey. That could be important."

We exchanged cell numbers before he left.

My initial flush of excitement faded, replaced by throbbing hands and a frisson of unease. If word of what I was doing ever got out, Mother would trip.

As if on a mother-daughter psychic connection, she called. Intellectually, I comprehend that she doesn't really know when I've done something wrong, but this happens often enough that it's spooky. Given my family, anything is possible.

"Pick up, Portia. I know you're there. This is your mother," she added unnecessarily. "We never finished that conversation."

I slouched over to the phone and did what I was told. "Good morning, Mother."

"What was that little crack about working with Ellie during dinner?"

"I never said anything about working with Ellie. I said I was giving the dog to Ellie." I glanced around to make sure Corinne wasn't hovering. She still thought I was keeping Billy.

"And why were you over at Ellie's house?"

"She's my cousin."

"You've never been close. You two have nothing in common."

"Okay, I needed an in with the police. I took them what I heard about the girl who died in my hospital room. Only we pretended that Ellie had gotten some vibes. That's the extent of my working with her."

This was true. Ellie was still furious over my little stunt with the file. She had agreed to an object reading, but I filed that away as Too Much Information. I didn't lie to my mother. I just didn't tell her everything.

After I soothed Mother and convinced her I would not be appearing in any episodes of Ellie's *Psychic Investigators* show and promised to choke down another desiccated pot roast on Sunday, I hung up and went to start my shower.

Corinne huddled by the commode, a far cry from her high-flying self that had been swooping around. Her eyes were dry, but red and swollen. "What was that thing last night?" she whispered.

I crouched down next to her and wished I could pat her shoulder. How much could I tell her without screwing things up? "That was a demon. I burned it, but it could come back. Better to stay inside and stay hidden. Better still, cross over and let me handle things."

"Not yet," she insisted. "I want to go to work with you once or twice. You might need me."

"That would be fine. We'll go tomorrow."

If she wanted to be suicidally brave, who was I to argue?

* * * *

My first day at Wollencroft Agricultural Research started off as any new job. I had a photo ID made, filled out my tax information and Duncan Werner showed me to my cubicle. There were fewer people there than I had expected. Apparently Woll Ag had multiple facilities.

This was a relatively small one since the scientists here did mostly field research. And the field research was done primarily, well, in a field. The first and second floors belonged to the laboratories where research assistants and folks in white coats ran around doing goodness knows what with machines that simply went by acronyms such as GSMC. The secretaries were on the third floor. We provided support to the various scientists, RAs and lab techs as needed. Administrative types were on the fourth floor. Third and fourth floor didn't mix. Likewise, the first two floors required special clearance passes to enter. There was one place where they all came together: the break room in the northwest corner of the third floor.

Duncan Werner sashayed down the hall and pushed open double swinging doors. "This is where you will take your lunch. Woll Ag is a closed campus, so to speak." He waved a languid hand at the bank of gleaming stainless steel appliances along the far wall. "There's a microwave, coffeepot, espresso machine, and a little fridge with sodas and bottled water, which are free. Don't abuse the privilege. There's the water cooler, and paper cups are in the cabinet. If you're a coffee drinker, you can leave your own mug here. You have thirty minutes for lunch. Bring your own or take your chances with the vending machines."

On the short wall to my right were three machines stuffed with questionable sandwiches, ice cream and the usual chips, cookies, pretzels, fruit bars and gum.

He paused and lowered his voice. "You might want to write your name on your lunch in large letters. We've had a problem in the past with food disappearing."

There were ten small tables with metal and plastic chairs in two neat rows in the middle of the room. Each table had exactly four chairs. Someone had a fetish for symmetry and order.

Next was a tour of the cubicles and introduction to the other secretaries. The cubicles were around the edges in a big square. In the center was a work area with copiers, printers, scanners, etc. There was a single office in the corner with huge plate glass windows. Duncan stopped there and smirked. "That is my office. I'm your supervisor and boss. You work for me, not Dr. Tamaguchi. If you have a problem with any of the scientists, don't argue. Just take it up with me. I'm confident you won't have a problem with any of the girls. All of my girls get on extremely well." He clasped his hands together. "Ready to meet everyone? Of course you are."

We strolled down the row of cubicles. He touched each 'girl' on the shoulder as we passed. Most of the 'girls' were at least forty. Some were nearing on sixty. "This is Gayle." A grandmotherly type smiled behind pince-nez glasses. "This is Beth." Beth graced me with a sour grimace that probably doubled as a smile. And so it went, on around the square until we got to the last desk. "And this is my secretary." Since when did a secretary need a secretary? "She does most of the transcribing work and assists me in whatever I need." She had on a headset and was busily nattering away with her back to us. He tapped her shoulder and she turned. We locked eyes and her jaw dropped.

"This is Ruth." Duncan stroked his goatee.

"I've gotta go," she said into her wireless set. "What's she doing here?" She turned accusingly to Duncan, who surprised me by taking a step backward.

"This is Portia, the new girl. She's taking the vacancy."

"You mean replacing Corinne? Why? Why her?"

"I'm perfectly qualified, Ruth. Why shouldn't I be here?"

"Did she tell you that she knew Corinne?"

Duncan glanced around. "Maybe we should go into my office."

Ruth leapt to her feet and strode down to his office. Her beady eyes were furious. I wondered idly where she got her nice Anne Taylor twin set and pencil skirt. It fit her a lot better than Corinne's sweater had. If I wasn't mistaken, her shoes were Jimmy Choo. I ought to know. Cruella had been seriously addicted to Jimmy Choo. If he made it, she bought it.

Duncan closed the door. "Now what is this about? I take it you two know each other?"

"She came to my apartment and forced her way in, claiming to be friends with Corinne."

Duncan cocked his head, reminding me of Billy. "I'm not following."

"I did know Corinne," I said. "After she died, I went to get her dog. I promised to look after him."

"I told her I gave him away, but she forced her way in." Ruth's face flushed. "She was very unpleasant. I don't know what game you're running here."

"There is no 'game.' I was keeping a promise. As for working here, Corinne always said it was a good place to work. We didn't talk that much about it, but I was looking for a new job and there was one open here. That's all there is."

"I bet she didn't tell you she knew Corinne. Did she? Huh? Did you?" Ruth's eyes had taken on a wild light. She had a fresh haircut, and were those new highlights?

"I don't think it came up. I didn't want to get the job that way. I let my credentials speak for themselves."

"I'll handle this, Ruth. That will be all." Duncan waved his hand. Her squinty eyes bugged in an unattractive way at being dismissed, but she was careful not to slam the door on the way out.

"I don't know what's passed between you and Ruth, but is there going to be a problem with you two working together?"

"Not with me. I'm surprised she feels so strongly about it. I don't really know her." But I hate her. "No problem at all."

"Excellent."

He showed me back to my cubicle and piled on a stack of work which consisted of turning handwritten correspondence into something resembling the English language. There was a reason these guys were scientists and not English teachers.

After an hour, I needed to stretch; a nice woman who told me her name was Dawn pointed me in the direction of the ladies' room.

"She's such a mean girl. I should have listened to Billy. He never liked her."

I checked under the bathroom stalls before answering Corinne. "So other than Ruth being more hateful than you thought, have we learned anything yet?"

"No," she said wistfully. "I've been wandering around. I wish I could say goodbye, especially to Dr. Seleman."

The door opened and another girl came in, effectively cutting off the conversation. We gave one another polite smiles. I busied myself washing my hands.

"I'll keep my eyes and ears open," Corinne whispered.

* * * *

My cubicle sat by the opening into the center of the square housing the community copiers and fax machines. I had read the same paragraph three times when a man wandered by who absolutely had to be a scientist. He had a friar's bald spot surrounded by frizzy gray hair and glasses perched so far down on the end of his nose that he was forced to tilt his chin upward to look through them. He wore stained khakis, appropriate for field work, but his most striking feature was his footwear: one blue sneaker and one gray one. Perhaps he was colorblind.

He seemed lost.

"Can I help you?" It was doubtful since I knew less of the layout than he did, but it seemed the polite thing to say.

"No...I'm sure...here somewhere... I... Oh. There it is. I was looking for the room with all the faxes and such. Can't understand why they insist on hiding it."

I held out a hand for the papers. "I can do that for you."

"I don't mind," he said cheerfully. "It's only two pages." He went into the copy room, but was back out a few minutes later. "The fax machine doesn't seem to be working properly."

"How about I take a quick look? Maybe it needs toner or something." I got to my feet. "I'm pretty good with most fax machines."

"No, no, no. I can actually repair it myself. Not helpless, you know. Be right back. I'm very good mechanically." He said this with great confidence.

True to his word, he was back a few moments later with a small leather pouch of gleaming tools. I rose out of my chair with alarm. "Sir?"

"Why, I haven't introduced myself. I'm Dr. Seleman."

Of course. Corinne had been right. No way this man could be a crazed poisoner. "Portia Mahaffey. Pleased to meet you. How about I call facilities?"

"You must be new."

"I took Corinne Simpson's place."

"Ah, yes. Sad. She was so young."

"How about I call the repair company directly?"

"No need," he said airily.

I rushed back to my desk, hunting for Duncan's extension as Dr. Seleman removed the faceplate off the fax machine.

When he delved into the guts of the machine, I gave up and ran for Duncan's office. Duncan looked up in alarm as I bolted into his office.

"Dr. Seleman is fixing the fax machine," I gasped.

"Oh, shit!" Duncan sprang to his feet. "You left him alone?"

"What else could I do? I couldn't stop him."

We raced around to the far corner to gain access to the copy room. By the time we ran in Seleman had already dismantled the fax machine into little bits and pieces.

"I've almost got it completely apart," he said triumphantly. He had a huge black smear of toner across his face as he held up a glass tube that looked vitally important. "I'll have it right as rain in no time."

"I'm sure that will be a great help to the service rep." Duncan bent over and gently took the man's screwdriver away and replaced it in the leather pouch. "Thank you, Dr. Seleman, but I'm sure you have important things to do." He helped him to his feet.

"It was no trouble, really." Dr. Seleman seemed pleased, but a little bewildered at his tools being put away. "Glad I could help." He wandered off.

Duncan pointed upwards with his index finger. "Rule number one. Never, ever let one of the scientists near the fax machine. Or the copier. Or the scanner. They may be brilliant in their fields, but they can't resist fixing things."

"I'm sorry, I--"

"I know. I know." He put his hand up. "It was your first day. I should have told you. Your cubicle is guardian of the electronics. You have my permission to do anything necessary to stop them. I don't care what you do. You work for me, not them. Got it?"

"There wasn't anything I could do short of grabbing him."

"Next time tackle him. And don't forget to wrap up."

Chapter 11

I managed to keep the rest of the electronics intact until lunchtime. My reward was the tuna on wheat I'd packed because I sure wasn't eating anything that came out of the fridge here.

At the threshold of the break room I had a moment of anxiety. I was back in junior high, going to a strange school and I had no one to sit with at lunch. A group of the 'girls' saved me from slinking into the corner. They busily disrupted the careful order of the room by pushing the tables together and dragging over chairs. They waved me into a spot and introduced themselves, not that I would remember many of the names.

I checked up and down the row at everyone's lunches. Not a burrito in sight. There were salads in cute little plastic bowls, a variety of frozen diet meals and a scary container of mystery leftovers that smelled faintly of cabbage when Dawn heated it in the microwave. Gayle and Beth locked eyes and rolled them. Two distinct cliques were starting to emerge. The seniors versus the freshmen.

Gayle smiled winningly at me. "Corinne always sat with us," she said. The younger ladies were at the far end of the table. Everyone looked at me expectantly as I dropped into the empty chair at the older ladies' end. I had the feeling I had just been told which team I was playing for. Interesting that Corinne, in spite of her age, had spent more time with the older women. She probably didn't have much in common with her thinner, hipper counterparts.

Ruth swished in and carried her lunch down to the younger ladies' side. She had to get her own chair and wedge in. Beth and Ruth traded glares. Ruth ignored me, and that was fine. Invisible was good in this circumstance.

A gaggle of men strode in, and all went to the fridge to pull out lunches. Beth leaned over. "Research assistants," she muttered. The guys took a table by themselves down at the end. "Ted, Tom, Trent and Trey," Beth said. They were as interchangeable as their names. Brown hair and eyes, khakis and a blue shirt with the Woll Ag logo. I watched them spread out their lunches. Again, no burrito.

I stood up. "I need a drink from the fridge." I strode over and opened the door. There it was. A small stack of burritos waiting to claimed and heated. "Whose are these?" I demanded. Blank stares all around. "Whose burritos?" More blank stares and a few uneasy shrugs. "Well, who isn't here?"

More stares. I was obviously breaching etiquette, but I pressed on. "Could they belong to one of the scientists? Do they eat with you guys?"

Finally Beth spoke up. "They eat whenever their schedules permit. I don't know who those belong to. Did you want one?"

My shoulders sagged. "Never mind." I grabbed a bottle of water and turned back to the table.

I was dealing with an actual murderer here, someone who had been desperate enough to kill, but patient enough to wait for poison. If someone had poisoned one burrito from the stack, they would have to wait until the right one was selected. If they had poisoned all of them, then they didn't care who might get hurt.

Ruth stared at me with wide eyes; her whole wheat sandwich paused halfway to her lips; her mouth hung open to receive a bite that hadn't arrived.

She knew.

The look in her eyes said it all. She knew about the burrito.

And she knew that I knew.

I had just put a huge target on my back.

* * * *

The air outside was still and cold, with that sharp expectant feel that promised precipitation tonight. I was going out anyway. I had a follow-up date with Ethan, and after a tense day looking over my shoulder, I deserved a reward. Poking at a murderer is bad for the nerves.

Harry was late of course. I was the last person there, a human Popsicle by the time Harry pulled up in the blue van.

"Sorry," he said as I climbed in. "I had a pickup on the way. Old Man Biddle finally had a heart attack. Can you believe it? I thought the old freak would live forever."

Old Man Biddle had lived down the street from Mother and Walter. He was the stuff of childish nightmares: the old man who lived alone in his creepy house, ranting and raving at anyone who set foot on his lawn. If your ball went over his fence, you could kiss it goodbye. As we got older, a favorite dare was to ring the doorbell and run. Of course the legend was that his house was haunted, but Mother insisted it wasn't and I believed her. She ought to know.

He was nothing but a cranky old man, but I shifted uneasily in my seat. "He's back there now?"

"Yeah, he's in the cooler. The weird sisters are going to work on him tonight. His niece is in a hurry for the funeral. Not a lot of warmth there. But first, there's something I want to show you."

He smoked his tires leaving the lot, taking the curve fast enough to fishtail the van.

"Harry, I need to get to the train station. I want to catch the five-forty."

"What? You've got a date tonight?"

He laughed like it was funny. I braced myself against the unexpected lane swerves and held on tight. "As a matter of fact, I do. With the doctor."

"Yippy-skippy for you. This will only take a sec."

"You shouldn't drive like this with a body in the back. It could bounce him around."

"Like he's going to complain."

"Whatever it is, you can show me another time. Take me to the station and Old Man Biddle to the funeral home."

"Don't sweat it, Portia. I'll get you there in time." He stomped the accelerator, and the van leapt forward. I closed my eyes. "And Old Man Biddle's got nothing but time."

"Says you," yelled a querulous voice from the back of the van. "Damn kid. Always driving like a maniac." I sagged back into my seat. Of course he would be a ghost. Biddle was that type of man.

The tires smoked again as the van screeched to a halt.

"Jeez, don't be so dramatic," Harry said. "Open your eyes." It was a construction zone, still all wooden beams and large machines. But there was a big blowup picture of what the building would look like when the renovations were done. I looked around. "Well?" Harry said impatiently. "Nice neighborhood, right?"

It was. "This is where you want us to live?"

He was already climbing out of the van. "C'mon. Come see the building. If the front office is open, you can look at the brochures."

Fighting Harry when he's set on something is like resisting a force of nature. Hurricane Harry. I trailed after him.

"Hey! What about me? You can't leave my body here. What if somebody steals me? You didn't even lock the van. Piece of shit Mahaffeys. I'm goin' back to guard my body, since you brats couldn't care less." Biddle groused all the way up the steps. I ignored him, pretending not to hear. Maybe he would go away. I wasn't about to befriend the old bastard.

The front office was locked, so I had to settle for tromping around the edges. It looked pretty nice, with a castle motif going on. The front entry had two pseudo-towers, and the roof was crenellated. "New construction, you say?" I made the mistake of asking about price and gagged. "You have got to be joking."

"It's okay. Mother said she could help with the down payment. We can get the financing down to something affordable. I already talked to Richard."

"Ellie's husband Richard?"

"Yeah, he says we can do it. What do you say?"

"The same thing I said yesterday. I'll think about it. I want to come back and see the plans and crunch the numbers for real. Then I'll decide." My eyes narrowed slightly. "What was here before? Was it residential? Did they knock down a bunch of old houses?"

"It was commercial. I think maybe a warehouse or something."

That sounded safe. Down the street was a cemetery and church, but contrary to popular opinion, Mother swears they aren't especially haunted. Ghosts tend to stay somewhere important to them, not where their bodies came to rest. With demons roaming, I could see benefits to living near sacred ground.

* * * *

As always, I was on the lookout at the train station, but I saw neither the demon nor the missing Mr. Lester. Even Corinne had deserted me. When I opened the door to my apartment, Billy reclined on the couch with his chewed-up bed and Dingo, both of which he had dragged up there. I'd forgotten to put him in the bathroom. He wasn't the least bit embarrassed to be caught on the couch and actually jumped up on the back of it, snorking joyfully.

"It's nice to be wanted," I said. "Anyone else here?"

No answer.

I hadn't seen Corinne since this morning. More worrisome, I hadn't seen Starla since the demon attack.

I took Billy out to add to the turd pile and pee on some tires. I had agreed to meet Ethan at the hospital. Even though it was threatening rain, I refused to wear a hat and squash my curls. I debated between practical boots and the ones with stiletto heels. The train doesn't go near the hospital, and I would have to hike three blocks from the nearest bus stop. Vanity won out, and I wore the stilettos. By the time I got to Our Lady of Mercy Hospital, my feet shrieked in pain, my ears were completely numb and I was wondering how long it took to get frostbite.

I walked through the double doors to find Hephzibah kicked back in one of the vinyl chairs in a red velour tracksuit. "How you doing, doll? Here to see that yummy doc?"

I looked around the room. There was at least one ghost for every human. "Holy shit," I breathed.

"I warned you about this place. Hospitals are the worst."

Heads turned. "They think I'm talking to myself," I whispered, dropping into a chair next to her. The orange vinyl squeaked.

"I can take myself out of invisible mode." She blinked. "How's this?"

"You don't look any different," I said.

"Not to you." She turned to the woman next to her whose mouth had dropped open. "How you doing, hon? They got you checked in yet?" The woman nodded, her jaw still slack. "That's real good." Hephzibah turned back to me. "All better."

The poorly lit orange and blue waiting room reminded me of a Howard Johnson.

"Can you see me?" A stringy-haired teenager floated over me.

"'Course she can. You can see all of us, right? Can you deliver messages?" a woman asked.

"Not now," Hephzibah said. "We're in a full room." The woman seated next to her got up and moved four rows away. "Good. Now everyone go away and leave this girl be. She ain't here for you."

I swallowed. I had no idea so many ghosts could exist in one place. "There's so many of them."

Hephzibah nodded solemnly. "Now you know why the Reclaimers were called forth. Things were getting crowded. Used to be that everyone was eager to cross over, but people ain't got faith no more. They don't believe, doll."

From the corner of my eye, I saw a shadow move. One minute the shadow was part of the wall, the next it was part of a rolling cart. I tried to fix on the image, but the shadow melted into the other shadows in the waiting room and I lost track of it.

"See something, doll?" Hephzibah asked sharply.

"I thought I saw a shadow walk."

Hephzibah closed her eyes. "Oh, damn. I was hoping you wouldn't have to see this for a long time."

"See what?"

From the other side of the room, another shadow moved so quickly I barely had time to register the shape of a man with too-long arms, more gorilla than human. It loped along on its hands and feet.

"Reclaimers!" shrieked a woman. "Reclaimers!"

Chapter 12

Ghosts screamed, fleeing in all directions, and the shadows moved. Shady figures crawled from every crevice. They swarmed the room, grabbing for ghosts with their thick arms.

Reclaimers swarmed the stringy-haired ghost in front of me, wrapping their arms completely around him. Dark shadows covered his mouth and arms. He was immobilized, but his eyes bugged with fear.

The Reclaimers made a noise, deep inside their featureless faces. I felt the rumble in my chest before I heard it. It started as a low hum that made everything vibrate and tremble. The tile floor cracked, splitting open, melting away tile until it was a hot maw with jagged tiles like teeth, spewing a weird, deep blue fire. The indigo flames seemed to have a life of their own and reached up like grabbing hands. More Reclaimers poured from the hole.

It might not look like any fire I'd seen before, but the heat searing my skin was real enough to make me draw my feet up into the chair. Blue flames raced across the floor, crawled up the walls and over the lights until everything was darkness and heat and sound.

A woman wiggled loose enough to scream, but her mouth was quickly covered again as Reclaimers dragged their thrashing prey into the hole. One youngster, barely more than a teenager, made a break from his hiding place. He skimmed the ceiling, heading for the back wall. A hand lashed out of the pit and snaked around his ankle with a hideous popping sound.

The low hum rose to a shattering wail. I clapped my hands over my ears, unable to bear the building decibels. The sound hammered at me like a fist. Two more hands caught the boy around his knees and waist. The teenager scrabbled helplessly on the floor as he was pulled down into the dark flames. I couldn't hear his screams, but his mouth was locked open with terror.

An absolute silence blanketed the chaos. The floor tiles stretched like closing lips until the crevice sealed.

Oblivious, the living walked, read, chewed gum, checked watches.

"It's over, doll. Sit up," Hephzibah said. I had curled into a fetal position on the chair.

I gradually uncurled. "That's what will happen to Corinne?"

"She has until midnight tomorrow. Then the mark will fade."

I shivered. "What about Starla? How long does she have?" Tears collected in the corners of my eyes, threatening to spill. I couldn't let this happen to Corinne after she had been through so much.

"Starla's time is up, doll. She died before Corinne. She's in play."

I couldn't let it happen to either woman. "I've got to warn her. Have you seen her? Do you know where she is?"

Hephzibah shook her head.

"There you are. Hope you haven't been waiting long." Ethan crossed the same floor that had been a gateway to hell only moments before. "Who's this?"

"Oh, shit," Hephzibah muttered. "Forgot I'm not invisible."

"Not too long," I said. "This is, uh…"

"Helen. I'm an old friend of Portia's mom. Me and her family go way back. I'm here visiting friends. Got to go, doll. See you soon." She tottered off down the hall. Fortunately, Ethan turned around and didn't see Hephzibah walk through the back wall.

"I need to finish marking a few things on a chart and sign off on something and I'm done." He glanced around. "Sorry for making you wait. This place can be pretty grim."

You have no idea. "Just hurry. I'm starving and I need a drink like you wouldn't believe."

"Great." He looked up at me. "I can't wait to hear about your first day with the new job."

A nurse in pink floral scrubs walked up. "One more, Ethan?"

"I haven't even finished the paperwork on the last one, Lisa, and I need to be going."

The nurse looked at me with pleading eyes. "Can you spare him for a few more minutes? We're really shorthanded."

I had made reservations at a very nice French place. I glanced at my watch.

"Excuse me?" A frazzled woman in a baggy coat tapped the nurse on her shoulder. "How much longer?"

"I'm working on it. If you'll have a seat over there, someone will be with you shortly."

Behind the frazzled woman, a girl with enormous eyes had a dish cloth wrapped around her hand.

"Is this your little girl?" Ethan crossed over to her and knelt down. "What's your name?"

"Lucy."

I could barely hear her soft voice.

"Nice to meet you, Lucy. My name is Dr. Ethan." He glanced over at me and I nodded.

"Do what you need to," I said.

"What seems to be the problem, Lucy?"

"She was helping me in the kitchen and her hand slipped. We were cutting vegetables," the mother said.

Ethan smiled. "Do you like vegetables, Lucy?"

"No, but I like to cook," she said.

Ethan peeled back the dish cloth a little. It had a lot of blood in it. "That's a yucky cut on your thumb. It's going to need stitches. But we can take care of you right away." He looked up at the pink nurse. "Do we have an empty room, Lisa?"

It was another two hours before we left. The ghosts who had escaped the Reclaimers never came back. I read the magazines and then wandered around chatting up the nurses. The consensus was that Dr. Ethan Feller was quite a catch, which left me to wonder why such a catch was still on the market.

Nobody said anything, but I could see the smirks and half smiles as the nurses noticed my height.

I called Le Cuisine and cancelled the reservations, despite the snooty man on the other end who informed me that no one ever cancelled *Le Cuisine.*

"Well, let me be your first. Something's come up. An emergency." That was sort of true. "We won't be there."

I was half-asleep, curled in one of the vinyl chairs, when a hand on my shoulder woke me. Ethan squatted down next to my chair. "Sorry about that. Things always take longer than you would think."

"It's okay," I said, and it really was.

"I know a great Mediterranean place right around the corner," he said. "It's not fancy, but the food is good and it's open late."

"Sounds perfect."

He looked down. "Your feet must be killing you in those heels. How about I bring the car around and pick you up?"

* * * *

The Mediterranean place was fun. Lounging on the oversized pillows piled on the floor around low tables made me feel like a character in *Arabian Nights*. Waitresses in belly-dancing costumes brought platters of meats and mysterious sauces with pita breads and salads.

I steered clear of the onions and feta cheese. Not good date food. But we enjoyed feeding each other grapes and dates and giggling.

We also consumed a great deal of a milky drink called *ouzo*. It was vile the first time I tasted it, but on each subsequent drink, it tasted better. Either that or my tongue was getting numb.

Byblos was dimly lit, and we took full advantage of the soft lantern glow to cuddle as I told Ethan in hilarious detail about Dr. Seleman fixing the fax machine. Well, he did laugh, but maybe it was the *ouzo*. I skipped all mention of Ruth, but described the other secretaries in savage detail.

I took a long drink of *ouzo*. "I don't know what's in this, but I don't think I can walk."

He leaned both elbows on the table. "Me either. And I definitely can't drive. We're gonna have to call a cab."

"You look good in the lamplight." He had a warm skin tone anyway, but the flickering light made him glow. His hair was a little too long and starting to curl at his collar. I reached up to touch it absently.

"Time for a haircut," he said.

I traced the strong curve of his jaw. "Why aren't you married?"

He pulled back from my hand. "Should I be?"

I dropped my head onto the table with a thunk. "That isn't what I meant to say." My voice was muffled against the table.

He pulled my head up gently. "I almost was."

"So what happened?" I so did not want to be having this conversation, but I couldn't stop myself. This was why I rarely drank. Blabbermouth.

"She got tired of sitting home alone while I was working. I guess I was gone too much. So she found someone else."

"That is so sad."

He looked down. "A little. She didn't want me anymore."

"My last boyfriend wanted me," I said.

"But you left him?"

"He wanted every other woman he met too. He was a drummer," I added as if this explained it.

"We can want each other."

"That would be nice."

It was a drunken kiss, a little sloppy, but very enthusiastic. He lurched to his feet and found our waitress, who had been hiding discreetly in the kitchen. A flash of plastic took care of the bill and got us a cab ride to my apartment with my head resting on Ethan's shoulder. I had to scooch down a little in my seat, but it was still nice.

The cab smelled like the restaurant we had just left. Actually, the cab driver had the same accent as our waitress. She probably called a brother or brother-in-law or cousin or friend to come and take her drunken patrons home.

Billy needed to pee. He didn't care that I was drunk and horny. After tending to the dog, I was a little less inebriated, but no less needy.

Ethan let me get inside the door and hang Billy's leash on the peg that usually held my jacket. He helped with the removal of said jacket and drew me over to the couch.

Instead of sitting right next to me, he sat at the other end and lifted one foot into his lap, unzipping the boot and sliding it off. He massaged the arch of my foot with practiced hands, sliding up my calf. "You shouldn't wear heels that high. It puts a strain on your toes." He caressed them. "The balls of your feet. Your ankles." His hands slid higher. "Your calf muscles." He released my leg. My eyes opened. I didn't remember closing them.

He lifted the other foot and repeated the motion. This time he didn't stop at my calf. I lay back on the couch and groaned.

The phone rang and time stopped.

I blinked. "I won't answer that."

"Are you sure?"

"I'm not a doctor. I can ignore my phone for a little while."

"Or a long while." A slow smile spread across his face.

"Oh, wow."

The phone kept ringing. The machine picked up. "This is Susie Simpson. Corinne's aunt?"

I flew across the room and snatched up the receiver. "Hello? This is Portia." I smiled weakly at a befuddled Ethan. "Um, sure. I can pick you up at the airport. It's no problem. When?" I wrote down the flight information and hung up. "I'm sorry. My friend is coming into town. I had to take that."

He crossed the room to me. "You're a good friend."

"She's not from the city. I hate the idea of her here alone, not knowing anyone."

He took my hand. "Where were we?" He stretched up to kiss me. I leaned in and met him halfway, lips stroking lips. His tongue slipped in, caressing mine and starting a sweet ache.

I should have dated a doctor a long time ago. He knew what he was doing with his hands. There was no fumbling as he kneaded my neck, shoulders, back and lower. Magic hands.

We pushed and pulled one another back to the couch, moving clothes aside. I pulled my sweater over my head. We unbuttoned his shirt together as I trailed little kisses down his chest, following the trail of hair down until he gasped.

Ethan pulled me up to him and took me in his arms. The first skin-on-skin contact was electric.

"You're so beautiful," he murmured against my breast.

I think I would have taken him right then and there on the couch. His mouth was doing incredible things to my breasts and stomach, trailing lower until I was the one gasping and sighing. And the hands.

Have I mentioned his hands?

A small inkling of common sense reminded me that we were hardly randy teenagers. We didn't have to settle for fumbling on the couch. I stood up and pulled him to his feet, then led him to my bedroom, remembering to put the dog out of the room and close the door.

* * * *

I went three days without unmasking the owner of the burritos. I did narrow it down to management or one of the scientists, and something about the cheap, frozen burritos didn't say upper management to me. They had to belong to one of the scientists.

During this time, I started to slip into a workable rhythm. I also received flowers from Ethan. Pink roses. Very nice. I managed to keep the scientists from completely dismantling the equipment, although I did find Dr. Tamaguchi trying to unjam the copier. He had pulled out the paper drawers and spirited the sorter shelf away from the main unit, but no real damage was done. At least he was very tidy about it, the complete opposite to Dr. Seleman. Dr. Tamaguchi never went anywhere without a crisp white lab coat that never seemed to wrinkle, a white shirt and gray slacks. He never had a hair out of place.

I never did learn to tell the differences in the research assistants. Ted, Tom, Trey and Whatever were still interchangeable to me.

But Friday was Friday. I was cheered by the thought of a date with Ethan and only slightly stressed about Sunday dinner with my family.

I like a super hot, borderline scalding shower, and my bathroom was a steam chamber. I stepped out, wrapping one thick towel around my body and a smaller one around my hair. When my hand wiped the moisture off the mirror, I peered into Starla's face.

"Agh! Don't do that!"

"Someone hasn't spent enough time on the Stairmaster lately," she said.

"How dare you? I haven't seen you since the demon attack and you just show up playing peeping Thomasina in my bathroom?"

"I've been busy."

"Get out."

She pouted. "You don't mean that."

"I do. Get out of my bathroom. I'll speak to you in the kitchen."

"I'll do what I want."

"Fine. If you aren't interested in what the detective had to say..."

"You spoke to him?"

"Kitchen," I said.

She flounced as much as a ghost can. I didn't have too much time. I needed to get ready for work. I dressed and combed through my wet hair.

Starla hovered sullenly in the kitchen. "Happy now?"

As if. "Fierro went to talk to Joby."

"That's the detective guy? What did he say? Joby, I mean. Did he admit anything?"

"Joby claims you called him from California and that he sent you your stuff."

Starla is creative when it comes to swearing. I never would have thought to put the words *kangaroo* and *dick* together like that. Not wanting to waste time, I moisturized while I waited for her to finish. Then I pulled out my stand-up mirror from the cabinet and sat down at the table to put on makeup. The light in my bathroom is cruddy, so I always get ready in the kitchen.

By the time she finally wore down, I had on base and blush and was working on my eyes.

"Don't worry. Fierro isn't a fool. He knows Joby is lying, but it's not enough for the warrant. We're still working on it. I need information. First of all--" I paused to make the dopey, openmouthed face necessary for putting on mascara. "Where have you been for the last several days?"

"I've learned a new trick."

I was almost afraid to ask. "A trick?"

"Watch." She swiped her hand through my coffee mug. "Shoot." She did it again. "Dammit! This should work." She slapped the mug for a third time and it crashed to the floor, splattering the last teaspoon of liquid left over.

"There," she said smugly. "I'm a poltergeist now."

I rolled my eyes. "Nice. But you're not a poltergeist."

"I am so. I'm haunting them."

"You're just an angry ghost. I take it you've been haunting Joby?"

"And his little whore. Joby's so twitchy he's called in sick to work and Wanda's gone to visit her mama."

I recalled seeing Lincoln swat the cup at the police station. "How do you do that anyway?" I puckered up to put on lip gloss.

"I don't know. I concentrate real hard and think 'solid.' I have a talent for it."

"You shouldn't waste time playing spook. This is serious."

"Yeah, my murderer is getting away."

"I mean it, Starla. If you see the shadows move, run."

She pursed her lips. "You're creeping me out."

"Just because you're dead doesn't mean bad things can't happen to you. You aren't safe until you cross over. Got it?"

"I'm getting my revenge where I can."

I put down my mirror and turned to face her. "Fierro has questions."

She drifted closer. "Like what?"

"Like when exactly did you die? And where?"

"I told you. I was in a car. And it was a Saturday. I died the Saturday before Corinne did." She sighed. "Joby was so sweet when we started dating. I never had a man so nice. It was two whole months of heaven. Then we got hitched.

"I noticed he was working a lot but didn't have spit to show for it. Then I noticed my money was missing. I started digging and there it was. Receipts for places we never gone to and for stuff I never got. So I waited and followed him after work. He went right to her place. I watched him go in and I just sat there, getting madder and madder.

"I went up, but I didn't knock on the door. I had a key. See, me and Wanda used to be roommates. We used to be friends. Hell, I helped her get a job at the bar even though she ain't got any real skills other than a tight little ass and big floppy tits. They didn't even have the decency to do it in the bedroom. He was banging her right there on the kitchen table. I started screaming and yelling and I think I scratched Wanda and maybe Joby too."

"That's when he strangled you?" It was starting to sound a little like self-defense.

"Naw, I just broke some stuff and left. Joby chased me out to the car and hollered at me to stop. Like a fool I let him in the car. He was all *honey, baby, sugar, I'm so sorry.* He was crying and I started feeling sorry for him. He said, *Let's go somewhere and talk, darlin'*, and I was so stupid." She looked around like she wanted something else to break.

"Fresh out of coffee mugs," I said. "What happened next?"

"I let him drive me someplace. It was dark. I don't know where we was. Someplace up by the industrial park where the overall factory is. He started kissing me, and I kissed him back and I couldn't breathe. I fought him, but..." She looked away. Her lower lip trembled. "He put me in the trunk and you know the rest."

I stood up. "I'll call Fierro tonight. I've got to go to work now."

She gave me a nasty little smile. "Me too. Joby ought to be good and hung over after last night."

* * * *

I borrowed the older black hearse after work. Mother couldn't spare one of the vans because they were busy with bodies. This gave me a little time without Harry breathing down my neck about the condo.

I parked the hearse outside the police station, and the looks I got almost tempted me to leave it unlocked. Even the wild-eyed man carrying on an animated conversation with himself crossed the street to get away from the death car.

I sat there for a minute, formulating a plan of attack, when I realized I had a visitor.

"Good evening there, Miz Portia. Did you come to visit little, old me?"

"Hello, Lincoln. I guess I did. I'm going in to see Detective Fierro. But I'm looking for a little inside information."

"Are you now? What can old Lincoln help you with?"

"I heard that Fierro was supposed to be a skeptic and nonbeliever, but the first thing I know, he's beating down my door, telling me he knows I'm clairvoyant and wanting to work with me. I can't figure that."

"So Fierro came to you? He ain't said a word of it 'round here."

"Really? Not to anybody?"

"Not even his partner, who is Vic Tessler. Ain't that just like a man? He's keeping any credit, that's for sure."

"Lincoln, have you heard the name Starla Mueller?"

"Now that you mention it, Fierro's been yammering about her and how he's all suspicious of the husband. Tessler thinks he's nuts. Did that come from you?"

"It did. And I asked him not to tell anyone about me. I don't want to make a name for myself."

"Gotcha. Life on the QT."

"Exactly. So you think Fierro's on the up-and-up?"

"Seems that way. I've never known him not to be."

"Thanks, Lincoln. That's good to know."

"There he is now."

Fierro exited the building from the side, striding for the street. I opened the door and stepped a foot out. "Detective, could I have a word?"

He turned to me, his face weary. Then a small smile as recognition dawned. He looked both ways before trotting over, surprisingly agile for a man his size. I don't mean to imply that Fierro is fat; he's big in a solid, NFL kind of way. Today's suit was marginally better than the upholstery I last saw him wearing. It was a decent fabric, but it still didn't fit. A man with shoulders like that needed a good tailor.

Fierro slipped in the passenger side and slammed the door, stretching his legs appreciatively. "Lotta room in this old thing. They don't make cars like this anymore."

"I finally talked to Starla."

"What did she have?"

I gave him a rundown of our conversation, minus the sarcastic cracks. He took dutiful notes. Then it was my turn to question him.

"Tell me about Corinne Simpson. Have you got anything on her case?"

He hesitated. "I'm still not completely convinced it was murder and not some kind of accident."

"I'm convinced, and so is she. Listen, her roommate is living really well. She's wearing expensive new clothes and such since Corinne died. And she's being totally uncooperative with Corinne's Aunt Susie. She practically threw me out of the apartment. And she had a fit when she saw me at...um...at the office." I hadn't meant to let the last part slip. Fierro's expression didn't change, but he had gone still.

"Tell me you haven't been playing Nancy Drew."

"I didn't mean to. It just sort of happened."

"You'd better tell me everything you've done. And let's drive for a while in case people start staring."

I looked out the window. "It's a little late for that."

"Just drive," he said.

As I drove, I told him about rescuing Billy from the pound and demons and Reclaimers and taking the job at Woll Ag. And my search for the owner of the burritos.

To his credit, he listened thoughtfully.

"So you're thinking what? That the roommate is selling her stuff?"

I shook my head and turned left near Chatterly Park. Kids swarmed the swings and slide in spite of the cold. They reminded me of the Michelin man with their big puffy jackets. "I don't think Corinne had much worth selling. I'm telling you, Ruth freaked when I mentioned burritos. She's involved in this."

"It might not be related to the girl's death. Could be a sugar daddy."

"Could be." I parked and killed the engine, staring at the shrieking children, pink cheeks, glowing eyes.

"But you don't think so."

Tears pricked the corners of my eyes. I almost never cry and the idea of crying in front of Fierro made me angry. I hate to look weak.

"Portia." He touched my shoulder. "I don't have any right to tell you not to do this, but you need to understand what you're playing for. This is dangerous. If someone killed Corinne, you could be putting yourself at risk."

I swallowed hard. "I have to do this. I made a promise."

He leaned back in his seat. "So how does this work? Do you get premonitions or what?"

"No, I'm not like Ellie. I don't see visions or pick up info from objects. I'm not precognitive or telepathic. I just see dead people."

"Is that all?" he said dryly.

"Pretty much." He was smiling. "It's not funny."

"I didn't say it was."

"It's damned inconvenient."

"I can only imagine."

"The dead have no respect for anyone trying to have a life."

"Which is understandable."

"They eavesdrop and peep on you and show up at the worst times and try to talk in your ear. Some of them aren't very nice."

"So these Reclaimers. Where do they take the souls they collect?"

I shivered. "I don't know. I understand they're like mercenaries. It depends on who they work for."

"Do you believe all that church stuff about heaven and hell?"

I was quiet for a long time. It was snowing lightly now, little flakes that faded away as they hit the ground. "I think I do. My mother believes, and she's been doing this a lot longer than I have. She's at Mass every Sunday."

"Maybe I should give church another try."

"Funny. I've been thinking the same thing." I felt cold and started the engine again.

"So your mother is psychic too?"

"Clairvoyant. All the women in my family are and have been for centuries. It's sort of the family curse."

"Sounds like a gift to me."

"They call it the 'family gift.' But we're not all like Ellie. Mother says she's proud of her gift, but it's a big secret with her. She'd freak if she knew I was discussing it with you."

"She can't like what your cousin does. You couldn't be much more public about it than she is."

"No kidding. Mother hasn't even told Walter she's clairvoyant. Walter is my stepfather. They've been married since Harry and I were little."

"Harry is your brother?"

"My twin brother."

"So is he gifted too?"

"No, just the women, although Harry does have this uncanny ability with women. It makes me wonder sometimes."

"And your father?"

"Dead," I said more abruptly than I had intended.

"I'm sorry. I shouldn't have pried. Occupational hazard for me."

"It's okay. He died before I was born." According to my mother, but something about the way her eyes slid away when she said it always gave me pause. Maybe Dad was just a rolling stone gathering honey but no moss. "Walter's been a father to me. So have you discussed me with anyone?"

"I haven't told a soul. Didn't want to sound crazy. I haven't even told Tessler. That's my partner."

· "I'd rather it stay that way." The light was fading and the kids gradually thinned away. "What made you believe I was clairvoyant?" I turned to face him. "I thought you were supposed to be the skeptical one."

"I was. I am."

"So why, then?"

"I don't know. I just did." That wasn't an answer. Fierro asked a lot of questions, but didn't answer many. "I think I'm going to Mass tomorrow."

"Me too," I said. We locked eyes and something sparked for maybe a second. Then it was gone.

It was dark by the time I deposited Fierro back at the PD. I'd intended to call Ethan and see if he wanted to meet for drinks, but the weather gave me the perfect excuse. Now all I wanted was a hot bubble bath and an evening without ghosts.

I got my wish.

Chapter 13

On Sunday I planned to meet my mother for Mass and then stay for the meal as promised. I had a brilliant idea for the next week, but needed Corinne to make an appearance. I wanted her to stake out the fridge at work and watch to see who helped himself to a burrito.

But on this Sunday, there was no Starla and no Corinne and I didn't go to Mass. I thought about saying a prayer, but I wasn't sure how to begin, so I decided that God would understand. I was doing something important by solving murders so the victims could cross over. Surely that was what he wanted me to do.

Starla had given me a pretty good description of the bar where she worked. A quick cruise by the Peppermill revealed it was not only open on Sunday, but would actually open at nine. Who goes to a bar on a frosty Sunday morning?

I circled the block and finally parked around the corner. I wasn't sure exactly why I had come, but I wondered if Starla had any friends at the bar and if they knew anything helpful. I was lost in thought when someone knocked on the passenger side window. I started and then sheepishly unlocked the door. Fierro climbed in.

"This is police work," he said. "Not psychic work."

"Good thing I'm not a psychic."

"Clairvoyant. Whatever. You might want to drive something other than a hearse if you want to stake out a place."

"This isn't a stakeout," I said. "I was just thinking."

He shifted in his seat and turned toward me. "I thought you were meeting your mother for Mass."

"I was. I thought you were going to church too."

"I was. In one hour we can both go in and see who wants to talk about Starla."

"I get to go too? I thought you had a partner."

"He doesn't share my enthusiasm for the Starla Mueller case. In fact, he doesn't think there is a case and officially there isn't a homicide. What about you? I thought you had a boyfriend. What's he going to think about you hanging out in bars on Sunday morning?"

I stared. "How did you know I had a boyfriend?"

He turned to face ahead. "You must have mentioned it."

"I did nothing of the kind. You've been checking up on me." I wagged an accusatory finger.

Fierro unbuttoned his jacket. "I had to make sure you weren't some type of nut, that you didn't have ties to the case."

"You said you believed me."

"I did. I do. But I checked you out first."

"That's not fair. You know more about me than I do about you."

"Come on," he said. "Pull out and turn left."

"Why should I?"

"Because there's a good Spanish bakery around the corner. Esperanza's. Coffee and a pastry, my treat. Plus you can grill me. Deal?"

"Fine." I put the hearse in gear. "But I don't know where you get off thinking a boyfriend gets any say about where I go when. And he's not my boyfriend. We just started dating."

"So what does that make the good doctor?"

I cut my eyes over. "It makes him none of your damn business."

"Does he know you see dead people? Right there. Pull in."

"It says *no parking*."

"I can handle that. One of the perks. So does he?"

I parked and glared. "No, he doesn't know. I don't want him to think I'm weird."

Fierro thought for a moment. "Good choice."

We sat by one of the windows with coffee and pastries. He was right. My pastry was a pink shortbread with icing. Amazingly good.

"All right," he said. "Shoot." I raised an eyebrow. "Not literally of course. I'd haunt you."

"Is there a Missus Detective Fierro?"

"There was."

"How long have you been divorced?"

He took a long drag of coffee before answering. "I'm not. Gracie died. Cancer." He put up a hand to stop any embarrassment. "She's been gone for four years. I'm okay with talking about it."

"I still feel like a heel."

"Ask me more questions."

"Now I'm afraid to."

"I'll fill in the blanks. No kids. No pets. I've been a detective for six years and a cop longer than that. I joined the force when I was twenty-one. And yes, I played college football until I blew out a knee. How's that?"

"It'll do."

At nine o'clock the doors to the Peppermill were unlocked. The interior was dark and smoky. There were no windows, and for all I could tell, it might have been nine at night except for the lack of people. That's not to say that the bar was empty. There were two people sitting there drinking. One of them was the bartender. A woman stood off to the side polishing glasses with a dingy towel. Her smudged eyes and tousled hair gave rise to the suspicion that she didn't sleep in her own bed the night before. She eyed us with a lack of interest.

"Help you?" she asked in a throaty, smoker's voice.

Fierro flashed a badge. "Looking for Lurlene Hooper."

"Found her," she said. Compared to Lurlene, Starla looked fresh and dewy eyed.

"Talk to you over here?" Fierro gestured over to a table at the far corner.

Lurlene shrugged and followed us.

"I'm looking into the disappearance of Starla Mueller," he said.

Interest flickered in her dull eyes. "'Bout time someone gave a damn. Me and Dean reported her missing. That bastard she married don't give two shits."

"I hear you. Thing is, we don't have much to go on. I'm looking for anything you can tell me about Starla and her husband."

"Like what?"

"Like, how would you describe their marriage? Would you say it was in trouble?"

She snorted. "Trouble? Did the *Titanic* run into a little trouble with some ice? That marriage was beyond trouble. Starla was pretty sure Joby was running around on her. She said she was gonna follow him and find out. That's what she said the last time I talked to her. She never showed for her shift. Me and Dean got worried. We started calling, but ain't nobody seen Starla. That bastard husband of hers cussed us and claimed she run away with Dean's cousin, but Dean and me knew better. Starla ain't the type to run."

"Why not?"

"She just ain't. Starla never run from nothing in her whole life."

Fierro nodded. "I hear you. Here's my card." He pulled a little gold case from his pocket and handed one to her.

Lurlene's eyes grew canny. "This here card says *Homicide*. You think she's dead?"

Fierro hesitated and then nodded. "It's a strong possibility."

Lurlene stared at the card. "Shit," she said, blinking back tears. "That's what I think too."

When we got back in the car, I said, "So where does that leave us? Lurlene didn't do anything but confirm what Starla already told us."

"It leaves you keeping your date with your mother. It's bad enough skipping church, but you better not miss lunch. And it's nice to confirm what Starla told us about going to confront Joby, especially from a living witness who can actually testify in court. But that's enough freebie work on behalf of the dead for one day."

I decided Fierro had a point, so I swung by my apartment and grabbed Billy, who spent the ride racing back and forth between the dash and the passenger window. He never settled down into his seat. Halfway there, I remembered to drive with the window cracked. When he finished this bag of dog food, I was buying something cheaper. Hopefully it would make Billy less gassy.

I didn't bother putting Billy on the leash at Mother's. He had gotten used to staying on my heels. "Be good," I said. "Don't pee on anything."

He snorked along the front door with too much interest.

"I mean it," I said.

"Ooh, it's a little doggy. Looks like a tasty snack." Old Man Biddle hovered over me, grinning.

"You're still here?"

"'Course he's here. He won't cross over," Hephzibah said. "Be careful, doll. Don't let him pollute you."

Mother whipped the door open. "Stay out! You're not wanted here!"

I recoiled in shock.

"Not you," she whispered. "Him."

"Hee hee." Biddle zoomed down the street, cackling.

I followed her inside, shucking my coat and draping it over an armchair. "Why won't Biddle cross over?"

"Because he doesn't want to." She picked up my coat and opened the closet door. "He knows where he's going."

"You mean hell?"

"Amen, sister," Hephzibah said. "He's just hanging around trying to cause as much havoc as he can before the Reclaimers get him. Personally I'm rooting for a demon. If anyone deserves to get eaten, it's that old bastard."

Mother shuddered. "Enough about Old Man Biddle. Where were you this morning?"

"It was the weather. I wasn't sure if the streets were good."

"You're such a bad liar." She patted my cheek. "It does a mother's heart good."

"What did Old Man Biddle do that was so awful?"

"Never you mind. It's being handled. Once the place goes through probate," Mother said, giving Hephzibah a worried glance.

"Don't look at me. I don't meddle in matters of the living," Hephzibah said. "I've got business of the dead to tend to." She walked through the front wall.

"I figured now that you saw concrete evidence of the spiritual world you would come back to church with me."

"I meant to," I said. "I had things to do. And the weather really was bad last night."

She raised an eyebrow. "Were you meeting someone perhaps? How is your doctor?"

"He's not my doctor, but he's fine. His name is Ethan. If things stay good, I'll let you meet him."

"You say that like you're ashamed of us." Walter entered the room, stamping mud from his feet. Harry's arms were laden with firewood.

"Oh honey, that's too wet to burn," Mother said.

"It's not bad. Just a little damp," Harry protested.

Mother made a face. "That makes it so smoky, and it takes forever to catch. Portia's not ashamed of us. She's cautious. Doesn't want to jinx a new relationship. Right, dear?"

"That's it," I said.

"I mean," Mother continued, "there isn't anything wrong with him, is there? Something we should know?"

I rolled my eyes. "No, Mother. He's very nice. Nothing for you to worry about."

The meal was a disaster and not because of the rubbery lemon chicken or a broccoli rice casserole with the consistency and flavor of paste. It was the poltergeist-style antics of Biddle, who'd found his way back into the house. Walter prayed over the meal and I joined in. I don't know if it helps, but I figured that little things like saying grace couldn't hurt and if they helped, well, so much the better.

Grace was interrupted by the bread pudding flying off the table and onto the floor. Mother looked up and saw Biddle cackling and hovering over her table. Her jaw tightened. Harry and I leapt up to clean the mess.

"It's no great loss," Harry whispered. "There's a pie from Perulli's in the fridge."

"Leave it somewhere safe," I said.

He gave me a funny look. "You know, a lot of strange things have been happening around the neighborhood lately."

We went into the living room to see Mother red-faced and Walter holding a squirming Billy, who had been doing his best to clean up the pudding by himself.

"I didn't think he needed to eat glass," Walter explained.

"Little piggy," I said. Billy wiggled with delight, then his eyes bugged over my shoulder.

"Ar-ar-ar-ar."

"Your dog is weird," Harry said, but he had a thoughtful expression as he stared at the place Billy was looking. "You know, all this started when Old Man Biddle died."

"That's ridiculous," Mother said, but she got up and lit her incense candles that she gets from Father Mike. She has a little shrine to the cross in the living room. I think the candles smell foul. Fortunately, Biddle seemed to agree. He hacked and wheezed and recoiled from the smoke before disappearing.

* * * *

I had a good excuse for leaving early. I needed to pick up Aunt Susie at the airport. Billy was pitiful when I left him in the car with the windows cracked.

I recognized Susie Simpson, although I had never laid eyes on her before. She was Corinne, three decades older. Same round face, long blond hair and wide blue eyes. This was how Corinne would look if she had matured, raised her niece, then buried her.

Susie greeted me like an old friend with an enormous hug. "I'm not usually a hugger," she said. "But I feel like I know you."

I helped her gather her luggage. Susie recoiled at the hearse. "Oh my." Her carry-on fell to the ground.

"I should have warned you. My family owns a funeral home. I had to borrow a car. Don't worry. I won't put your stuff in the back."

Bug eyes and frantic scrabbling paws on the window told me that Billy had spotted us.

"Billy," she exclaimed, rushing to the hearse. "He looks so good." She cuddled the wheezing pug trying to lick her face.

I eased us back into traffic and turned toward downtown. "It's a longish ride. Do you want to stop for a bite or a Coke? I can pick you something up."

"Thanks, but I'm fine. I'm anxious to get to the apartment."

"You want to go now? I thought maybe tomorrow after work..."

"Oh." She sounded disappointed. "That would be okay."

"Are you sure? You don't mind?" I turned to look at her.

"That would be fine. I was planning on staying a couple of days. I'll get a hotel room."

"You could stay with me. I don't mind."

"That's so sweet, but I wanted...well..." She seemed embarrassed. "I don't get down to Dallas very often."

Something clicked. "You want to go shopping."

"That seems awfully shallow, doesn't it? Poor Cori." She sniffled. Fortunately I was armed with tissues. I had expected this.

"Of course not. You have to go on living," I said. "Corinne will understand."

Susie looked at me oddly. That hadn't come out right. "I guess she would. I'll just get a hotel room and take a taxi. It's no problem."

"At least let me make dinner for you tomorrow," I said.

"That would be nice."

"Good. Tomorrow I'll pick you up and we will go get Corinne's things and then we can have a nice meal."

"I'd like that. I'm glad Cori had a friend like you. I didn't think she had any gal pals here. She didn't get along with other women her age."

"I'm not so good at that either."

I helped Susie check into the XYZ Inn and took Billy home. He whined when I took him from Susie's arms. "Sorry, bud," I said and wondered if I should offer to give him to Susie. Maybe they belonged together.

I had plans for the night. Ethan wanted to make dinner for me at his place, and considering how well the last date had gone, I wanted to shave my legs first. Corinne flitted around my bedroom. She had been jumpy since the demon attack.

"Your Aunt Susie is at a hotel," I announced.

"I thought she would stay here."

I flopped onto the couch. "I offered, but she wanted to stay at a hotel. It's understandable. I'm a stranger. She's coming here tomorrow."

Corinne clapped her hands and brightened. "I'm so excited."

"Then it will be time to cross over."

Her chin trembled. "But...but..."

"I'm working with the detective. He's all over your case now. We've got some leads. One last goodbye with your aunt and then it's time." *Before it's too late*, I thought. She turned away, her shoulders shaking. "It will be okay," I said softly. "You were a good person. I can tell."

"I'm scared anyway. Do you believe in heaven? There's a church over on Sela Street. I liked going there."

"Then that's okay, isn't it?"

"It was supposed to be. Why am I still so scared?"

I didn't have any good answers, but I was in a somber mood when I left for Ethan's place.

I left the hearse parked. The thing guzzled gas and the train was too convenient.

I stayed alert for demons, but only foul smell wafted up from the sewers. When I got off at Bellingrad, the neighborhood smelled noticeably better. Rows of classy townhomes lined the streets with cute little yards for kids and pets.

Stop that. Don't think that way. Third date. Think third date.

Of course, I had gone all the way on my second date, which was unusual for me, but when Ethan answered the door I remembered why.

He didn't say anything, just leaned in and kissed me long and slow as the blood deserted my brain, rushing downward. My awkwardness melted away.

"Hey there."

"Hey there yourself," he said, drawing me inside.

Ethan's two-story townhome was unspeakably cute. It was so warm and homey that I suspected a woman's touch. Then again, he could have hired a decorator. Maybe that's what doctors did. Something smelled wonderful. I said this out loud.

"Cooking is a hobby of mine."

Score. "Smells like my lucky day."

"Pinot Grigio?" He held up the wine bottle.

I accepted a glass and a tour of the town house. It was a two bedroom completely done in harvest colors, like an advertisement for the Pottery Barn. "It's beautiful," I said.

I followed Ethan into the kitchen. "Do you mind eating in here?" he asked. "It's less formal, but it's my favorite room in the house." I could see why. Buttery yellow plaster walls, Italian tile. I'd live in that kitchen too.

I perched on a padded barstool near the granite island. "Can I help?"

"I've got it covered. How was the rest of your week?"

I sipped the wine. "More of the same. I managed to keep the scientists from taking apart the electronics. There's a lot of transcription involved. I had no idea. It's a little like learning to read hieroglyphics. Some of those scientists are as bad as doctors when it comes to writing."

"I hear that complaint all the time. The nurses claim mine looks like a five-year-old wrote the chart notes."

"So tell me about your week."

"More of the same. Lots of car wrecks with this weather. Lots of homeless people with cold-related injuries. Flu. Pneumonia." He shredded field greens into a tangerine ceramic bowl.

"That's sad. Why don't they go to a shelter? Surely there's enough room."

He added whole pear tomatoes and sliced cucumber to the salad before answering. "There probably are enough beds."

"Then why don't they go to them?"

"There are reasons a lot of them are homeless aside from the obvious economic ones."

"Like they're addicts?"

"And mental problems or alcoholism. Some are too proud to go for help. Others have been banned from the shelters because of violent behavior."

I touched his arm. "Sounds like a sad week."

"Just a typical one. At least I do something to help." He caught my hand and kissed it. "It's all better now."

"Do you go to church?"

"Sure. St. Matthew Cumberland Presbyterian. It's right around the corner from the hospital. The head administrators go there. It's a smart move."

"So more of a career decision than a religious one?"

He shrugged. "Only partly. How about you?"

I drained the last of my wine. "Lapsed Catholic."

"Hand me those?" He gestured toward the beige oven mitts. A quick check in the oven assured him that dinner was ready. The chicken was flavorful, and the veggies barely blanched. The salad was healthy and organic, but it all left me wanting something more. We adjourned to the cozy den. I would have to find my own dessert.

Ethan dimmed the lighting, adjusted the music volume and sank down next to me on the couch.

He pulled me close. "Portia?"

"Hmm?" I leaned back against his chest, entranced by the crackling fire.

"You asked me once why I was single and unattached. What about you?"

"No mystery. I date inappropriate men." This made us both laugh. "Or I did in the past. You, on the other hand, would make my mother squeal with delight."

His hands kneaded my shoulders and neck. "I hope to meet her soon. I'd like to meet your parents. Oh, there's a knot."

Forcing away the little bits of panic, I reminded myself I was the new and braver Portia Mahaffey. I could handle ghosts, face down demons, and date a nice guy without running away. "This girlfriend you had. How long ago did you break up?"

His hands paused and then continued. "Last year." I relaxed a bit. That was long enough. "Confession," he said. I tensed again. This was where he admitted he was a closet transsexual or that he had been married three times, or-- "We lived together." That wasn't so bad. "For three years." Oh crap. That was almost like marriage.

"That's a long time," I said.

"I know. But sometimes things don't work out. Or sometimes they work out for the better," he whispered against my ear. He nibbled the lobe and trailed kisses down the side of my neck. I tilted my head, exposing my entire throat.

Ethan slid lazily around to the front, in no great hurry. I needed him, though, and pulled him up to my mouth for a long, deep kiss. Running my hands up the inside of his shirt caused him to groan. Just a third date. I'd feel slutty if he wasn't Mister Perfect, if he wasn't right for me in every way.

He rose up and crossed his arms, stripping off his shirt. I trailed an admiring hand down his hard abdomen. He leaned over me, propping himself up on his arms, teasing me with little butterfly kisses until I couldn't think anymore.

* * * *

The rotten thing about having a dog at home is it made spending a night away almost impossible. Much as I loathed the idea of dragging myself out of the warm bed and away from Ethan's arms, the thought of cleaning dog pee out of the carpet was enough to leverage me upright. He spread sleepy kisses down my back and I rationalized that maybe it wouldn't be so bad to have my carpet steamed.

"I need to get up and shower," he groaned. "I have an early shift."

I pushed away from the bed. "If you don't stop fondling me like that, we'll both get fired."

He laid back and grinned at me. "It might be worth it."

"Says the doctor who can get another job and make wads of cash." I pulled on my clothes.

He was singing opera with his beautiful baritone in the shower when I trudged out into the cold. Was there anything the man didn't do well?

Chapter 14

I found it hard to concentrate at work. I was thinking about perfect men and sneaky roommates and crossing over into the unknown. On a break, I opened the fridge to find the burritos all gone. "Damn it. Damn, damn, damn."

"Problem?"

I turned to look at Duncan. "There was some food here and now it's gone."

"Again? I thought the problem stopped when..." His face blushed until it matched his rose colored jacket.

"Corinne ate people's food, didn't she?"

"She liked to eat."

"You mean she was a cow." Beth leaned against the doorjamb. "I'm going out to smoke."

"She wasn't a cow," I said.

"Of course she was," Kelley said, hand on her skinny hip. "You've sat in her chair. They had to order a special size." The girls snickered. "They kept breaking."

"Not funny," I said through my teeth.

"Why? It's not like she cares. She's in the great beyond."

"Hope they had a big enough cloud."

This caused them to cackle with laughter. My face felt hot and I turned away. I desperately hoped Corinne wasn't hovering close by. There was a time I might have engaged in the same mindless cruelty, laughing about the chubby spinster from Omaha with pictures of her dog on her desk.

"Enough," Duncan said. "Fifteen minutes and not a second more. And don't smoke out front. It looks bad. And I better not smell anything in the stairwells."

Beth and Kelley slunk off grumbling.

"Sorry," he said. "They don't know she was your friend. Now about your food..."

"It wasn't my food. I was wondering whose it was." My mind reached for a plausible answer. "Those burritos looked good. I was wondering where they bought them." Weak, but the best I could do.

"Really? Those beef and bean monstrosities?" He gave me a strange look. "They're disgusting. I would think you could find them at any supermarket. Why Seleman buys them is beyond me."

"Dr. Seleman eats them?"

"All the time."

"But where did they all go?"

Duncan shrugged. "Maybe they got old and he threw them out. I don't keep up with it." He tapped his watch meaningfully.

"I know," I said. "Back to work." A sudden thought occurred to me. "I haven't seen Ruth today."

"She went on a trip. She was due some vacation time."

Sounded like a good way to spend some money. "When will she be back?"

"A few days. So enjoy it while you can."

* * * *

As soon as I could grab Aunt Susie, I would whisk her off to search Ruth's place. I concentrated on the city streets. I had driven more this week than in the last two years, and the roads were slick. Seleman bought the burritos. I was wrong to think he couldn't be involved because he seemed harmless. His medicine. His food.

"I know about the burritos."

I almost drove off the road. "Shit! Corinne, you scared me half to death. Yeah, they belong to Dr. Seleman."

"I thought they belonged to Tamaguchi."

"Why would you think that?" I couldn't picture the uptight scientist in white eating cheap burritos.

"Because he took them all from the fridge. I staked out the fridge like you suggested. He came up there midmorning, put them all in a sack and left with them."

"But Duncan said that Dr. Seleman buys them."

"I know what I saw." She crossed her arms.

"How long did you stay?"

"Until I saw Dr. Tamaguchi take the burritos. I followed him. He took them out back and threw them in a dumpster."

"Maybe they were all tainted. I need to go get them." I looked for a place to turn around.

"Too late. They emptied the dumpster already. Tamaguchi put them in a few minutes before the trash people came."

"Did he know when to expect the trash pickup?"

"I don't know. I'm just..."

"Telling me what you saw. I'll pass it all on to Fierro."

"Who's that?"

"The detective handling your case. He'll know what to do."

"My, aren't we chummy? Is that where you were last night?"

"Of course not."

"Must have been that cute doctor."

I allowed myself a little smile. "He looks even better with his clothes off."

Corinne gasped. "I don't know whether to be shocked or envious."

"You can be both if you want to. I think Ruth is out of town. Either that or she's holed up in your apartment and pretending to be gone. Where is the key again?"

"First step of the staircase. There's a key holder taped in there. Will you go in the apartment if she's not there?"

"Of course. I want to search it without Ruth there. And if she comes back I can act all righteous on Susie's behalf."

"I can't wait to see her. There she is!"

I had called ahead. Susie Simpson was standing in the vestibule near the glass doors. I pulled in and she ran out and got in the car. The wind had started picking up around three, and the skies were full and heavy.

Susie was understandably nervous. "Did you get ahold of Ruth?"

"Aunt Susie looks so good." Corinne began crying immediately. It took effort to ignore her sobs.

"Ruth wasn't at work today," I said.

"What if she's not home?"

"We don't need her. We have a key."

Susie's face was creased with worry. "Can we do that? Are you sure?"

I had pondered how much to tell her. Looking into her guileless blue eyes, I knew that the answer was nothing. I couldn't spoil her vision of the world. "I'm absolutely sure. It has to be legal. I have a key."

"But is it right?"

"The right thing to do would have been to pack Corinne's things up and send them to you. The right thing to do would have been to return your calls. The right thing would have been to give you Billy, not drop him off at the pound as soon as Corinne died. I don't care what Ruth thinks." The vehemence in my voice surprised even me.

Susie sat back in her seat. "Oh."

I parked right in front of the apartment. "Corinne told me the key would be here," I said, feeling around under the stair. "Got it." I held up the key case. "Just in case we need it."

As I expected, Ruth didn't answer. I unlocked the door and flicked on the lights. The place was empty.

Which room was Corinne's? I hesitated. There was a main living area and then rooms that shot-gunned out. Bedrooms, a bath and a kitchen.

"That one." Corinne sniffled and pointed.

"This way," I told Susie, following the direction of Corinne's finger.

"Look at my room!" Corinne said. I hurried to see. Boxes were ripped open and items spilled out. Dresser drawers hung open. I stepped around a broken lamp.

"What a mess! Who would do such a thing?" Susie followed me in.

"I don't know." This was hardly what I had expected. I stopped by the dresser and slipped a hair scrunchie with strands of blond hair into my pocket. "We'd better check around the apartment," I said, uneasily turning back to Susie. "Corinne's things could be scattered all over."

"I'll check the bathroom." She went out.

I paused to add a tiny little pug figurine to my coat pocket, then hurried after Susie.

Susie wandered out of the bathroom, her eyes glazed over. "I think I'm going to be sick." She put a hand on the wall to steady herself. Then she threw up.

"Aunt Susie?" Corinne said.

I shoved past the dazed woman and hurried into the bathroom. Ruth Yeshu was more than out of town. Ruth's body lay half in the shower. Copper-scented blood painted the walls in smeary handprints, like she had repeatedly tried to rise up.

"Sorry, doll," Hephzibah said. "You're too late. Ruth's already crossed over."

I wanted to close my eyes, but I couldn't. She didn't look real, more like a rag doll that had been flung down. She was wearing a bathrobe and nothing else. The dark edges around my vision closed in and I felt lightheaded, dizzy.

I swallowed hard. "When?" I whispered.

"About fifteen minutes ago. It took her a long time to bleed out."

Don't panic, I told myself. "How was she?"

Hephzibah cocked her head. "Confused and sad. But she crossed over without a fuss."

"Did she say anything about Corinne or who did this to her or... anything at all?"

Hephzibah shook her head. "Sorry."

I stumbled backward, but before I left the room, I picked up Ruth's lipstick and charm bracelet.

* * * *

I had the presence of mind to use my cellphone to call 911, which is how Susie and I ended up sitting outside on the stairs trying to convince a Sergeant MacAllister that we had nothing to do with Ruth's death.

"I told you already." I pulled my coat tighter. I was shivering even more than I had earlier. Probably shock, although it was quickly giving way to anger. "I brought Susie to get her niece's things. We had a key."

"Sergeant, why aren't these ladies in someplace warm?" The gruff voice flooded me with relief.

"Fierro." I stood and was surprised that my legs felt rather wobbly. He put a large hand on my shoulder to steady me.

Sergeant MacAllister put his notebook back in his pocket. "She claims you can vouch for her."

"Of course I can. I'll take Ms. Mahaffey's statement. You make sure the crime scene is secured."

"They stomped all over the place," he said in an accusatory voice.

"We didn't know it was a crime scene." My stomach contracted as I thought about the items I had collected. It was hard to look Fierro in the eye.

"Thank you, Sergeant. I'll handle this portion of it."

"I take it you've met?" A short, swarthy man who was a good fifteen years senior to Fierro stood behind him looking on with some amusement.

"Yeah, this is Portia Mahaffey. She's sort of a witness in the Corinne Simpson case. Portia, this is Vic Tessler. He's my partner and a big asshole, so let me apologize up-front."

"Nice mouth you got there, Fierro. Mahaffey. I don't remember no Mahaffey in the Simpson thing."

"She's more like a concerned party. She was a friend of the deceased."

"Which deceased? Seems to me we've got two dead roommates." Tessler popped a stick of gum in his mouth.

"I'm Corinne's friend," I said. "Not Ruth's."

"You didn't like Ruth much," he said.

"There wasn't much to like."

"Mahaffey. You any kin to Eleanor Mahaffey? I heard she came to visit Fierro."

"She's my cousin."

"Ah," Tessler said as if that explained things. "You resemble her is what made me think of it."

"So how about you see to that lady over there." Fierro gestured to Susie. "Take her statement and see she gets to her hotel safely. She's a nice lady so don't give her none of your crap. Susie Simpson. She's in town to get her niece's stuff."

"Sure. No problem, boss."

"Don't call me that."

"Whatever. I guess you'll be making sure Ms. Mahaffey gets home safely?"

Fierro ignored him. "And keep an eye on the crime scene. Make sure they get everything. I'm not sure I trust MacAllister to run it."

I had another guilty twinge that no one had thought to search me, but I kept my mouth shut. Tessler set off to tend to Aunt Susie. I pulled my coat tighter.

"You're freezing," Fierro said. "Sit in your car with me. I'll drive you home."

My teeth were chattering, but I stammered out. "I c-c-can d-d-drive m-m-myself."

"Unh-huh." He held onto my elbow and steered me toward the car. I fumbled in my pocket for the keys and handed them over. The car blew cold air for a minute as he put the hearse in reverse and backed us out.

"You gonna tell me what's really going on here?"

"We really did go to get Corinne's things."

"Unh-huh. Where'd you get the key?"

"Corinne told me where to find it. Oh hell, I was also going to search the apartment because of the way Ruth was acting. I was sure she had something to do with Corrine's death."

He mulled the thought over. "She might. She just might."

"She died about fifteen minutes before we got there."

He was startled. "You talked to her?"

"I wish. She had already crossed over. It took her a long time to bleed out, though. I don't know when she was attacked. Just when she died."

"And where did you get this nugget of info?"

"From Death. But she prefers to be called Hephzibah."

He stared at me. "Holy shit," he muttered.

"I found out something about the burritos too." I filled him in on the conflicting information. "So they could have belonged to Dr. Seleman or they could have belonged to Dr. Tamaguchi."

"And Tamaguchi disposed of them?"

"That's what Corinne said."

"Interesting." We both fell quiet. "You talk to Death?"

"Yeah." I glanced over. "You believe me?"

"I always have."

"Why? Don't get me wrong. I'm grateful and all, but *why*? It sounds crazy."

He nodded. "Sounds crazy. It is crazy. Could be the craziest thing I've ever heard. But you aren't crazy. Everything you've ever told me has checked out. That says something."

"I think you're better with the idea of solving cases with ghosts than I am."

He kept his eyes straight ahead. "I've seen a lot of bad things. Maybe I want to believe. I want there to be something more out there. I need it."

I sat back and closed my eyes, feeling worse than ever about lifting things from the crime scene. Fierro's trust mattered to me, and I'd just abused it. No amount of rationalization would make that right.

Chapter 15

Fierro came inside my apartment with me. "I'm supposed to be getting a statement from you. I need you to come downtown tomorrow and give a formal one on paper."

"An edited version?"

"You might leave out the part about having a conversation with Death."

I puttered around making tea. Fierro dropped onto one of my kitchen chairs. "I was starting to think that Ruth had killed Corinne," I admitted.

"She might have. Hey, buddy." He scratched Billy's head absently. Billy raced off to get his Dingo. "Just 'cause she got killed doesn't mean she wasn't involved in Corinne's death. Tell me what you saw."

When I closed my eyes I could still see Ruth, lying half in the shower, her dark hair spread around. Blood everywhere. I could smell the room.

"Maybe I should rephrase that," Fierro said. "You're looking kinda gray. First body?"

"No, I've seen dead bodies all my life."

"But not like that."

"No," I agreed. "Never like that."

"Tell me about the rooms. Anything stand out?"

I thought for a moment. "When I went into Corinne's bedroom, I had the feeling it had been searched. Things had been pulled out of boxes. Someone must have been in a hurry. I didn't go into any other room except the bathroom." I placed the kettle on the stove and sat opposite him.

"It would help if you pretend not to know me tomorrow."

I drew back. "Excuse me?"

"I meant at that research place. The one they worked at. We'll have a search warrant by tomorrow morning for their work areas. Don't acknowledge that you know me. It could be dangerous for you."

"I hadn't thought of that."

"You don't think that way. Which is nice," he added. "But it could be dangerous. That's two dead girls. I don't want to go for three. Even with Killer here to protect you." He threw Billy's Dingo for him. Billy bounded after it and returned it to Fierro, who dutifully threw it again.

"Congratulations. You just became his new favorite person."

"We've got to talk, doll." Hephzibah stood by the fireplace. The grim look on her face made my stomach lurch.

I stood up. "I've got to take this."

Fierro looked puzzled. "The phone rang?"

"Not exactly. Excuse me a minute." I went back to the bedroom and closed the door.

Hephzibah followed me by walking through the door. "Corinne's mark may already be gone. She's in play. There have been Reclaimers working the area, and I mean heavily. And demons. There are two demons patrolling the city. Brothers. Demons usually hunt alone, but these two hunt as a team. This is in addition to the demon you've already attracted. I don't know what you did to him, by the way, but he's royally pissed."

"I burned him."

"I'm sure you had your reasons."

"He attacked the girls in my apartment."

"That's a good reason."

"Is Corinne here?"

"She can't be far. I want you to call her."

I sat on my bed. "I didn't know I could do that. Does that work?"

"Sometimes. If they're tied to you, like she is. You gotta yell real loud."

"I'll try." I snagged Billy's leash on my way out the front door.

"You're leaving?" Fierro said.

"Just taking the dog out. I've got to call Corinne up and get her to cross over."

"I didn't think it worked that way."

"Apparently I just need to yell loud enough. I'm gonna try it outside." I opened the door and Billy darted out. I decided he wouldn't go far and stuffed the leash into my pocket.

Big fat flakes drifted down, cozying the landscape, softening the hard edges of the city. It's an illusion. We aren't far enough north to maintain the snow blanket. By rush hour tomorrow morning it would be gray slush again.

Billy didn't care. He was charmed by the cold mouthfuls. He chased the floating flakes, gulping greedy bites of snow.

Feeling slightly foolish, I stood outside and yelled Corinne's name. Just before I was ready to quit, she materialized.

"He'll get cold." Corinne hovered over Billy.

"Looks happy to me," Hephzibah said. "Anyone ever tell you you're a fussbudget?"

"You know nothing about dogs," Corinne said.

"Damn things are always barking at me. Cats. Now that's an animal I could live with. You know. If I was alive." Death snorted laughter at her own joke.

I felt vulnerable and exposed standing there with Corinne. Every shadow made me twitch. Were the Reclaimers lurking nearby, waiting for the last vestiges of the mark to fade? Was there a demon around the corner? "Have you told her?" I whispered to Hephzibah.

"Told me what?" Corinne flitted closer.

Hephzibah shot me a warning look. "Nothing to worry about."

I took a deep breath. "Corinne, you know how seriously the police are taking things now. Fierro's on the case and he won't give up. You've seen Aunt Susie. Billy is being cared for. You can go now."

"But..."

"No buts. You can't stay here. Don't you want to see your parents? You've done everything you can here. The loose ends are almost all tied up. It's time. Look around you. Isn't this the image you want to go with?" I gestured at Billy, who was still chasing snowflakes.

"She's right," Hephzibah said softly. "Let me take you across."

Corinne flitted over to Billy and hovered for a moment. He ignored her and plowed face-first into a shrub. He popped out, sneezing. His tongue lolled out the side of his mouth.

She closed her eyes and bent her head. Her long hair slid in front of her face like a curtain. I gave her a minute. Finally she lifted her head. "All right. I'm as ready as I'll ever be." Her chin trembled.

"Good girl," Hephzibah said.

"Thank you." Corinne turned to me. "Thank you so much." She waved at Billy, who was too busy playing to notice. "Be a good doggy."

I was surprised to blink back tears. In a funny way, I would miss my first ghost.

I watched Corinne and Hephzibah move together and then, they were gone, like someone had flicked a switch. Billy trotted over to me, the bristly hairs on the back of his neck raised; his eyes were wary. I knelt to rub his cold little ears.

"It's okay, boy. She had to go."

But he wasn't looking at me. His eyes were fixed over my shoulder. He growled. I froze, then slowly turned my head.

Red beady eyes were close to mine. Its fetid breath was overpowering. The demon roared, and I fell backward on my rump. Billy rushed forward, barking as ferociously as anything weighing twenty pounds could.

The demon sat back, studying the little flat-faced dog curiously. It drew its lips back exposing jagged teeth in a grimace that was part smile, part snarl. A noise rumbled deep inside, which enraged the little dog further. At first I thought the demon was growling, but its sides shook. It was laughing.

Billy miscalculated. I'm not sure if he equated the thing's appearance with Corinne leaving or if he was protecting me, but he lunged, snapping.

The demon moved so quickly it was just a blur. A single swipe sent Billy airborne. He landed in a tiny snowdrift piled against a car tire. The demon gave a last sniff of the air and snorted. In a whoosh it was gone. I rushed to pull Billy out of the snow. He shook his head slowly, bemused, while I felt him all over. He licked my face, none the worse for his demon encounter.

"Were you protecting me?" I rubbed his ears, which were now like ice. He grunted happily, closing his eyes. "Ellie's gonna have to get her kids their own dog. Any dog brave enough to tackle a demon is mine."

I carried my dog inside.

Fierro was pouring tea into the blue willow cups. "You want milk or sugar?" When he saw my face, he set the kettle down. "What's wrong?"

The tears came flooding back. I blinked furiously, but they spilled over, running down my cheeks.

Fierro was across the room in an instant or maybe I met him halfway, but he was warm and solid. He felt like a wall between me and the rest of the world, with his arms around me like that. "Corinne crossed over," I said against his coat.

His hand smoothed my hair. "Isn't that a good thing?"

I nodded and raised my face. "It's the right thing. She's safe now."

"How about you? You okay?"

I swallowed hard. I couldn't find my voice to say the things I was thinking. His hand touched my cheek. "I'm okay," I whispered.

We were eye-to-eye. He smelled clean, like soap. "Letting go is hard sometimes." His voice was husky.

"It helped her, you know. Knowing that you're taking her case seriously, that you're going to solve it. That's really all she wanted. That and for Billy to be taken care of."

His hand cupped my chin for a moment, then he released me, stepping back. "You're keeping him?" Fierro cleared his throat and sat down at the table. Billy hopefully bumped his knee with Dingo. Fierro tossed it.

"He's my dog. Now all I need is a place to live. I'm being evicted. They don't allow pets here."

"That's dedication."

"Not really. I used to love this place, but I think I'm buying a condo with my brother. New construction. No ghosts."

"Owning is better than renting."

"You own?"

"A little house in Queensland Estates."

"That's a nice neighborhood. Very trendy."

He made a face. "I lived there before it was trendy. It was my parents'. When Dad died, Mom moved to Florida."

I took a sip of the tea and wrinkled my nose. It had sat too long and was very strong. "Needs milk. You want anything?"

"Nah. I'm good." He stood up. "That search warrant isn't going to write itself. I'd better go before Tessler puts out an APB on me. Remember, if I can pull this off, you don't know me."

"Got it. And then after work I know you again and I need to do a statement."

"See you tomorrow. Lock the door after me."

"Jeez, Fierro. It's not my first night in the city. Don't you need me to call a cab or something?"

He raised his hand, showing me a cellphone. "I called for a black-and-white to give me a lift while you were outside. They'll be here any minute."

I stayed awake for a long time after Fierro left, unable to sleep. Billy didn't suffer from the same problem, and I found his snoring strangely reassuring.

* * * *

Pretending not to know Tessler and Fierro was the weirdest thing I've done in a long time, which is saying something. There was a big hubbub, and Duncan rushed out of his office instructing everyone to lock their desks until the legal team arrived. Then he collected keys and sent everyone to the break room.

"What's that all about?" Beth said.

Kelly shushed her. "He said no talking."

"God, I need a cigarette right now."

"It has to be about Ruth," I said.

Kelley glared and moved to the next table, but Beth and Gayle scooted their chairs closer.

"What did you hear about it? I heard someone cut her head off and left it in the sink." Gayle's eyes were alight with excitement.

"Ghoul. Try not to look so happy." Beth gave her a withering stare and adjusted her glasses. She glanced sideways at me. "Ruth told me that you knew Corinne."

"Not that well."

Tim and Tom and Ted or whatever the hell their names were wandered in looking confused. "What's all this about? Why are the police here?"

"Because of Ruth," Beth said. "Duh."

We spent the entire morning in the break room. Finally, we were herded out like cattle into the hallways. Police crawled over the place. Duncan and a man in a blue suit-- whom I took to be the lawyer because no one else would wear a suit that boring -- stood over to one side. Duncan wrung his hands in distress as our desks were searched. The contents of Ruth's desk were packed up and carried away under the watchful eye of the lawyer. Duncan kept yammering on about proprietary information.

"We aren't interested in that sort of thing," Fierro said patiently. "We're looking for personal information. But yes, we will need to know what Ruth was working on."

"She wasn't working on anything. I told you. The girls aren't assigned to any particular scientist or research assistant. I assign them work as needed. Beth is the receptionist." Duncan worked himself into a tizzy.

"We'll need to interview everyone separately," Fierro said. His eyes swept down the line of 'girls', but skittered away from mine. I looked at my shoes to keep from making eye contact.

"You can't think that anyone here is involved," Duncan said.

"At this point we're seeking information," Fierro said. "That's it for now."

We were herded back into the break room. This time an officer stayed with us to keep everyone from talking.

It was a long, boring day. I couldn't wait for it to be over so I could grill Fierro about the case.

The parking lot was jammed as everyone tried to rush out at the same time. Sitting in line, I finally took the time to check my voice mail.

"We need the black hearse back. One of the vans is in the shop. Call me." That was from Harry.

"Portia, it's Ethan. I'll be finishing up my shift, and all I can think about is you. Dinner? Call me."

"Yeah, this is Fierro. I got questions. You got answers. So call me already. You know you want to."

Of all the presumptuous men in my life, Fierro had to take the prize. The line started moving.

The first call I placed that night wasn't Harry or Ethan or Fierro. It was Ellie.

"I need your help," I said. "I've got some objects I need you to read."

"I'm busy right now," she whispered. "PTO. Call me later. After eight, okay?"

I toyed with the idea of calling Fierro versus calling Ethan.

Hmm. Information or hot sexy doctor with food? I was hungry. And information could wait.

Chapter 16

I should have known better than to plan an evening. These things never work out for me. There was no hot sex. There wasn't even any cold sex. Ethan sent me an urgent text that he was pulling a double shift, so I called him back and insisted I didn't mind at all.

I'm getting better at lying.

The next message humbled me. "Portia? This is Susie Simpson. I was wondering if you had heard anything from the police. You seemed to know that detective. I'm supposed to fly out tomorrow. Do I get to leave?" She sounded shaky.

I had forgotten poor Susie. I called her and promised to find out the answer. I also promised a ride to the airport. She sweetly declined my offer of dinner. She wasn't feeling so hungry, she said. I couldn't blame her.

I should have called Mother or Harry, but I chickened out. I didn't want to talk about hearses, condos, or the events of the last twenty-four hours. At least not with them. Mother doesn't find bloody bodies in the bathroom. She only sees embalmed and reconstructed corpses after the sisters have worked their magic.

So I called the newest number on my cell, which is why I was sitting in Mancuso's Grill eating bruschetta with Fierro. It wasn't the evening I had planned, but lately my life was nothing if not unpredictable.

"Why would Ruth have copies of a scientist's notes? Is that normal?"

I stopped eating. "Copies? Like from the copy machine?"

"Did I stutter? Yeah, like pages were stuck on the copy machine. Handwritten notes and stuff like that. So is it normal for you guys to keep that sort of thing?"

"No, it isn't. We transcribe notes sometimes, but mostly we do correspondence and stuff. From what I've seen, all the scientists are pretty protective of their work. I've never been asked to transcribe anything like that. Each scientist seems to have his 'pet' that he trusts to transcribe stuff. But Ruth is Duncan's secretary. I can't imagine why she would have something like that."

"What exactly do they research?"

"Something about plants and plant growth. Farming stuff."

"Is there big bucks in that?"

"Someone spends money on it. What are you thinking?"

He leaned forward conspiratorially. "I'm thinking industrial espionage." He sat back. "How's that for a motive?" He crammed the rest of his bruschetta in his mouth and chewed.

"You mean like spying?"

"I mean like maybe Ruth was selling secrets to a competitor. That would account for the money."

"Then why kill her? Wouldn't that make her more useful alive?"

"Not if she had passed on everything she could. Maybe she was about to blab. If this competitor took out Corinne, that could make Ruth wig out."

"But why Corinne? You never met her. There's no way she was involved in anything like that. That doesn't make sense."

"The medicated burrito probably wasn't intended for her."

I thought back. "Ruth knew about the burrito. I'm sure of it. She freaked when I started asking about the burritos in the fridge."

Fierro started on another bruschetta. "So Ruth knew about it before or after the fact? Maybe she threatened to out someone. Blackmail might explain her sudden turn of fortunes."

"Whose notes were they?"

"Don't know yet, but I will. I don't want to go waving that info around. Don't mention it to anyone. I need someone who'll recognize the handwriting, but I don't know who to trust." He looked at me hopefully.

"I don't recognize that yet. Heck, I don't even know which RA works with whom."

"RA?"

"Research assistant. They all look alike and their names are Ted, Tom, Tim... Heck, I don't know. They're interchangeable as far as I'm concerned."

"Who would you consider the most likely candidate for trust?"

I thought for a minute, chewing bread and drinking my Diet Coke. "Not one of the secretaries. And I don't know the scientists and RAs at all. Maybe Duncan Werner."

"That head secretary guy?"

"He knows everyone, and he's been with the company a long time. I'd bet he's loyal to them."

"I'll give him a shot."

"Anything interesting in the apartment?"

"Do you really want to know?"

I shuddered. "No. Tell me anyway."

"Ruth was stabbed multiple times. She bled to death. We think she was attacked and died right there in the bathroom. The place was definitely tossed, but this was no burglary. No electronics taken except her computer and her cellphone. There was a bunch of cash still hidden in the kitchen in a canister. But Ruth's desk was cleaned out. There wasn't even an address book left behind. No prints. Nothing useful that way. Everybody knows to wear gloves. Our killer couldn't have gotten out without being bloody and there were some smears in Ruth's bedroom, but not Corinne's."

"So what does that mean?"

"I'm thinking this way. Killer is in the house. He's looking for something. He searches Corinne's room. No luck. He's in there when Ruth comes home. She goes into the bathroom to take a shower and puts on her robe. Killer surprises her in there. Stabs her. Ruth lies dying in the bathroom while he searches the rest of the house."

"That's horrible!"

"Did you think it wouldn't be?"

My shoulders slumped. "I guess not. I haven't been around anything like this before."

"I should hope not."

"So how did he get in?"

"No signs of forced entry. He probably had a key. If we're talking about someone who knew Ruth or Corinne well, it might not be unreasonable to have made a copy or simply stolen a key."

I cleared my throat. "There was a key under the stairwell. I used it to get in." I explained about Corinne's instructions.

"So anyone could have known this?"

"A lot of people hide a key."

"Where is the key now?"

"I don't remember." An image came to mind. "Wait. Yes, I do. I left it on the entry table beside the front door. There's a little tray there. I set it there and forgot to grab it on my way out."

"I'll see if CSSU collected it. You realize that you've probably destroyed any evidence by handling it."

"Which I did on purpose because I knew that Ruth was dead inside." I looked down at my plate. "I need cheesecake."

"Where do you think she is?" Fierro said it so quietly I could barely hear him.

I knew whom he meant. "I don't know. I'm sure Ruth was involved in Corinne's murder."

"So she's in hell?"

"I'm the wrong one to ask."

"I went to Mass."

I set down my drink. "How was it?"

"Weird. I felt like a fraud. I haven't been to church since Gracie died. I think I believe everything the priest was talking about, but I just wasn't... into it. I can't explain it."

"I thought about praying," I said. "But it felt strange. I couldn't do it."

"Yeah, this was like walking into a new school. Nobody noticed me, but I felt so exposed."

"It was always easier with Harry." I brightened. "That's what you need."

"I need a twin?"

"No, but you need a buddy. You need someone to go with you."

He raised an eyebrow. "You volunteering?"

"Well...maybe..."

"Because it sounded like you were volunteering."

"Maybe I was. Sure. If you want to." I placed both palms down on the table and exhaled. "Okay. I'll do it."

"You act like I just talked you into robbing a bank."

"Stage fright. I'll do it."

"Good."

The silence was awkward. The waitress saved us by delivering piping hot parmesan-artichoke dip.

"Oh, I'm taking Susie Simpson to the airport tomorrow. If that's okay, I mean." I spooned some dip onto a plate.

"Why wouldn't it be?"

"I wanted to make sure she could leave town."

He laughed. "Of course she can leave town. Why? You think the nice librarian from Omaha offed her niece's roommate?"

"No, of course not."

"Me, neither. Why on earth would you ask that?"

"I don't know. Because that's what they always say on TV. *Don't leave town.*"

"She can go. You watch too much TV. What?"

I froze, my hand halfway to my lips with a chip. A blob of artichoke fell onto the table. There was something wrong in the room, something that made the hair on the back of my neck stand up. "Did it just get cold in here?"

"I don't think so." He looked around. "Maybe the door was open."

"That must be it." The cold reminded me of someone, and I knew just how to draw her out. "So, anything new in Starla's case?"

Something blew through the room. Candles on the tables flickered. I looked around, but saw nothing.

"I've worked the neighborhood, but got a lot of nothing. When I get the chance, I'll take another run at it. Shake up the husband again. See if he slips up. I don't got a lot of time to spend on Starla seeing as no one thinks it's murder yet. I've got two related murders on Corinne's case. I've got help there." He shoveled a chip in his mouth.

"Starla's out of time," I said.

"What do you mean?"

"She's in play, unclaimed. Reclaimers could grab her any minute."

It was a sobering thought. Fierro raised his beer. "To Starla."

"To Starla," I agreed. *Clink.*

"Don't I feel all warm and fuzzy?"

I sipped my beer. "How long have you been there, Starla?"

"Long enough. So my case goes to shit while Corinne is so fucking important."

"Stuff has been happening on Corinne's case," I said. "He's been working on yours when he can."

Fierro was sitting very still, cradling his beer. "I'm missing a vital part of the conversation here."

"Fierro, meet Starla. Starla, meet Fierro."

"Charmed, I'm sure," he said to an empty chair.

"Wrong chair." I pointed to the other side of the table. "Actually she isn't in the chair. She's sort of hovering over it."

"Sorry. Anyway, I'm glad you're still safe," he said in Starla's general direction.

"Fuck off, pig. Like you care." The bread basket went flying off our table. I hadn't even seen Starla move.

"Starla says it's nice to meet you," I said.

"Fuck you too, Portia." The candle on our table went out.

Starla and I glared at one another. "Starla's a little cheesed that her case isn't getting as much attention right now as Corinne's."

"Damn straight," she said.

Fierro put down his beer. "Not getting attention? Excuse me, but I spent all yesterday morning working on her case. I knocked on doors and talked to every single neighbor. I'd have kept at it, but I got called away when you tripped over the dead girl."

"I didn't trip. And you don't have to justify yourself to me." I turned to Starla. "Corinne crossed over."

She made a sound like sucking in air. "When?"

"Last night. I promised her I'd see her case through."

"What about me?"

"You could cross over too."

"Maybe I ain't ready."

"So how's the haunting business?" I turned to Fierro. "Starla is haunting Joby and Wanda."

"Interesting," he said. "Learn anything new?"

Starla gave a nasty grin. "I learned that Joby can't keep his pencil dick up anymore. Some flickering lights and a few pictures tipped over, and he wilts like week old celery." She cackled.

"No, she hasn't," I said. "She's indulging in parlor tricks."

"I ain't got no parlor. And these ain't just tricks."

"Know that people do care," Fierro said.

"Yeah, you're real noble that way," she snarled. My fork flew off the table and landed near my foot.

"Cut it out," I said through clenched teeth.

"Make me." Starla's hands were balled into angry fists.

"Fine. Be demon food. I don't know why I bother."

Customers clutched their sweaters and jackets. Drinks on the counter tipped over in the sudden gust that blew out about half the candles. Starla sure knew how to make an exit.

"Darn wind," groused a waitress. "Don't worry, hon. We'll take care of this."

Fierro looked around with interest. "Is she gone? That was bizarre. I've never seen anyone argue with a ghost before."

I retrieved my fork and set it back on the table. "Somebody is turning into a nasty poltergeist."

"That's one word for it."

"The worst part is I don't think Starla was that way before."

"Before what?" He leaned back to allow the waitress to relight the candle.

"Need anything?" she asked.

"More cheese sticks. I'm a growing boy."

"You're an eating machine," I said. "Nothing else for me."

"That's 'cause you'll eat half my cheese sticks and you know it."

I waited until the waitress was gone. "I meant that right after Starla died she was angry."

"Understandable."

"Sure, but she didn't seem so *malicious*. She isn't getting nicer. She's getting angrier and crueler. I don't think staying here has been good for her. She needs to cross over before she goes truly evil."

"That's a cheery thought."

"Come to think of it, Corinne changed too, but not in this way. She sort of came to terms with things. I don't think Starla is."

"Mmmmm. Cheese sticks," Fierro said.

* * * *

I called Ellie after her PTO meeting and begged her to meet me. She wasn't thrilled but finally agreed. Ellie didn't want to come into the city and I didn't want to drive out to Addison, so we compromised on a coffeehouse in between. It barely touched suburbia, which made it neutral territory.

I wasn't looking forward to a reading in public with Eleanor the drama queen, but I was determined to see this through.

First came the curious looks when I parked the hearse, which were followed by the whispers as people recognized Ellie. We chose a booth way in the back corner by the restrooms.

"Coffee and a cheese Danish," I told the waitress.

"Nothing for me." Ellie stowed her jacket on the seat next to her.

"She'll have coffee and a Danish too, with half-and-half, please."

Ellie glared as the waitress walked away. "I didn't want that."

"So don't eat it."

"And I certainly don't drink coffee at this time of the night."

"Did you want her to spit in my coffee? You don't take up space in a booth without ordering. Take the damn cup of coffee and tip the lady."

She folded her hands primly. "You have something for me?"

I carefully placed the little pug statue on the table.

"How sweet. Now don't tell me anything. You know I like to go in cold." Her eyes blazed with excitement. She reached out with one finger and touched the statue.

"Anything?"

"Patience is a virtue, Portia." She picked the figurine up, turning it around in her hand. "This belonged to a woman."

An obvious guess. How many men had little doggy figurines sitting out? I shifted impatiently in my seat.

Ellie sighed. "Are you ready?"

The waitress delivered our coffees and pastries. "Anything else?"

When she left, Ellie closed her left palm around the statue. The effect was instantaneous. Her right hand slid down to her side and her head lolled backward against the padding. Her eyes rolled back in her head. Her lips worked silently for a moment before she spoke.

"Woman...she loves him...loves...her dog...not fair...not fair at all... Fat girl...called me fat girl... Hate her...not fair...pain." Her voice sharpened. "Pain...my heart pounding...shouldn't...shouldn't have done it...greedy... greedy. I always knew food would kill me." A tear slid down her cheek. "Fat girl."

Her eyes sprang open, and she wiped the tear away. I had forgotten how disconcerting it was when Ellie switched from reading impressions of the object to channeling the persons last living moments.

"That wasn't so bad," she said. "Just a little sad. She was a very unhappy person. Was it helpful?"

"Not really. Try one of these." I placed Ruth's lipstick and charm bracelet on the table. Ellie studied them a minute before choosing the charm bracelet.

"The more personal the item, the more intense the impressions," she said, jingling the little silver charms. I hadn't bothered to study them before. A horse head. A tennis racket. A music note. A high-heeled shoe. A teddy bear. I wondered what they meant to Ruth. I was going to have to return something this personal. The charms were probably gifts.

Ellie's hand closed around the bracelet and she again slumped back in her seat. "A man...she steals...she steals for him...money...but love... guilty...I feel guilty." Her breath came faster. "He gave me this...he gave me...wasn't my idea... I'm so sorry... Didn't mean... Done with me? Just like that? But I did it for him... I stole for him... I killed for him."

Her voice was rising. She swatted the air as if at a fly. "Get away. I didn't tell them anything. You're so paranoid." She swatted the air again, fighting off a phantom attacker. "Stop it. Stop it. Aaagh! Aaagh!" Her hands flailed. "Aaagh!"

I grabbed both Ellie's hands to stop her from screaming. Ellie bolted upright, eyes wild. "Don't ever do that to me again," she gasped. "Those girls were both murder victims." She rubbed her face with shaky hands.

"You said you wanted to go in cold."

"Please tell me that one was useful. That was not fun."

"That one was very useful. It confirmed what Fierro and I were thinking. Ruth killed Corinne for her partner."

She arched her eyebrows. "Working closely with the detective, are we?"

"It isn't like that."

"Why not?" She smoothed her bob as if a hair were out of place. "You're both single people."

"I'm seeing someone."

"Ooh, dish."

I gave her the PG-rated version of my relationship with Ethan Feller.

"A doctor? Nice. You should marry him."

"You haven't even met him yet, Ellie."

"What's there to know? A handsome, single doctor who digs you? Don't let him get away."

"I already have a mother, thank you. Oh, speaking of, we have a new ghost and he's wearing Mother to a frazzle. Remember Old Man Biddle?"

"That creepy guy down the street? Ugh. Who could forget him? I thought he died years ago. Remember all those rumors?"

"About the house being haunted?"

"Not that kid stuff. I mean about his wives."

"I don't remember a woman living there."

"You never heard? I guess we were kids, but you never paid attention to the adult conversation," Ellie said.

"I still don't. What happened to his wife?"

"There isn't much to tell. She just vanished one day. He went around telling everyone that she up and went home to her mother, but no one ever saw her again."

"That's it? That's the big rumor?" It was uncomfortably close to Starla's story, but not all missing wives were dead.

"That was his first wife. He had a second one, a Russian mail-order bride. I remember her. She was young and kind of pretty. Well, he told everyone she left him too and went back to Russia. Didn't say goodbye to anyone. Some of her friends raised a big stink for a while because they never heard from her, but nothing ever came of it."

"Two wives who vanished? What do you think he did with them?"

She sat back. "I didn't say I thought he did anything to them. Don't go putting words in my mouth. If you were married to Old Man Biddle, wouldn't you run as far and as fast as you could?" She sipped the coffee she hadn't wanted. "Anyway, my mother always said that he hit them, that they probably were in hiding from him. That's what she always thought, anyway."

I shivered. "He won't cross over. He's sure he's going to hell and figures that they'll have to come and get him."

"Good riddance."

"But if he's hanging out at the funeral home, he's pretty safe. It's built on sacred ground. I don't think they can go there."

"Are you sure? I know demons that can't go onto sacred ground, but I think Reclaimers can go anywhere they please."

"There's a lot to learn about this gig. I wish there was some kind of manual out there."

"Can't you ask your mother?"

I gave her a look. "Of course. What was I thinking?"

* * * *

Duncan grumbled about my coming in late, but he could hardly complain about my delivering Corinne's aunt to the airport without appearing churlish. Sure, I was playing loose with my new gig, but worst case was that they fired me. I wasn't sure I was staying anyway.

Susie Simpson was as glad to get on a plane as anyone I'd ever seen. Her stay had simply confirmed what she knew about Dallas. It was a big city full of dangerous criminals just waiting to murder you in your own home. Fierro promised to have Corinne's property shipped to her as soon as it was released. He was footing the bill personally, but I wasn't allowed to tell Susie that. He wanted to do it.

I had a parting gift for Aunt Susie. As she was ready to make her escape from the hearse, I instructed her to hold out her hand.

"Where did you get this?" She turned the pug figurine over in her hand. "This looks just like..." Her voice choked off.

"It is."

"But how? When?"

"Don't ask." Because I palmed it while you were finding a dead body. "It isn't important. But it's Corinne's."

She threw her arms around me for a parting hug.

Chapter 17

As I walked into the office, I could feel eyes on me. There was something about the mood, some shift of tension in the air. Nobody looked up as I walked past their desks. There were no hellos. Beth finally looked up, gave me an icy stare and then looked away.

I sat down and tried to work. It was no good. I couldn't concentrate, so I marched myself into Duncan's office.

He was busy at his desk and didn't look up. I stood there with crossed arms. "I'm getting a weird vibe."

Sighing, he took off his reading glasses. "Close the door." I did. "You don't read the paper."

"No," I said. "It's depressing."

"Plenty of other people do. Something you want to tell me about Ruth's murder?"

A knot of tension formed in my shoulder. "Like what?"

"Like you stumbling over Ruth's body? And that photo of you being all chummy with the detective who searched us? What the hell is going on?" He lowered his voice. "Are you under cover? You could tell me, you know. I know the agency didn't send you to that job interview. I called Stephanie and she'd never heard of you, but when I checked your references, they were good. So who are you?"

In my experience, secretaries are the worst gossips God created, but I needed Duncan on my side. "I'm not police, but I am helping the detective."

Duncan raised his sandy eyebrows. "Go on."

"Listen, Fierro, that's the detective, is going to ask you some questions, but I have a few of my own."

Duncan sat back and picked up a pink message slip. "Detective Fierro? As a matter of fact, he called earlier."

"Who did Ruth usually type notes for?"

"She worked for me."

I shook my head. "She typed notes. I've seen her do it."

"The girls aren't assigned to anyone in particular."

"The scientists all have their pets. So who did she usually type notes for?"

He steepled his fingers and stared for a moment before reaching a decision. "I suppose anyone could tell you. Tamaguchi usually gives his notes to Ruth. She's the only one who can read his writing. Seleman gave his work to Corinne. Ball and Harrison do their own." He ticked off the rest of the scientists and secretaries on his fingers. He still spoke of Ruth as if she was alive.

Ruth typed for Tamaguchi? I could have slapped my forehead. In my mind I had Ruth stealing secrets from Seleman's research and attempting to poison him so no one would discover. I had imagined her sleeping with the buyer, who then had Ruth whacked once she was no longer useful. But Ruth didn't type for Seleman. Had she been selling Tamaguchi's notes? I considered the possibility of in-house espionage. Maybe Tamaguchi had a reason to get rid of Seleman and Ruth. They could have been stealing from him.

"What type of research do they do?"

Duncan arched his eyebrows again. I needed to learn that trick. "Hybridization. New strains of textile producing plants. More drought-resistant. More prolific. More disease-resistant. It's the new frontier in agriculture."

"And there's money in making new types of plants?"

"Big money. Billions. It's intensely competitive. Even within Woll Ag they compete against one another."

"You mean they don't work together?"

"Not at all. Each one works independently. That's why they get funny about who types what. Ball is so paranoid, she writes everything in code. She won't use the secretarial pool for a letter to her dentist. Don't let the false bonhomie fool you. No one is a friend in this business."

"Knock knock," said an overly cultured voice with a hint of a British accent. I wasn't surprised it belonged to Ken Tamaguchi, who looked like an ad for *Upscale Tennis Today*. He was wearing whites and carried a racquet. As he got closer, I noticed that the racquet seemed different.

"Do you play tennis?" I asked.

He looked surprised, like a bug had spoken to him. "Squash," he said before turning away. "Do you have a moment, Duncan? I have an issue to discuss."

"Not now, Ken." Duncan stood.

"This won't wait." They both turned to look at me. I know when I'm being dismissed.

* * * *

Morning was a miracle: cold, but bright and sunny. After weeks of gray skies, it drew everyone outside. I felt like I had too many balls in the air, so I called in sick. Let them fire me. I wasn't in the mood for Woll Ag. I gassed up the hearse and returned it to Mother.

Mother was with a client. "I am so sorry, Mrs. Finklestein."

Mrs. Finklestein was dead. She was also very angry. "How dare he? My poor Levi should not have to put up with such nonsense."

"I am so sorry. He isn't usually here. Hopefully, he'll be gone after his funeral. I assure you, it won't happen again. Rest assured that your Levi will be allowed to grieve properly."

I jingled the keys. Mother looked up at me, perilously close to tears. "Excuse me, Mrs. Finklestein."

From down the hall came the thunderous strains of Beethoven's Fifth being butchered on the organ. Boris played like a fiend at a breakneck pace.

"I've got a migraine coming on." Mother put a shaky hand to her forehead. "I'm so glad you're here. I need help."

"What's going on?"

From the other side of the wall came the sound of a crash followed by maniacal laughter. "Dear God, I hope that wasn't Mr. Potter's ashes," Mother said. "I agreed to bury Bartholomew Biddle. He still won't cross over. I'm hoping that after tomorrow he'll move on somewhere else." She closed her eyes. "I don't know how much more I can take."

"What can I do?"

"I hate to get you involved."

"But?"

"But his niece brought over a key. I need you to go down to his house and pick out an outfit. I was going to have Harry do it, but he's tied up and we have to bury Mrs. Finklestein today. Walter is at the airport picking up a body that was shipped. The sisters are as busy as can be. I can't leave. Lady Hildegard won't come out of hiding. Boris won't play anything other than Beethoven. I never thought I would long to hear *Roll Out the Barrel*."

"I'll go," I said. "I don't mind."

Her shoulders slumped in relief. "Thank you. Thank you, Portia."

I pocketed the key to Biddle's house and got back in the hearse. Biddle must have been listening in because he was waiting in the passenger seat. I resolved to ignore him.

He leaned over the seat and leered at me. "I'd love to give you a personal tour of my house. You were too afraid to come and visit me before."

I kept my hands on the wheels and my eyes straight ahead as if I couldn't see him. He got closer.

"I know you hear me," he crooned directly into my ear. "I'm so close you can almost feel me."

I gritted my teeth and kept staring ahead.

"You would have liked my house. We could have been friends. We can still be friends."

I parked in the street and walked purposefully to the front door. The two-story Cape Cod had been neglected for a long time. Faded blue paint peeled off in strips, and the smell went beyond musty.

According to Harry, Old Man Biddle had lain dead in the house for three days before anyone found him. The kitchen smelled of old fish.

"Don't you want to ask about my wives? Hmm? It's what everyone wants to know about."

A quick look around assured me that downstairs only contained the kitchen, a den, and a room crammed with junk. No bedroom and no clothes here.

Biddle followed me down the narrow, dim hallway. He zipped ahead and spun around. We were eye-to-eye. "You want to know where they are? What I did with them?"

"Are they here?"

"I'm not going to tell you."

"So they aren't here." I passed him and headed for the stairs.

He swooped closer. "They might be. I didn't say they weren't."

"I don't believe you killed anyone." The first door I opened was a half bath.

"I did. I murdered them."

"I doubt that."

"It's the truth."

"I think they both left your sorry ass. You just wanted people to think you were a killer."

"Oh no, they didn't. No woman ever left Bart Biddle. I killed them and three girlfriends nobody knows nothing about. So there."

I felt sick. "I'm calling bullshit on you. You're all talk and you always were. You're nothing more than a dirty old man."

Bitch," he snarled. "I'd have killed you too, but I'd have made you beg first."

Having eliminated the other doors, that left the room at the end of the hallway as his bedroom, his lair. He was dead, I reminded myself. He couldn't do a thing.

He whispered in my ear all the way down the hall. "Where could they be, Portia? Under the stairs? The basement? Back yard? Under the floorboards? In my room?"

I flung open the door and stepped over the rat's nest of magazines and food wrappers. I reached for the closet door.

"In the closet? Hmm?"

I ignored him and selected a pair of pants and a shirt. Reaching a decision, I faced him squarely. "If you did all that you claim, why not go down in history as a serial killer who got away with it? It's not like they can do anything to you."

He pulled back. "You've got a point there."

"Why not claim your fame? Why not let them have the bodies? Otherwise you'll be forgotten, a nobody."

His eyes glittered. "Maybe I should. Follow me."

I put the clothes I had selected in a hanging bag. "Like I said. I'm not interested in helping you."

"You know you want to."

"I don't."

"Do."

"Don't."

"You'll follow me. You can't help it. You know you will." He zipped down the stairs. I had no choice but to go after him. I had to go down the stairs to get out.

"In here," he called from the back of the house. "I'm by the back door."

I stuck my head in the room. "I'm leaving."

"No! Wait. Let's play. Guess where they are."

I walked to the front door. I wanted him to tell me, but I wasn't going to play his guessing games. It wasn't worth it. I put my hand on the front door, but a foul smell stopped me.

I turned back to Biddle. "You'll have to give me a clue. How many bodies total?"

"Five," he said with a grin. "Five bodies are somewhere on the property."

"Names," I said.

He wagged a finger. "First you have to guess."

"No, I get three clues. That's only fair." The goatish smell grew stronger.

"Oh, all right. My first wife was Helen. The second was--"

"The girlfriends," I said. The stench was almost overpowering. "I need their names."

"Okay, Katherine and Lorna."

"You said three."

"I lied. One wasn't a girlfriend, just a hooker I picked up. I don't know her name. Holy shit! What is that?" His eyes grew wide.

The demon was fast. Biddle didn't have a chance to move before it had him. Grasping him with claws and fangs, it bit deeply into his neck like a vampire and sucked. I've never heard anyone scream the way Biddle did. His voice was high and hysterical. The demon shifted its hold and bit him on the opposite side of his neck.

Biddle's scream turned into a hoarse gurgle. He struggled in the demon's hold, but the claws had impaled him. He reminded me of a fish on a hook, thrashing, growing weaker and fainter. Finally the screaming stopped and the only sound was the horrid sucking noise made by the demon's mouth. Biddle faded to an insubstantial wisp.

The demon released the pale husk that had been Biddle. The old man's image flickered and then dispersed. He was gone.

The demon sneered at me. Sated, it oozed out the doorway and was gone.

Chapter 18

I couldn't think of anyone who more deserved to be eaten by a demon, but I was disappointed Biddle hadn't told me where the women's bodies were. They deserved a decent burial in hallowed ground.

Harry was home when I handed off Biddle's clothes to Mother.

"About time you brought the hearse back," he said.

"You never use that old thing." I dropped the keys in his hand. "And... er...problem handled," I said to Mother. "Things should be more peaceful around here."

"What problem?" Harry asked.

"Problem client," Mother said. "Really? He's gone?" She looked at my face. "You look a little pale. Did he give you a bad time?"

"I'm fine. I think I'm quitting my new job."

"Not working out?"

"Just not for me. I'll go back to the temp agency."

"You can fill in here whenever you want."

"No, she can't." Harry had his hands on his hips. "Portia, you can't quit your job until we get the mortgage for the condo."

"She can use Mahaffey-Ringold as her primary employment."

"I don't remember agreeing to this," I said. "I never said I definitely would buy the place with you."

"You have to. It would be good for both of us."

"I'll help pay the down payment," Mother said. "It's my Christmas present to both of you. I think it's a wonderful idea."

"But Billy comes with me. Love me, love my dog."

"I thought Ellie was taking that dog," Mother said.

"Change of plans. I'm keeping him."

"Bring the dog. This will work. I'll get us something to celebrate with." Harry bounced out of the room over Mother's protestations that it was working hours.

"You must really want him to move out," I said.

"I think Walter and I have earned some alone time." She lowered her voice. "How did you ever get Biddle to cross over?"

"I didn't."

Harry burst in carrying wine and plastic tumblers. "This is all I can find."

Mother gave me a quizzical look.

"Demon attack," I whispered in her ear.

* * * *

Harry took me back to the train station. As we hurtled along he smirked.

"What?"

"You're lucky she doesn't read the papers."

"Excuse me?"

"You're lucky that Mother doesn't read the newspapers. I do." He changed lanes abruptly, passing a Volkswagen Beetle.

"Oh." Not witty, but all I could think of to say.

"Did you really find a dead person?"

"I was helping someone get stuff from her niece's apartment." I omitted the part about Corinne also being murdered. "We found this girl I worked with dead in the bathroom. Don't tell Mother."

"Is that why you're quitting?"

I clutched the armrest as he merged on the freeway. "Part of it. The rest of what I said was true. I don't like the people."

The car in front of us was too slow for Harry. He laid on the horn and whipped to the right, then back into his lane, nearly separating the car from its bumper. "But you stuck it out with Cruella de Vil for years."

"I'm never doing that again. Life is too short. So how is whatshername? The couch girl."

"I don't know. She stopped calling me back."

"Who's the new girl?"

"What makes you think…"

"Hickey on your neck."

"Aw, shit. Do you think Mother saw?" He crossed three lanes of traffic and hit the off ramp without braking.

"It's the size of Idaho. Of course she saw. What's her name?"

"Violet."

"Like the flower?"

"She's an artist."

"Cool. I want to meet her."

"Double date?"

"I'll show you mine if you show me yours? It's a deal. One thing you have to know."

"He's not really a doctor."

"Yes, he's really a doctor. He's a short doctor."

Harry glanced over in amusement. "How short?"

"Short short." I crossed my arms. "But he's a doctor and he cooks and sings and does just about everything well. Tell me about Violet. What kind of art? This is not funny." I cuffed him on the arm.

"It is so funny. You're dating a short guy. Violet is different from my usual type too."

"Omigod, is she ugly?"

"No, she's not ugly. She's hot. But she's...you know...all crunchy-granola earth-mother. Just different."

I grinned. "I can't wait to meet her."

The light ahead changed from green to yellow. Harry mashed the accelerator.

* * * *

I couldn't face going back to Woll Ag, so I made good on my threat to quit. Besides, I needed the time to box up everything I owned and move back home. Harry and I signed the papers on our condo, but we still had months before we could turn the key. I'm not sure how Richard, Ellie's husband, made the financing work, but he swore it was okay.

Since I was on a roll, I also called Ellie and told her I was keeping Billy. Things were more peaceful for Mother with Old Man Biddle gone, but this left the problem of what to do about the bodies buried somewhere on his property. Fierro and I had played a little phone tag, but I needed to see him in person to discuss things.

Violet was everything and nothing I expected. Her long brown hair hung in beaded braids. She had huge dark eyes and a too-large mouth that was always smiling.

Moving my possessions out of my apartment wasn't the double date Harry and I had envisioned, but a yellow notice from the manager stepped up my moving plans. If I wasn't out by tonight, the manager would go to court and have me forcibly evicted.

Violet had access to a horse trailer she used for hauling her pottery and sculptures around. We had a hearse, a van and Violet's trailer, which meant only two trips.

"What's in this one?" Violet held up a marker over the box I had taped.

I thought for a minute. "Hell if I know."

"You just taped it," Harry said.

"I know. I can't remember what's in there. Maybe books. Or dishes. It could be dishes."

"I'll write *fragile*," Violet said. "Just to be safe."

Ethan hoisted the box up. "Oof. Feels like books."

"Hold the bottom," I said. "I don't want them dumped out in the parking lot."

"Hearse or trailer?" he asked.

"Trailer. Those are going into storage." I hated being without my books for a month, but there simply wasn't room in Mother's house for most of my things so I had rented a storage unit.

Harry smirked at me as Ethan staggered out with the box. He hadn't made a crack about Ethan's height, but he took every opportunity to tweak me about it. I ignored him.

My lovely apartment was almost empty. The few big items I owned--table, couch, bed, armchair--were already in storage.

"Ar-ar-ar." Billy raced back and forth across the seats of the hearse. I took him out so he could deposit one last turd in the shrubs.

Harry and Violet brought the final boxes out. "Meet you at the storage place," Harry said and tossed me the keys to the hearse.

Ethan checked his watch.

"Go," I said. "I don't want you to be late for work."

"I won't. I have plenty of time to shower and change before my shift."

"Good to finally meet you. See you Sunday." Harry and Ethan clasped hands and did the manly shoulder thump thing. Harry had to bend down to do this.

I crossed my arms and turned to Harry. "Sunday?"

"I invited him to dinner," Harry said.

"You should have checked with Mother first." *And with me.*

Harry smirked. "It was her idea."

"Great." I pasted on a smile. "You get to meet the family."

"Is it okay?" Ethan asked.

"Of course. It's great. Terrific." Yikes. Deep breath.

Harry and Violet waved and drove off in the van. Ethan hooked a finger in my waistband, pulling me to him. "Are you sure it's okay? You seemed a little..."

"Surprised. I was surprised." I slipped both arms around him. "It takes bravery to face my entire family at one time. If you're ready, I'm ready."

I leaned down to kiss him. He pulled away slightly and glanced past my shoulder. "We have an audience."

I turned to see Fierro sitting in his car. Talk about bad timing. "Oh. He's a friend of mine. I'm sure he's here to--" Think. *Think.* "--talk," I concluded. And I had thought my lying skills were improving.

Fierro unfolded himself from his front seat. Ethan kept an arm around me. He couldn't have marked his territory more clearly if he had peed a circle around me.

"Hey, looks like moving day. This must be the boyfriend. Arthur Fierro."

"Ethan Feller."

The handshake lasted a little too long, as did the stare-down.

"Ethan was just leaving for work. It's okay," I said to Ethan more quietly.

Ethan leaned in for a possessive kiss. He gave Fierro a look before driving off.

"Didn't mean to set your boyfriend off."

"He's not usually like that."

"It's okay. I get it. Short man syndrome."

I put my hands on my hips. "Did you need something?"

"Boyfriend doesn't know shit about what's going on, does he?"

"No, and you'd better not tell him, either."

"Got your message about quitting the job. It's a good thing."

"You have something new?"

"We've identified the pages from Ruth's desk. The bootleg copies."

"Tamaguchi, right?"

"That's what we thought, too. But no. They belong to Dr. Seleman." He put a hand up. "I know. I know. That secretary guy said that Ruth typed Tamaguchi's papers. But I showed them around and got a second opinion. Seleman confirmed it. He gave his notes exclusively to Corinne to type."

"So Ruth took them from Corinne? That means..."

"Her accidental poisoning may not have been so accidental. Ruth could know about Corinne eating other people's food."

"I don't think it was a big secret. Duncan Werner told me about it. But that was a big gamble to take. Why not some kind of accident at home?"

"The same reason Ruth used Seleman's heart meds. She probably wanted to keep suspicion away from her."

"You can't be positive it was Ruth."

"I can," he said smugly. "There was a print on the drawer to Seleman's desk. Oh, she was careful to wipe the bottle, but not careful enough to get the whole desk."

"She could have left that print anytime. It could have been when she was stealing his work."

I didn't think it was possible for him to look even more smug, but he managed. "This was the drawer he keeps personal items in. It was the meds."

I was more confused than ever. I just wasn't cut out for the detective thing. "But we still aren't any closer to knowing who Ruth was giving the pages to."

He smiled and leaned against the van. "Closer than you think. You're a smart girl. Use your head. Who is doing the same type of research? Who is she already handing typed pages to?"

It finally clicked. Well, *duh*! "Tamaguchi! Ruth and Tamaguchi were in it together!"

"Think about it. Multiple scientists all chasing the same scientific discovery? At the end is international acclaim, not to mention Woll Ag has promised a huge cash bonus to the first one. So Tamaguchi persuades Ruth to steal the papers from her roommate's desk, copy them and replace them. Then Ruth simply includes the information in Tamaguchi's own field notes as if he did the work."

"She was in love with him," I said. "Ellie did a reading. Ruth was in love with her killer. She stole for him."

Fierro was still for a moment. "And what sort of object did she read?"

I couldn't meet his eyes. Instead I dug the bracelet out of a box. I had put it with my good jewelry and knew exactly where to find it. I handed it to him without a word. "It has a racquet on it. Tamaguchi plays squash. I think he gave it to her."

"Can you explain this?" He dangled the bracelet on the end of one finger.

"I took it from Ruth's apartment."

"How could you do this? I vouched for you with the other detectives. This could be evidence. How am I supposed to explain my having this bracelet?" His voice rose.

"Say you found it."

"You mean lie?"

"Is that so bad?"

"This is a murder investigation. I can't do that."

I faced him, hands on hips. "So you've been open about everything? About working with a clairvoyant? About where you get your information?"

"This is different. You took a piece of evidence."

"I didn't know it was evidence." I flapped my arms in frustration.

"Jesus, Mary and Joseph. I don't know how I'm gonna smooth this one over."

It was too late for contrite. I told him about the pug figurine too and what I did with it. When he was good and angry, I told him about Old Man Biddle. That stopped him.

"Are you serious? Bartholomew Biddle? Geez, I know that guy. They were always sure he killed his wives, but never could find a bit of evidence. His picture is up in the break room so guys can throw darts at it."

"Well, those bodies are someplace on that property, and I think I can get you access."

"I sure would like to close those cases. At least he got what he had coming."

I grimaced. "Yeah, I'd have to say that he did. It was horrible, yet strangely satisfying."

"Anything more from Starla?"

I shook my head. "Not a peep. I'm afraid we've lost her."

"That's too bad."

We stood there in silence.

"So you're not mad anymore? Ellie had good information."

He sighed heavily. "Not that I can use any of it. You've put me in a bad place, a real bad place."

"But it confirms your theory, right?"

"It's not just theory, Portia. We've got an arrest warrant out for Ken Tamaguchi. We searched his house and found a shirt with Ruth's blood on it. He just rinsed it and put it in with things to be laundered. Arrogant shit. I wanted to warn you off so you could stay clear of that place."

"I have to pick up my last check."

He caught my elbow. "I don't think you should be there for any reason. I'll call you when he's in custody."

"Tell that to the bank. I'm picking up my paycheck."

"I'll go with you."

"That's ridiculous. I don't need an armed escort."

"I'm telling you that place isn't safe."

I jerked my arm away. "Who are you to tell me anything? Besides, the place is crawling with security." I figured the fat guy watching his soaps counted. He could be armed.

"Can't you get a direct deposit or something? Maybe they could mail it to you."

"I'll call them." I had no intention of doing that, but lying was easier than arguing.

His eyes narrowed.

"What? You win. I won't go."

"That was too easy. I know you."

I crossed my arms. "You don't know me at all."

"And for the record, I'm still mad at you. You put me in a bad spot."

I drove off with Billy and left him there, glaring at me from the parking lot. Fierro had no right to get so involved in my life.

Did he?

There was true panic on his face when I mentioned going back to Woll Ag. I glanced over at Billy, who stood with his front paws up on the dash. He grinned at me, his tongue lolling out the side of his mouth. "Oh boy," I said. "This is a complication I don't need."

* * * *

First thing Monday morning, I drove to Woll Ag to pick up my last check. Fat Carl was behind his console taking in *The View*. I guess it was too early for his soaps. He hitched his belt at the sight of me and lumbered to his feet. "Duncan said to call him when you came in. Ya can't go up." He leaned on the counter. "Security, ya know? Nothin' personal."

I smiled to show no hurt feelings here. "I understand."

I only waited a minute before Duncan swished off the elevator. His eyes were red, and his goatee needed a trim. Even worse, his puce pocket handkerchief clearly did not complement his aqua suit.

"Everything okay?" I asked.

"Other than being shorthanded?" He glared. "Why wouldn't it be? Christ, I need a cigarette!"

I held out my hand for the beige envelope he was holding. He started pacing back and forth, stroking the soul patch on his chin. "You know, right? You know they're looking for Ken Tamaguchi?"

"I heard that. My check?"

He slapped it in my hand. "Hope you're happy." He spun on his heel and stalked off into the waiting elevator.

Fat Carl raised both eyebrows. I shrugged.

Chapter 19

Mahaffey-Ringold was much more pleasant without Old Man Biddle. Boris reverted to his ebullient self, butchering *Tin Pan Alley* and tormenting Lady Hildegard. I was in the break room when I heard the strains of *Ain't We Got Fun* trilling down the hall. Since Mother had a living client in her office, this seemed particularly inappropriate. As I stepped into the sanctuary to admonish Boris, I ran into a painfully thin woman. I mean, ran into her literally, sending us both sprawling.

"Hah! Bit of a collision, what?" Boris stopped playing and zoomed upward for a better vantage.

"I am so sorry," I said. "I was going to turn the--"

"You have the oddest music system in this place." The woman brushed herself off and straightened the crocheted doily pinned to her hair, the kind little old ladies sometimes cover their heads with in church. "Is that one of those automatic organs? Like a player piano?"

"Yes, that's it exactly. Sorry about that piece. It shouldn't have..."

"Doesn't matter," she said. "I'm not a mourner. Well, I was. Except not really. My uncle's funeral was here last week, but I barely knew him. I had to pick up his property today. We didn't want the cuff links cremated, if that makes sense. They weren't his. They're my husband's."

Something clicked. "Biddle was your uncle?" I almost said '*Old Man.*'

"That's right. I'm Bootsie Bosch." She held out a hand. It was like shaking a limp, bony fish.

I went with the direct approach. "How much do you know about your uncle?"

"Nothing," she said flatly. "We never associated with him. Mother always said he was a filthy pig, even as a little boy. She kept me as far away from him as possible."

"Did you ever hear rumors about his wives?"

"Wives?" She frowned. "I heard about how his first wife vanished. I didn't realize he ever remarried."

"A lot of women went missing from his house."

"I don't want to talk about it." She tried to push past me.

"The police want to search the house."

"That's not a good idea." She shook her head. "I don't like that at all."

"I have reason to believe that there are women's bodies buried in that house. Five of them. And you're the owner. You could give the police consent to search."

"I said no." She clutched her handbag. "You're blocking my way."

"Why not?"

"I'm selling the house. My husband and I could use the money. The last thing I want is for it to be some notorious--"

"You can still sell the house. They won't destroy it." Much.

"It isn't just the house. I have children. I don't want people to know. It isn't fair to them for people to know their uncle was a *you know what*." She leaned forward and whispered.

"A serial killer?" I whispered back.

She straightened. "That is so presumptuous. You don't know anything of the kind."

"But we would if you let the police search. Knowing the truth won't change anything."

"It will for me."

I studied the old-fashioned head covering. And here we were in the chapel. "Don't you think those women deserve better? Don't you think they deserve to be buried in hallowed ground? What about their families?"

She looked down at her hands. "I can't promise you this won't be on the news, but no one has to know he's your uncle, right? Different names and all."

She was quiet for a moment. "I guess so. There wasn't any reason for this, you know."

"Reason for what?"

"There wasn't any reason for him to be a monster. My grandparents were nice people. It wasn't that kind of family. His wife came over once or twice when I was little. She seemed...nice." Bootsie Bosch shuddered. "Tell the police they can search the place. Just keep my name out of the papers. I don't want anyone to know. If they find something, let me know. I'll make certain those women are buried in hallowed ground."

I stepped aside to let her go.

"Whew, I thought she'd never leave. So the old crackpot wasn't just a braggart, what?" Boris swooped closer. "Did he really murder five women?"

"Apparently so."

"Good riddance to bad rubbish, I say. Care for a little sing-along? Hmm? Maybe a little canoodle?"

"No, and Mother has living clients in her office, so lay off the Cole Porter. I need to call the police before Biddle's niece changes her mind."

"Suit yourself, but you don't know what you're missing. I know how to treat a woman," he called after me.

I ignored his halfhearted advances. Flirtation was like breathing used to be for Boris, second nature. Fierro's cell rolled automatically to voice mail, so I left a message about Biddle.

I tried to put Biddle out of my mind. I had more stressful things to worry about. Ethan was having dinner with Walter and Mother tonight, which meant ghosts and killers would have to take a backseat.

This was real terror.

* * * *

When I opened the front door, the house was spotless. The couch had a fresh slipcover on and all knickknacks were dusted and polished to a shine.

"In here," Mother called out. "I need your help." I could hear the clatter of pots and pans. I followed the sound into the kitchen. Something smelled overcooked. Tonight she was roasting a succulent chicken into a hunk of jerky.

"I'm not much help for that." I pointed at the doomed bird as she brushed it with margarine.

"Not that. Her." Mother pointed over her shoulder. "This is Mrs. Bierstock."

"Good grief," I muttered. Mrs. Bierstock was impossible to ignore. Pink and round, with an upturned nose, she reminded me of a little piggy, a very *sad* piggy. Mrs. Bierstock perched on the beige linoleum counter weeping ostentatiously.

I cleared my throat. "Pleased to meet you, Mrs. Bierstock."

For some reason this made the woman bawl louder.

"Mrs. Bierstock is having a difficult time adjusting," Mother said. She stirred a gelatinous goo that bubbled sluggishly in a sauce pan. Gravy? At least the salad looked fresh. It was still contained in its plastic bag on the counter.

"Hiya, doll. How's tricks?" Hephzibah reclined on the window seat, both legs stuck out in front of her and crossed at the ankles. Her bony calves poked out of her burnt orange velour tracksuit, reminding me of a boiled chicken.

"What gives?" I asked her, sidling closer.

"Like your mother says. Mrs. Bierstock seems to be having a difficult time adjusting."

"I see that. But what can I do?"

"Talk to her." Mother brushed stray curls away from her face. She was beet-red and sweating in a way that had little to do with the hot stove. Menopause had snuck into her life, and this meant we would all get to enjoy the pleasure of a house that felt like a meat locker. "Try to reason with her," she said.

"I'm guessing you've already tried."

"Mrs. Bierstock don't seem willing to communicate." Hephzibah uncrossed her legs, rotating her ankles. "She won't talk."

"Waaanh!" Mrs. Bierstock wailed.

"And you think I have ways of making her talk?" I intended to take a shower and primp, not run interference for Mother's latest project. "Couldn't you have left her at work?"

Mother yanked the meat thermometer from the chicken carcass. "Don't think I didn't try."

Mrs. Bierstock cried harder.

"Sorry," I said loudly. "I didn't mean that. Why don't you come into the living room with me? It's nice in there."

"Ding-dong," sang out Violet's sunny voice.

I looked at Mother in panic. "You invited Violet? Don't tell me you invited..."

"This is a family dinner. Everyone is invited. Don't you like her?"

"Of course I like her. It's just...never mind. I'll go say hi." And hope she brought wine.

She did and we immediately uncorked it. "Where's Harry?" I asked as Violet poured the zinfandel.

"I thought he would be here. He said something about a late run to the crematorium, but he should be here by now."

"Waaanh!"

Mrs. Bierstock had followed me out of the kitchen. She was likely the reason for the late run.

"He had a pickup at Our Lady too, but that was earlier. He said to be here around six-thirty." Violet tucked a braid behind one ear and chewed her lip.

"Waaanh!"

Violet wrinkled her nose. "What's that smell?"

"It used to be chicken," I said.

"I don't eat meat. Is that going to be a problem?"

"I don't know if I'd still call it meat, but it did used to be alive. I know there's salad and probably mashed potatoes and stuff like that. How about some fruit? I saw apples and oranges on the counter."

"I can make do."

"Harry called. Said he's running a bit late. He just left the crematorium." Mother came into the room, wiping her hands on her apron.

"Waaanh!" *Didn't the woman ever shut up?*

Mother avoided my eyes. "I'll take some wine too. Fill it up," she instructed, then knocked back half the glass in one swig. She held it out for a refill.

"Thought we'd make some screwdrivers for cocktails." Walter emerged from the back porch carrying orange juice and vodka and some little plastic sacks. French bread poked out of one. He stopped at the sight of us. "Or we could drink the wine."

"Save the vodka," Mother said. "I may want it later." I wanted something stronger than wine, but drunk might not be a good thing. I probably needed my wits.

I was saved by the doorbell. Ethan looked yummy as ever in chocolate brown slacks and a buff shirt that showed just the right hint of muscular chest without delving into Hasselhoff territory. He stood on tiptoe to kiss my cheek.

If Mother was startled at his height, she was graceful enough not to show it. Ethan held up a bottle of Cabernet Sauvignon. It was unanimous. Everyone had determined that alcohol would be necessary for the evening. "I brought a little something to share, but perhaps it won't be needed."

"Oh, it will," I assured him under my breath.

He also produced a lovely bouquet of gardenias, freesia and white baby roses for Mother. She inhaled the heavenly scents.

"These are so beautiful. What a thoughtful man. Look, Walter. The doctor brought us flowers." She winked at Walter.

"His name is Ethan, Mother."

"Of course it is." She opened her arms wide as if to hug the room. "I'll just put them in some water."

"I'll go," I interrupted, snatching up the flowers and heading for the kitchen, where Mrs. Bierstock had retreated. She sat cross-legged on the kitchen table. Hephzibah studied her impassively.

"So what happened to her?" I asked.

"Car wreck. Her and two kids."

"Kids?" I sucked in my breath. My lower lip quivered.

"Teenagers, but yeah, kids. She was talking on her cell and eating a hamburger."

"Then where are the kids? Did they..."

"They crossed over, doll. Kids almost always do. They're used to following orders. Then again, the kids died on the spot, but she didn't. That makes it harder. When she passed, she jerked away and has been damn near hysterical ever since."

My feelings softened. Mrs. Bierstock had accidentally killed herself and her two teenage children. Her sorrow was understandable. I made a mental pledge to hang up when I drove.

I located a nice crystal vase under the sink. I took a moment to arrange the flowers and carried them over to the kitchen table where Mrs. Bierstock was still noisily mourning the life she had so casually disregarded.

"Mrs. Bierstock? Mrs. Bierstock?" She ignored me. "Mrs. Bierstock, don't you want to see your kids?" Her shoulders shook with the force of her sobs. "I know you feel bad about what happened, but staying here won't change anything. You need to go with Hephzibah."

Mrs. Bierstock turned her back to me, continuing to cry.

"She ain't listening, doll."

"Fine. Just stay in the kitchen until after dinner. I'll deal with you then."

I carefully snagged my wineglass with my left hand and hefted the crystal vase with my right. My fingers were just long enough to curl around the mouth of the vase.

As I pushed open the door to the dining room with my foot, a ghostly howl wafted down the hall that led to the bedrooms.

Aroooooooooooooooooo!

Great. Just great. All I needed was a Billy serenade through dinner. He was probably shedding in the middle of bed and trashing my pillow.

"There you are. Let me get that." Ethan took the vase and placed it on the table. "Do you need a refill?" He eyed my drink.

"Not yet." I smiled.

"The night is young." He winked and leaned in to whisper in my ear. "Don't worry. Moms love me."

"That's not what I'm worried about."

"I'm dating you. Not your family. Besides, they seem nice."

"Harry is coming."

Ethan grinned. "Can't wait to spend more time with your twin. I'm sure he'll tell me all sorts of gruesome stories about humiliating events from your past. It will be fun."

"Maybe I do want that refill."

His lips lingered on mine.

Aroooooooooooooo!

"Is that..."

"He'd be in the way."

Violet found us. "There you are. Is the table set?"

"Still no Harry?" I grabbed the stack of plates off the counter.

"No Harry yet." Mother crossed to the sideboard and uncorked the zinfandel again.

"Is everybody here already?" A voice came from the front of the house.

"Harry!" Violet bounced out to meet him.

Aroooooooooo! Aroooooo! Billy wailed at the sound of Harry's voice.

I lurked in the doorway. Harry bent to brush Violet's cheek, but she turned her head and enthusiastically kissed his lips. He looked up and we locked eyes. Both his ears blushed.

Mother knocked back another glass of wine. "I'll get the chicken," she said with a frozen smile on her face. She stood and tilted to one side. She steadied herself with a hand to the table before mustering her dignity and tottering to the kitchen.

Walter stood too. "I'll go help."

"That might be good." I turned to Ethan. "She isn't normally a lush. Nerves."

Unfortunately, Mrs. Bierstock followed Mother out of the kitchen this time and hovered over the table, weeping. My earlier wave of sympathy faded. I know the woman had suffered a tragedy, but she needed to get a grip. If she kept refusing all attempts to help her, she would end up Reclaimed, or worse.

Down the hall, Billy carried on his serenade. Even Hephzibah got lonely in the kitchen and came out to offer words of wisdom.

"What the hell is that?" She gestured at the desiccated chicken. "You ain't really gonna eat that, are you? Man, I wish I had a pot roast right about now. I love a good juicy cut of meat. Speaking of juicy meat, that boyfriend sure is some looker. Hang on to that one, doll."

Mother drank heavily. Walter eyed her rapidly emptying glass with trepidation, but when he looked at her face, he didn't say a word. She glared over the table at me as if was my fault that we had a crying ghost floating over the table, a pug howling down the hall and a running commentary on the dinner party courtesy of Death.

Okay, the middle one was my fault, but dinner hadn't been my idea in the first place. I had wanted Mother and Walter to meet us somewhere for cocktails where we could retreat to neutral corners. Now we were stuck with one another for the evening.

After dinner, as we trouped into the living room, the doorbell rang. Harry loped to the door and stepped back, grinning wildly before the guest could even get in a word. "Portia, it's for you."

Fierro stood in the doorway looking pissed. Over my shoulder, I could hear the agitation of an equally unhappy boyfriend.

I rushed to the door and Fierro stepped back. Ethan was right on my heels, but I turned, placing my palms on his chest.

"What's he doing here?" Ethan huffed.

"It's okay. He's here to talk to me about something that happened at work."

"He keeps showing up."

"It's okay. He's a cop. There was an incident at work. That's all. Please go back inside." I hated the wheedling note in my voice.

They glared at one another, but Ethan finally went back inside.

Fierro scuffed the stoop with his shoe. "Sorry about that."

"How about some pie?" I turned in disbelief to see Harry holding up a Perulli's box. "What?" he said. "Bring your friend inside and offer the man dessert. No reason to skulk around outside. Dr. Wonderful will get over it. So are you here to arrest Portia?" I was going wipe that grin off Harry's face.

"Why? Has she done something else I need to know about?" Fierro glanced over at me and I knew that he knew I'd been to Woll Ag.

Harry continued grinning like the idiot he was and looking back and forth.

"Harry, this is private," I said.

"Okay, sure." He was completely unabashed. "After your super-secret important conversation, at least have the decency to let the guy come inside and get a slice of pie. It's French Silk." He took the box inside with him. I slammed the door.

"So." I turned and found Fierro standing uncomfortably close. He was quick for a man his size.

"You just couldn't resist, could you?" he said.

"Resist what? Picking up my paycheck? You're annoyed I went to Woll Ag."

"Annoyed? That's a mild word for it. What the hell were you thinking? You couldn't wait a single day to let us pick Tamaguchi up?"

"No, Fierro, I couldn't. I have bills to pay, damn it. Half my stuff is in storage, and that isn't free. You don't get to tell me what to do."

"I didn't tell you what to do, but it was a reasonable suggestion, a pathetic plea on my part, really. I'm the bad guy for worrying about your safety."

I was acutely aware of how close we were standing, aware of his scent, of him as a man. I took a step back. "How did you know I went there?"

"For crying out loud." He ran a hand through his crew cut. "We have people watching. Hell, we've got people in the place."

"Then it's even safer than I thought. It's not like Tamaguchi has any reason to come after me."

"Stay away from now on. That place isn't safe."

If he was trying to keep me from Woll Ag, that was the wrong thing to say. It made me want to go there even though I had no legitimate reason to do so. Just because. I crossed my arms and stuck my hands in my armpits to warm them up. The cold was starting to get to me. "You don't think Tamaguchi would dare go back to Woll Ag, do you? I mean, assuming he knows you're looking for him."

Fierro's face darkened. "He knows." He didn't elaborate.

Another thought occurred to me. "You don't think he acted alone."

"Damn, you really are psychic."

"Seriously, Fierro. Did Tamaguchi act alone?"

"We're not sure. I have reason to believe that he didn't, and don't ask me 'cause I can't tell you. But someone helped him cover his tracks. That's all I can say."

"Wow. Okay, I'll be careful."

He shoved his hands in his pockets. "That's all I wanted. For you to stay safe."

A frantic scrabbling started at the door behind me, followed by muffled barks. The door cracked open and a fawn and black bundle burst out. Billy wound around our feet ecstatically.

"Hey, buddy." Fierro leaned down to scratch Billy's head. He snorked with joy, depositing his Dingo at Fierro's feet.

"Sorry." Violet poked her head out. "He was so pitiful."

She opened the door wider, and Fierro picked up the soggy Dingo and threw it inside. Billy tore after it. Violet closed the door again.

"We got the consent to search from Bootsie Bosch. We're gonna rip up Biddle's place tomorrow."

"Can I come?"

"Sure. It'll attract most of the neighborhood. These things always do."

"I hope you find them."

"So do I. I've pulled in a bunch of crime scene guys for this. It won't look good if we dig up nothing but a bunch of rusted cans." He shoved his hands back in his pockets. "I'd better go now."

"Don't you want that pie?"

"Better not. I think your boyfriend might develop an eye twitch." He turned and made his way down the walk.

"Fierro."

He turned back.

"Thanks for worrying," I said softly and went back into the house.

* * * *

Ethan sat between Harry and Walter on the couch looking grumpy. I rousted Harry and sat close, sneaking my hand into Ethan's. His expression brightened. "The situation at work is going to be okay," I whispered.

He gave my hand a squeeze and kissed my shoulder.

Billy ran to the door, hoping to be let out for more playtime. When rebuffed, he ran around trying to get everyone to play "Throw the Dingo." Dingo was a soggy mess after being savaged repeatedly, and folks became less and less willing to touch it.

I leaned over to Walter. "Shouldn't we clean up the dining room? The dog will get into the food."

"If we're lucky, he'll steal the chicken and there won't be any leftovers." Walter rubbed his belly.

I could see the wisdom in this. Maybe I would even push a chair closer to the table. Pugs have short legs.

Ethan was right about being good with moms. He was impressive. He was witty and charming. Not only had he eaten every bite of rubbery chicken without comment and even swished around the runny mashed potatoes and gelatinous gravy, but he helped clear the table later.

Billy insisted on sitting in my lap and snorking, which Ethan tolerated with good humor. He even played a cutthroat game of Trivial Pursuit and chased the dog helpfully when Billy stole the pieces. Mrs. Bierstock banished herself to God knows where. Walter told longwinded stories that went nowhere. Mother got quietly snockered on wine and sank into her easy chair, snoring softly. Only Harry seemed unaffected. His expression toward Ethan was distinctly cool.

"What is your deal?" I hissed at Harry while dunking dishes into the soapy water.

"I don't know what you mean."

"What is your problem with Ethan?" I handed him a plate to dry.

"Nothing. Golden boy is fine, okay?"

"You're jealous."

"I'm not." He dried the same plate again.

"You act it."

"Whatever." Harry set the plate to the side. "If he's so wonderful, why is he so needy?"

"Excuse me?" I dunked another stack of plates into the water.

"You heard me. Needy. Golden boy is as needy as a labrador retriever." A howl sounded from my back bedroom where Billy had been once again banished for savaging one of Mother's good throw pillows. "Or a pug. I don't care if he is a doctor. He's not right for you. I'm telling you this as your twin. You should dump him. That detective guy is hot for you."

"You deduced this after meeting Ethan twice and Fierro for all of ten minutes?"

Harry ducked his head, his ears burning red. "I'm saying it's really obvious. The detective guy likes you. And Doc isn't all he seems."

It was a strangely urgent speech for Harry. "I have no idea what that means. And how did you know Fierro was a cop anyway? When Fierro showed up at the door, you knew who he was."

"I recognized him. Newspaper. Remember that?"

"Oh. Sorry, but twinhood doesn't entitle you to pick my dates. Speaking of, I guess you and Violet are getting serious."

His eyes went wide. "She thinks so, doesn't she?" I thought he was going to hyperventilate.

I rinsed the last dish and dried my hands. "How would I know? She's *your* girlfriend. Is it serious? Should I be picking out bridesmaid dresses?"

"I like her and all, but I'm not sure I'm ready for what Violet is thinking."

"And what is she thinking?" I flicked him with my dish towel.

He turned away. "How should I know? But it's something serious." He shuddered.

* * * *

Walter bundled Mother off to bed, and Harry snuck Violet up to his room over the garage. I toyed with the idea of taking Ethan back to my bedroom, but the idea skeeved me. This was the same room that formerly sported pony posters and a yellow bedspread with daisies. Walter and Mother were down the hall. I just couldn't.

I settled for leading him to the back porch. Even wrapped in a heavy coat and Ethan's arms, I shivered. I snuggled closer to him, tucking my feet under myself. He gave the porch swing a little push with his feet. We swayed gently.

I tilted my face to him for a kiss.

"This is nice," he murmured against my mouth.

I explored his lips. "Mmm."

"I like your family. They're interesting."

"Interesting. Good choice."

He leaned back slightly. "I had fun."

"I'm having fun now. Or I was." I kissed him again, slowly and then with more energy, until the shivers got the better of me.

"We could go inside," he suggested, sliding a hand inside my coat.

"No," I groaned. "I can't do it in my mother's house."

His lips curved in a wicked grin. "My car has a heater in it."

"And bucket seats."

"The seats recline."

Giggling like teenagers, we ran hand in hand to the street where his car was parked. "Pull it around to the back," I urged. "By the garage. It's hidden by the neighbors' fence."

He fumbled his keys with eagerness, cranked the heater, then parked in the dark hollow between the garage and Mrs. Peeple's house.

He started to lean back his seat, but I pulled him to me for a long kiss. Then I pushed him back into his seat and straddled him. It was a tight fit.

He felt amazingly good pressed to me like that. He stripped off my coat and then shirt. The steering wheel pressed into my back. Ethan popped the seat and we both fell with bone-jarring suddenness. In a few minutes we had the car rocking with our rhythm. Afterward, we stayed there, listening to the radio. I rested my head on his chest.

"Come home with me tonight," he said.

"I can't." I placed a kiss in the crook of his neck and nuzzled his throat. "I've got a busy day tomorrow. The funeral home is slammed, and I suspect Mother's going to be hurting in the morning." Only part of that was true. I wanted to be there when Fierro searched Biddle's house.

Ethan laughed, his breath moving my hair. "I don't know what it takes to get you and keep you for the evening, but I'll find out. Just you wait."

Chapter 20

The morning sky darkened like an angry bruise. The perky blonde on my TV screen predicted yet more rain, but we had a viewing and a funeral scheduled. I clipped the leash to Billy, who snuffled with excitement, and took him for a quick run around the block. True, I couldn't really run with him. His little legs worked hard to keep up with my slow trot, but it was good for him to get out and do his business in someone else's yard.

He joyously inhaled scents off of everything we passed and hiked his leg a few times to contribute his own. Trotting past Biddle's house unsettled me.

It was only a house. Sure, the yard was choked with weeds since he no longer tended it. Winter meant it wasn't a jungle, just straggly grasses and Queen Anne's Lace. The paint was peeling, and one of the shutters on the upper story hung loosely. It rattled in the brisk wind.

I pulled my hat down tighter and gave the leash a tug. Billy popped out of the bushes, bright-eyed. Suddenly, he stopped and turned, staring straight at the house. My skin crawled.

"Come on," I said and tugged again. He hesitated, but followed.

We circled the block and made it inside in time to see Mother stagger down the hall cocooned in a chenille robe. She had showered, and her wet head was wrapped in a towel turban. She winced as I flicked on the lights.

"What time is it?" she said, her voice barely a whisper.

"Time to rise and shine." The daughter's revenge. How many times had these roles been reversed? "Would you like some coffee? How about scrambled eggs, nice runny ones?"

She groaned and staggered back down the hall. "Get things set up for me, will you? I think I'm going to be late."

"Can't. I've got an errand this morning. I told you last night. Remember? But I'll be there in time for the viewing. Cross my heart."

She whimpered and closed the door to her bedroom.

Ar-ar-ar-ar!

I found Billy in the kitchen. He had all four feet planted squarely, his head tilted back as far as he could without breaking his thick neck. His eyes bugged.

"Waaaaaanh!" Mrs. Bierstock was up near the fluorescent light.

It was clear that he could see her and he didn't approve.

Ar-ar-ar-ar!

"Waaaaanh!"

I snatched the vociferous pug up off the floor. He squirmed, trying to get a better view of the ghost.

"Cut it out. You'll wake the dead." This made me giggle. "Okay, maybe not, but you'll piss off Mother. If you keep barking at ghosts, you can't go to work with me anymore."

I set the coffeepot to brewing and went for my own shower.

* * * *

Biddle's place was barricaded off with yellow crime-scene tape. True to Fierro's prediction, neighbors had already gathered. Two news vans were ensconced across the street. The cameramen looked bored, stuffing their faces with breakfast sandwiches and checking watches.

"Isn't this exciting?" said Mrs. Peeples. She hadn't bothered to take the pink sponge rollers out of her hair, but she had powdered her face. "I always knew Old Man Biddle was a dangerous criminal."

The CSSU folks stood around in black Windbreakers and sensible shoes. Tessler ducked under the yellow line to meet me by the street. "Fierro says you talked the niece into signing the consent for us. We appreciate that." He steered me away from the crowd by my elbow.

"Glad I could help. I hope you find all the women."

He shifted his gum to the other side of his mouth. "You mean both women, right? The two wives?"

"There were rumors about something more, girlfriends. I thought there might be more bodies. Like...um...five of them."

"Really." He stared hard at me. "Interesting. We'll see what we see, I guess. Fierro's in the house."

"Could you guys use some coffee? I don't mind making a run."

"That would be great. Fierro was out late last night. Must have been with his lady friend." He nudged me with his elbow.

"Lady friend?"

Tessler shifted feet. "Thought you maybe knew her or something."

I shook my head. "No, but...but I'm glad for him." I felt a little sick.

"Yeah, he met someone recently. They've been going out. It's about damn time, too. It's the first time he's paid attention to a woman since Gracie died."

Of course Fierro had a girlfriend. Fierro and I were more like brother and sister anyway.

Like family.

Totally platonic.

Kissing him would have felt wrong.

This was good.

I made excuses and left to get coffee. I wasn't disappointed. Not at all. Why hadn't he mentioned it to me?

Stupid men.

I found things to do before I headed back to Biddle's place. Finally, I pulled up with Styrofoam cups in a cardboard cup holder.

Fierro was standing out front. I held up the coffee and his face brightened. He waved me under the tape. "Man, am I glad to see you," he said, taking one of the cups. "Tessler said you were going for coffee, but that was like an hour ago."

"Yeah, I was busy. Any luck yet?"

"Nada. We haven't found squat. Tessler is arguing with the lieutenant about getting geo equipment to check the grounds, but that's pretty expensive. I don't think we'll get a lot more time." He took a sip of the coffee. "Hey, cream but no sugar. Good call."

I smiled weakly. Of course I knew how he liked his coffee.

"Man, that place is nasty." Tessler came across the yard, hitching up his belt. "Coffee! My angel. Lou says it's a no-go with getting any equipment out here. We've got two hours tops. Then he wants CSSU outta here."

Fierro nodded. "Better let them know the clock is ticking."

Tessler hesitated for a moment. "Sure." He glanced from me to Fierro. "Sure. I'll do that." He raised a questioning eyebrow, but left us.

Fierro pulled me over to the side and lowered his voice. "Can you give me anything more to go on here? Anything at all?"

I closed my eyes, trying to recall my conversations with Biddle. "He admitted to five women and he said they were here. That's all I know. There aren't any spirits here for me to ask. I'm pretty limited. No Hephzibah, either."

"That's Death, right?"

"Yeah, but she's not here. I never thought to ask her for help in this."

"So maybe Biddle was lying."

"He could be, but I thought he was serious. I'm sorry. This looks bad on you, but it's all my fault."

"Naw, we've been trying to get in to search this place for ages. Lou isn't pissed at me. He just doesn't want it to cost a lot. But I've got one more card to play. I'm not ready to pack it in yet." He took a long drink of the coffee. "That's good stuff."

"So--" I kept my voice casual. "Tell me about your girlfriend."

"My who?" His face was puzzled. I told him what Tessler had said.

"Oh." He looked away. "Vic misunderstood."

"He seemed pretty sure."

Fierro sighed. "Look, I told him that 'cause he kept wanting to know where I had been. I couldn't very well say I was my checking on my psychic friend, so I tried to give him something vague. He's built this up in his head."

"So no girlfriend?"

He drained the last of his coffee and crumpled up the cup. "No girlfriend." He tossed it at the trash can, but the wind blew it to the side. He sighed and picked it up. "There's my ace up the sleeve right now."

Ellie's Suburban pulled in behind my car. Two more black SUVs pulled in behind her with heavily tinted windows and PIU logos on the doors. Four people bailed out of the darkened vehicles, all in matching black.

Tessler started over, but Fierro flagged him down. "It's okay," Fierro called. "I asked them to be here."

Ellie waved cheerily. Tessler whirled back to us. "You invited her?"

"And her whole team. Yes, I did. If there is ever a place for the Psychic Investigators Unit, this is it. I've promised them access. Lou knows about it."

Tessler's mouth hung open. "You called in psychics? You?"

Ellie ducked under the tape, followed by a woman with some sort of handheld device taking readings of God knows what. Two cameras tracked their every move.

"You agreed to this?" I recoiled from the camera trained on me. Ellie put a hand on the cameraman's shoulder.

"Give it a rest for a minute. How about some establishing shots before we go in? Set the mood a bit while I talk to them." He wandered away. She shook hands all around and introduced herself like everyone didn't know her.

"Do you know how Mother is going to react if she sees me in any of these shots? Is this for your show?"

"A special," Ellie confirmed. "I can try to keep you out of it. Or you can go."

"I was hoping you would stick around," Fierro said to me.

"Is she psychic too?" Tessler glared.

Ack! "Of course not, but I can help her." I rubbed my forehead. "I'll stay." Mother would flip, and there would be hell to pay when Aunt Bella got back from Europe. Mother would blame her for giving birth to Eleanor. "Don't worry about the filming. I'll deal with it, Ellie."

"Good. You're coming inside with me? In case I need help?"

I glanced over at Tessler, who was studying me carefully, his eyes narrowed.

"Sure," I said. "I'll do what I can."

We had the full attention of the CSSU folks. They congregated around the edges, muttering and laughing to themselves.

Ellie barked something and her cameraman scampered back. We proceeded inside. Ellie picked her way through the trash, wrinkling her nose as she stepped over the debris of Biddle's existence. Her hands stayed in her pockets so that she didn't touch things accidentally.

Tessler rolled his eyes, but got an elbow in the ribs from Fierro and a hard look. He sulked and hung back.

"Not much personal stuff here in the kitchen," Ellie commented. The room reeked of stale burgers and fries with an underlying funk of urine and sweat that permeated the entire house. I was anxious to be out of that room myself.

I pointed toward the stairs. "His bedroom is upstairs." Tessler raised an eyebrow. "I had to get a suit for him to be buried in."

Ellie looked at me. "Anything else I should know?" I shook my head. "Right, then. Upstairs."

Ellie was followed by her cameraman, then the two detectives, then me. It made the cluttered bedroom very crowded.

"That's his closet." I pointed across the room.

"What's in there?" Ellie gestured to another closet next to the one I had found his clothes in.

"I didn't tour the place. I got his clothes and left."

"Would somebody open it?"

Fierro snapped on gloves and opened it. It was stuffed to overflowing with crap. Just opening the door shifted things. A box started to slide. Fierro caught it and hefted it back into place.

"Open both closets, if you please."

Fierro did. Ellie studied them both, arms crossed. "That hat. He wore that a lot." She gestured to a worn Cubs ball cap.

Tessler removed the hat and held it out. Ellie circled it slowly. "Set it on the bed."

Tessler sighed and tossed it onto the frayed bedcovers, earning him a glare from Fierro.

She stared at it for a moment as if it might bite before cautiously making her way closer. She closed her eyes, taking deep, cleansing breaths in a great show of readiness, and then picked up the hat. For a moment, there was nothing.

Then her eyes rolled back and her head lolled. She grunted a few times, rhythmically. "Stupid bitch." Her head snapped back and forth. "Nobody leaves ... stupid ... make you sorry..." Her voice was vicious and low. A shiver ran down the base of my spine. I recognized the intonation. She sounded just like him. "Beg! Beg for it! Maybe I'll let you live! Beg me!" Her face mottled red with rage. "Stupid, fucking cunt! Should've done it a long time ago... What the...burns... Oh, shit." Ellie fell to the floor with a soft moan and was still.

"Cripes, she's passed out." Tessler knelt beside her.

"Just give her some air," the cameraman pleaded.

"Ellie? Ellie?" I cradled her head.

Her eyes fluttered. "He killed her in here. On the bed. Oh," she moaned. "He raped her and killed her. A woman with long dark hair. He strangled her. He made her beg for her life and loosened his grip like he was going to let her live. Then he tightened again." Her eyes searched wildly. "He was playing with her. Oh my God. The hatred."

"It's okay," I said uneasily.

"Something else happened to him," she insisted. "I saw him die."

"He had a heart attack." Fierro squatted on his heels next to me.

"No, something ate him," Ellie said. "It was big and smelly. It pierced him with its claws and sucked. It burned him from the inside out."

I felt faint myself. "That part doesn't matter," I whispered. "Old Man Biddle is gone. Really and completely gone." We locked eyes.

Tessler cleared his throat. "Are we done now?"

Ellie struggled to sit up. "No, I saw women's things crammed into that closet. Maybe I can get something that will help us figure out where they are."

"You sure?" Fierro helped her to her feet. "That was pretty intense."

"I got all of it," the cameraman said with satisfaction. "It was fantastic. Really good stuff, Ellie."

Ellie smiled faintly. "I'm fine. It's upsetting, but it doesn't hurt."

Tessler peered in the closet. "I see some women's clothes and a purse and..."

"I'll take the purse," Ellie said. "The more personal the object, the better the reading. Purses are great. Women hold them close to their bodies and take them everywhere. Does it look worn?"

"Yeah." Tessler drew out a battered black leather bag. "I'd say it got a lot of use."

"Bed," Ellie said.

This time he laid it carefully on the bed. Ellie went through her prep routine. Finally, she kneeled by the bed and took the purse in both hands. She was instantly in the slack-jawed thrall of her gift. "I don' wanna," she said thickly, her words slurring. "Wanna sleep. Go 'way. No." A soft sob. "Not again. Unh. Unh." She shook her head back and forth, gagging as if choking. Her eyes bugged open. Her mouth worked soundlessly. When she drew air in, it was loud and harsh. "Oh my." She spoke in her own voice. "Oh. My."

"Did you get something?" Fierro leaned in.

"That woman was drugged. She didn't know him. Biddle was a stranger to her. She was pretty confused, didn't know what was happening. I think he kept her for a while."

We were silent, absorbing the implications. They had expected wives and I had expected girlfriends, but no one had been prepared for the notion that Biddle might have held unknown women prisoner in his home. I'd thought the story about the hooker was just another boast. I was suddenly very, very cold. I wanted out of there.

I turned to go, but Ellie stilled me with a look. "Stay?" Her eyes pleaded her case. Finding out that the bogeyman of your childhood really was the bogeyman is deeply upsetting on a primal level. Just your friendly, neighborhood serial killer. How many times had we dared one another to ring his bell and run?

I turned back.

As the morning wore on, we had learned a great deal about Biddle and his house and the women who had lived and died there, but we were no closer to finding any physical evidence. Ellie would have one hell of a TV special, but that was about it.

Defeated, we trouped down the stairs. The CSSU had run out of time and begun to pack things up. I paused at the bottom of the steps, and then it struck me.

"I can't believe I forgot that." I smacked myself on the forehead. I could picture Biddle trying to lead me into the back room. "That room back there. We need to go there." Four sets of expectant eyes stared, waiting for me to explain. "I just remembered that he spent a lot of time back there. In that room and the back porch. We need to go there, as well."

Fierro sighed. "You heard the lady."

Ellie shook her head, worn from the emotions. How many deaths had she lived that day? "Let's start with the back porch. Now that you mention it, he spent a lot of time gardening."

"We've dug the back yard all to pieces," Tessler said. "It looks like the moon with all them craters."

"What about the porch?" I asked.

"Pulled up some boards. Nothing down there."

Ellie looked hard at me. "Can't hurt. Let's go out." She strode resolutely to the back door and grasped the knob. It doesn't matter how often I saw her do it. It always squicked me.

Ellie's eyes fluttered and rolled back until only the whites showed. "Heavy. The fucking bitch is so heavy... Too many of them under the tree...maybe I need to make the patio bigger...fucking cunt...ought to just burn it...I wonder..." Her eyes snapped open and gradually focused. "That's it. He put them under that stand of pine trees when the trees were little. Then he put them around the edges of the pavement and poured more concrete. They're under the slabs. He added those."

"Holy shit," Tessler breathed. "You sure?"

"'Course she's sure." Fierro rubbed his hands together. "She saw it. Hell, she lived it."

Tessler looked at the stand of trees in the back yard. "We're gonna need to get the equipment back here to yank those out. That ain't gonna be easy."

"What about the concrete slabs?" Fierro eyed them. They were about three feet by four feet slabs of concrete that lined the patio slab. They didn't look any deeper than an inch. He was already out the back door and pulling at the edge. It came loose and lifted. He dropped it back down. "Get CSSU back out here. Let's give it one more try."

I was sitting in the passenger seat of my car when my cell vibrated.

"Where are you?" Mother demanded. "I need you here. The viewing has turned into a vigil, and it's a little more complicated. I have to get over to First Baptist for the funeral."

I checked the time with a guilty start. "Sorry. I got caught up in something. I'll head in." I slid across to the front of the hearse regretfully. I could call and check on things later.

Chapter 21

"There you are. It's about time. Where have you been?" Mother had taken Billy to work with her. He trotted on her heels.

I shrugged vaguely. She would know soon enough, but her pissed-off face made me hesitate to mention it now. Her hair looked like she'd been running her hands through it.

She turned on her heel and stalked back into the sanctuary. Billy planted himself at my feet and watched her go. Boris only got four bars into *My Blue Heaven*.

"Give it a rest!" Mother snapped.

Harry brushed past me. "Lie low if you can. She's wicked hung over. Got a pickup." He vanished. Coward.

I followed Mother into the chapel. The coffin was in front. I could see it was top-of-the-line mahogany with platinum handles, no expense spared. Enormous flower arrangements clogged every available space. The smell of lilies was cloying.

"You knew we had a viewing today. You knew I needed help. I have a graveside in just two hours, and I can't be two places at once."

"Chill, Mother. There's plenty of time to get everything ready. Why are you so frantic?"

She fussed over the cushions, rearranging them, stepping back and then doing it again. "No reason."

"Do I look all right?" A matronly, olive-skinned woman of indeterminate age hovered over her casket, peering down. I looked at her corpse. She seemed in danger of bursting out of the plunging neckline of her couture gown.

"You look fine, Mrs. Jimenez. Doesn't she, Portia? The sisters did a good job."

"You don't think the necklace is too much? I can't believe Leo is going to bury me with it." She sniffed. "He always spoils me so."

"It's lovely," I said. "You look very nice." The sapphire on the necklace would have choked a horse. I could have retired on the amount of bling the woman was being buried in—assuming that the grieving Leo didn't have it removed before the casket was closed and lowered. It wouldn't be the first time.

"Oh, look at the little doggy. Aren't you a cutie?" Billy wagged his tail and flopped over to give Mrs. Jimenez a view of his belly.

"I've got to check the altar linens," Mother muttered, striding down the center aisle.

"Do you have blue?" Mrs. Jimenez traipsed after her. "Blue would match my eyes."

"Blue altar linens. Who's ever heard of such a thing? How's the love of my life?" Boris materialized at the organ and played *My Sweet Embraceable You*. He sang along, winking suggestively.

"It's been a long day, if you must know."

"I could wipe those lines of care from your lovely brow, my dear. I love all the many charms about you. Above all, I want my arms about you," he sang.

I laughed. "Don't you ever get tired of your womanizing ways?"

"No, actually I don't. Tell me about poor misbegotten Starla. What's her story?"

"Has Starla been here?"

"Oh yes, quite a bit as of late. She's endeared herself to Hilde, what? Thought they were going to have a slap about."

"Her story is more Nashville honky-tonk than Tin Pan Alley, something about drinking and cheating."

"Oooh, jealous husband? I know all about that."

"No, she was the jealous one and she caught him with her former BFF." His face was puzzled. I realized Boris didn't get the modern slang. "Best Friend Forever," I supplied. "Don't mention the name *Wanda* unless you want to see her go all poltergeist."

"Boris is something of an expert on jealous husbands, aren't you?" drawled the cultured tones of Lady Hildegard.

Billy startled and growled at her.

"Shut up, Hilde," Boris snarled.

"Haven't you heard the sad tale of how he died in the arms of his mistress?" Hildegard said.

"I said shut your yap." Boris played faster.

"Shot through the heart by a jealous husband. Too bad it was from behind while trying the exit the window. He left the poor woman there to face her angry husband alone and--"

Boris smashed the keyboard. "You're nothing but a vengeful bitch who never loved anything but yourself in your whole damn life. You're not even a lady."

Starla materialized above the organ. "You tell her, Boris!" I should have known that she would be drawn to drama like a moth to flame.

"I won't be addressed that way by a washed-up gigolo and a cocktail waitress."

"Oh gee," Starla sneered. "Sorry I ain't a mafioso's wife. Y'all get on real well."

"At least Mrs. Jimenez is a music lover," Hildegard said. "She appreciates opera. Her husband is a great supporter of the arts."

Starla laughed. "They're all a bunch of wise guys. That's your type."

"My type can't be found in a place such as this." Hildegard rose up near the ceiling. I swear she had actually swelled up like a toad.

"Then why are you here?" Starla rose to her eye level.

"That's the first intelligent thing you have said to me." With a crack like a gunshot, Lady Hildegard vanished.

My neck was going to snap off in a moment. "Come down here, Starla. What's that about mafia types?"

"Don't you know?" Hephzibah sat on the front pew. "It's a bona fide feud." She popped her gum. "The Kilpatricks and Jimenezes go way back to Prohibition. I bet Boris here knew some of them. They ran competing speakeasies. Things got real nasty when the Kilpatrick clan served some bad hooch. Rumor was that the Jimenez bunch diddled with it. Someone ratted Jimenez out to the revenuers. Grandaddy Jimenez did a stretch in the pen. Things got ugly and stayed that way for a couple generations. Then

Lisa Kilpatrick ups and marries Leo Jimenez over her father's objections. And trust me, nobody can object like Conan Kilpatrick. Things got kind of testy."

"How romantic, like Romeo and Juliet." Boris peered over the organ.

"Yeah, and everybody dies too." Starla settled on the organ like a torch singer.

"Conan Kilpatrick is good people. He keeps me busy," Hephzibah said.

I gasped. "You don't mean... Did he..." I searched Lisa Jimenez's corpse for bullet holes.

Hephzibah snorted. "Kilpatrick thought the sun rose and set on his only daughter. But Lisa had a booze problem. Took out a mailbox, a front porch and a poodle before burying her Dodge Charger nose-deep into someone's living room."

"Did anyone else die?"

"Naw, just Lisa and Mr. Puffy."

"Ixnay on the oodlepay," Starla said out the side of her mouth.

"Oh dear. It isn't time yet. I'm not ready." Lisa Jimenez pulled up short at the sight of Hephzibah.

"Relax, toots. You have until tonight, but then a deal is a deal."

Mother's tension became logical as mourners filed into the chapel, guys with names like Slow Eddie, Johnny One-Time and Repo Rico. It was the first time I'd had to ask mourners which side of the family they were on.

Slow Eddie bowed up at a little guy with jug ears. "You gotta lot of nerve showing up here, Peanut."

"Hey, Lisa was my cousin. I got a right." Peanut didn't back down.

Johnny One-Time didn't say a word, but lumbered to his feet to stand behind Slow Eddie.

"Oh, look," I said as loudly as I could. "Father Pat is here!"

Both sides reluctantly parted to allow me access to the center aisle. I fled to Mother's office and called Harry. "Get your butt back here right now."

"I had a pickup."

"*Had* being the operative word. I don't give a crap if you had a summons from the Pope. Get yourself back to home base pronto." I hung up on him. How dare he run off and leave me alone with these people?

The chapel was filling at an alarming rate. If things went bad, we would have a riot on our hands.

"Mother?" Where had the woman gone to? Had she gone off and left me too?

"Right here." She had a stack of programs. "I forgot to put these out and the guest book, too."

"Why didn't you give me the heads-up? I thought this was a viewing? When did it become a vigil? And why here? Shouldn't they do this at the church?"

Mother closed her eyes. I could see her lips counting silently to ten. "The church was booked." She crossed herself. "And so was Father Mike. Is Pat tanked?"

"Yup." I took the programs and guest book. "I'll put these out front."

Johnny One-Time grunted and pointed at Billy. "Whazzat?" I'd forgotten to put him up in the office.

"Sorry." I scooped Billy up. "I'll put him up."

Slow Eddie held up a hand. "Leave him. Lisa always liked little dogs, and given the circumstances of her unfortunate demise, it would be good karma. The dog stays." He looked outside and his eyes narrowed. "What the hell is he doin' here?" Slow Eddie gestured out the window. Johnny One-Time grunted.

Fierro had parked his car and started up the walk.

"It's okay," I said. "He's here about something else in the neighborhood. It's nothing to do with you. Go back in the chapel. I'll handle it."

"See that you do." Slow Eddie jabbed a finger at me. "I don't want him here when Leo gets here. Leo is *distraught*. Got that?"

"I got it."

Slow Eddie allowed himself be steered back to the chapel.

I could see the answer on Fierro's face: tired but jubilant.

I was pleased to see Fierro, but Billy spun in circles then tore off down the employees hall.

"I think he's going to look for his Dingo," I said. "How many?"

He grinned. "What makes you think I found anything?"

I punched his arm lightly. "Stop teasing and come back here." I grabbed his hand, dragging him down the hall. Billy was frantically snuffling around the break room. "I don't think Mother brought Dingo."

"It keeps him busy. Biddle lied to you."

"It wasn't five?" I shouldn't be disappointed that there weren't a bunch of dead women. What a ghoul I'd become.

"Twelve."

My jaw dropped. "Excuse me, but I thought you said twelve. Did you say twelve? My ears heard twelve."

"Twelve bodies. We're gonna have a heck of a time figuring out who they all are, but at least we found them. I'm hoping Ellie can help us with the identity issues."

"That's amazing. I'm so glad. Not that they're dead, but that you found them." I looked around.

Fierro leaned closer and lowered his voice. "Why are we hiding?"

"We're hiding from my mother."

"You didn't tell her yet? Don't you think she's going to find out?"

"Now isn't the time. Trust me on this. You don't know how rabid she is on this subject." I dropped into a chair.

He turned a chair backward and straddled it, leaning his crossed arms on the back. "So make me understand."

I sighed. "She always throws the name Elizabeth at me. It's like a secret code for how wrong things can go. Elizabeth was one of our ancestors who got hung for being a witch. Actually, if you look through the Mahaffey family history, there are always women being accused of witchcraft. Keeping it secret became a big deal in the family. You aren't even supposed to tell your husband."

"What about you? You've told me. And what about Ellie?"

"Aunt Bella isn't thrilled with Ellie's choices. I mean, you can't be much more public than that. Do you know about Agnes? My other cousin?" He shook his head. "She's in Europe, Romania to be exact, communing with the dead. That's where Aunt Bella is right now, visiting Agnes. Agnes is public too, just not in the way Ellie is. And sometimes Aunt Bella interprets visions for people. She's a visionary. She sees stuff, but she sucks at knowing what it means. It's sort of hit-or-miss. The thing is, not everyone is as fanatical about the secret as my mother is, but she's not trying to be a bitch about this. It really scares her to go public."

"The world isn't the same way," Fierro said. "A lot of people think psychics are cool. There's all those shows about paranormal stuff on TV."

"But others still think we're evil, that we do bad things or that we're in league with the devil. This is the Bible Belt."

"I think that without you those women would still be lying in shallow graves. You did a good thing. But I understand. I'll keep your secret for as long as you want me to."

"I appreciate that."

"So…" He swung his leg over the chair and stood. "You have dinner plans?"

I had an anxious twinge in my stomach. "I'm having dinner with Ethan."

"That's good. Have a nice evening."

His eyes slid away from mine, and I knew in that moment that Tessler was right about everything.

There was a woman in Fierro's life, and it was me.

My heart clenched. The last thing I wanted to do was hurt him. He deserved more than I could offer. Someone nice he could take to Florida to meet his mother. Someone who could cook. Someone who didn't have conversations with Death. Fierro was a guy built for marriage.

I stood there waiting for him to say something, to beg me not to see Ethan, but he didn't. He waved and left.

I should have been relieved.

Instead, I was disappointed.

Chapter 22

The viewing was a success as much as anything of that type could be. Maybe Father Pat was the perfect choice. I suspect he passed something around. All I know is that by the end of the afternoon, everyone in there was hugging and crying together like they were on the Dr. Phil Show.

Lisa Jimenez was so moved that she didn't even balk at leaving. She and Hephzibah were belting out *All You Need Is Love* as they stepped across the invisible threshold into the next world. It took a bit of wrangling to empty the place of mourners, but we had an evening funeral. Mother went for a nap in her office.

After the chaos of the day, Mahaffey-Ringold was impossibly quiet. Even the resident ghosts seemed to be absent. I flicked on every light in the place and plugged in the vacuum. It filled the void for a bit, but when I turned it off, the place seemed emptier than before.

Desperate for noise, I turned on the radio in the office and set the speakers to broadcast. This played music in the sanctuary while I gave everything a good dusting and placed the large photo of Mrs. Bierstock on the easel. Harry would bring the urn. So maybe Blue Oyster Cult wasn't the most tactful choice for a funeral home, but it was just me and the dog.

I turned to go back to the office and Mrs. Bierstock's photo attacked me. Actually, it fell off the easel and hit me, but I jumped like I had been attacked.

Deciding that the smell of fresh coffee would steady my nerves, I went back to the employee break room.

"Hiya, doll. Seen Mrs. B. around? I'm real hopeful I can get her at the funeral."

I was never so relieved to see Death in all my life. I dropped into the chair next to hers. "She was still in the kitchen, still bawling away."

"That ain't good. She's gonna have to get a grip. Her time's just about up."

"It can't be. Didn't she just die a couple of days ago?"

"Six."

"Oh, shit. I had no idea she was so close. Is the mark gone?"

"Fading," Hephzibah confirmed with a nod.

"So what about the kids, the ones who died with her?"

"Oh, they've been dead a long time. See, this lady was in a coma for months. It would've been easier if I could have crossed them all together. She might have gone then. Sometimes when they get stuck in limbo for as long as she did, makes it hard for 'em."

"Now I'm feeling sorry for her again."

"What is this caterwauling? This is worse than Boris!" Lady Hildegard sniffed with disapproval.

"It's classic rock. I'm guessing you're not a Clapton fan," I said.

"I prefer Wagner to anything recent generations have to offer."

"I keep telling you, he was a bloody Nazi." Boris materialized behind me.

"And I keep explaining to you that my admiration is for his understanding of a woman's voice and his dramatic use of rhythm. His Gotterdammerung is quite simply--"

"Absolute crap."

"How dare you..."

"You want rhythm? I'll show you."

They both vanished. In moments I could hear dueling voices in the sanctuary. *It's Delovely* vied with *Welches Unhold's List Lieges Hier Verhollen.*

With a sigh I turned off the radio and left them to it. Hephzibah was gone, and I started the coffee.

A sudden chill alerted me that I wasn't completely alone.

"Hello, Starla."

"Hi, yourself."

"What are you doing here?"

"Why shouldn't I be here? It's safe. Joby's at work anyway, and he ain't no fun there. I got nothing better to do. Until tonight. Then the fun starts again." She rubbed her hand and cackled, sounding for all the world like the green-faced witch in *The Wizard of Oz*. "I think he's about to crack wide open."

"Seriously. Why are you here? I thought you made your feelings clear the other night. You were rude to Fierro. He's put in a lot of time and effort on your case, and that's his own time and effort because the department doesn't think there is a case."

"That don't mean I don't need help." She lowered herself a few inches so that we were at eye level with one another.

"Would it have killed you to be polite?"

"That's funny. Real clever."

"You know what I mean. You could have at least said thanks or something. Instead you threw a hissy fit."

She swooped closer. "So he's pissed at me?"

"*I'm* pissed at you. Fierro is a nice guy who's trying to help you, and you treated him like crap!"

"I'm sorry," she muttered.

"You should be apologizing to him."

"I would if I could. Okay, so I got a little heated. Tell him I'm sorry. I won't do that again. I still need your help."

"If I help you, will you cross over?"

"No. No way. I don't want to be totally dead."

"You are dead."

"But that would be like really dead, like it's really over."

"It is over, Starla."

"No, it ain't. I'm a bona fide free mover now. I ain't never crossing over, and that's a fact. Will you help me?"

"Why should I? Give me two--no, give me *one* good reason I should help you."

"But, but..." she sputtered. "But I need you. You're all I've got. My husband killed me, and nobody wants to do anything about it."

"I'll think about it," I said, more harshly than I'd intended.

Starla began to cry and then vanished. I sat and hung my head in my hands, feeling lower than dirt. I started as something snuffled at my hands.

Billy licked me and then nudged a hand to be petted. I was starting to get why people have dogs.

I reached for a mug and my cell rang.

"Portia? It's me." Fierro's deep voice was a welcome sound.

"Hey, you. I was just going to call."

"You were?" He sounded pleased.

"Starla wanted me to apologize for her. She's sorry for her little tantrum the other night." I didn't tell him I'd read her the riot act beforehand for treating him that way.

"Tell her it's okay. I didn't take it personally. But my news is better. We've got Tamaguchi."

"That's fantastic. Where did you find him?"

"Actually he found us."

"Is he talking? Did he tell you anything? Does he have a partner?"

"No, I meant that he surrendered himself. He walked in all lawyered up. He hasn't said a single word. They've booked him, and his lawyer has been here trying to get a bond set but that ain't gonna happen. He's suspected of killing two women. With that purple shirt as evidence, no way is he getting out. It doesn't get better than greed as a motive and physical evidence."

I frowned. "Did you say purple? Is that the bloody shirt you found? I never saw Tamaguchi in anything but white."

"It was in his laundry. Who else could it belong to?" Hard to argue with that logic.

"So it's over."

He was quiet for moment. "I guess so."

"But he might still have a partner out there."

"This is true."

"And we still have to sort things out for Starla," I said. "She did apologize."

"Portia, I'm not going anywhere."

I exhaled. "That's good. I've gotten used to you being around."

"Like I said. I'm not going anywhere."

The pleasure in his voice warmed me down to my toes. "I'm counting on that."

"How about we try that church you talked about on Saturday night? Unless you've got a date or something else to do."

"I don't. That would be great."

* * * *

Mrs. Bierstock's funeral was the saddest thing. There were maybe a handful of people. I counted four before I had to excuse myself. Mr. Bierstock stood stoically by, and I was pretty sure the woman who held his hand was more than a friend. No one cried except for Mrs. Bierstock herself. Did they blame her for the kids' deaths? Had they been distanced emotionally by the time she spent in a coma?

Mrs. Bierstock sat in a corner, sobbing. She stayed there all day and was still there when I left.

* * * *

I prefer it when things are busy, but for the entire next week Mahaffey-Ringold was, well, dead. I cleaned the chapel for lack of anything better to do. Boris and Hildegard squabbled like siblings or an old married couple.

Mrs. Bierstock wept quietly in the corner where she had become a fixture. She hadn't left since her funeral and either sat and cried or prayed at the altar. I had given up trying to make contact with her. I couldn't help her. Perhaps she could help herself.

I found Hephzibah kicked back in Mother's office, yakking her ear off. "Hey, doll."

"Hey, yourself." I flopped into a chair.

"Don't you have a date?" Mother said. "Go home and get fixed up. It's been a long day."

I didn't need a second invitation. I fetched my purse from the chapel and headed for the door. The weeping sounds grew closer. I glanced over my shoulder. I was being followed. "Mrs. Bierstock? Mrs. Bierstock, you should stay here. You don't want to go out there with me." I was pretty sure her mark had faded, but I kept walking and she kept following me.

"Mrs. Bierstock?" I stopped and turned. "You need to stay here. You'll be safe."

She ignored me and kept crying. Finally, I left. If she followed me, she must have her reasons. Perhaps the woman wanted to be eaten by demons. There was nothing I could do for her if she wouldn't listen to me. I went home.

* * * *

I must have been in the kitchen for a good fifteen minutes before I noticed something was wrong. I had completely tuned out Mrs. Bierstock and was making myself a cup of tea, when I spotted the first one. I thought it was a shadow near the cabinets. I had to look twice to be sure.

There was no shadow, but a dim figure standing in my kitchen. The figure didn't cast a shadow as much as it sucked in the light. It was an absence of color and feature. A slight movement drew my eye to the fridge. Two more Reclaimers. My heart beat faster.

They almost blended with the wall, but not quite. I opened my mouth to warn Mrs. Bierstock, but nothing came out. I felt the vibrations in my chest before I heard the hum. The walls cracked from the intense vibrations.

For the first time, Mrs. Bierstock seemed to notice things around her. She lifted her head and looked around. "No," she said. "Oh no! Not this." They were the first words I heard her speak.

Her eyes roamed the room searching for escape. She made a break for the outside. The Reclaimers were on her the second she moved.

I rushed after them and opened the back door. Three had their arms around the struggling woman. No longer crying, she fought them viciously, but she was no match.

"No!" she screamed. "Let me go! I don't want to!"

When the humming became screech, I clapped my hands to my ears. The night sky split wide, and a light pierced my eyes so that I had to look away. I could hear the rumble as the sky continued to open. The wind had picked up, rushing from the gaping hole in the sky. My hair whipped my face, stinging me.

A swirling funnel of wind surrounded me, tugging at my clothing and sucking me toward the gaping hole in the clouds. My feet lifted off the ground briefly.

And then everything was still. And quiet. The crushing light dimmed. I was standing on the ground.

I carefully opened my eyes. They were gone.

I went back inside and canceled my date with Ethan. I wasn't feeling like company.

* * * *

I had the house to myself. Mother and Walter were always looking to expand their horizons. At least, Mother was. Making her happy made Walter happy, and so they had signed up for salsa dancing lessons. Harry was gone with Violet to one of her art shows. Just me and the pug.

The doorbell surprised me. A glance at the clock showed me it was eight o'clock. I left Billy on my bed, lovingly mauling his Dingo, and closed the bedroom door behind me. Frantic knocking quickened my step.

I peered through the peephole, then opened the door. Duncan Werner swished past me, running a hand across his head as if he had hair to muss. I stared in bemused silence at my former boss pacing my living room.

"They won't let Ken out. Did you know that? Why won't they let him out?"

It took me a moment to realize he meant Dr. Tamaguchi, who was still in jail. "Because he killed Ruth. Why are you here?" I closed the door, leaning back against it.

"Because you work for them undercover, right? You would know what's going on."

I swallowed hard. My lies had returned to haunt me. "How did you get my address?"

He stopped pacing and stared with red-rimmed eyes. "Your job application. You listed this address." He put his hand on his hip. "I don't even know why they arrested Ken. I took care of it." He began to pace again. "I was sure I got everything."

It hit me like a slap. Duncan was the mystery partner, the one who helped Tamaguchi clean up his messes. He must have told Tamaguchi I was asking questions about the burritos. Duncan's lip trembled. He was emotionally invested in this. Tamaguchi had been his friend.

I made my voice as gentle as I could. "Duncan, go home. There's nothing more you can do. You're not a bad person. You tried to help a friend, but he's already been arrested. There isn't anything you can do.

Tears leaked down Duncan's cheeks. "If Ken talks to them... If he has... Has he? Did he say anything?"

"Not that I know of."

He sighed and leaned against the mantle, wiping the tears on his sleeve. "I should have known he'd be faithful." He looked at me. "I've made mistakes. I should have handled everything myself. Ken counts on me."

"You don't have to help him anymore, Duncan. He made this mess, not you."

"Ruth made this mess! Ken may have been sleeping with that little slut, but it was me that he loved. I was the one he shared himself with, told his hopes and dreams to. She was useful to him, but he never should have fucked her. She thought that made her special." He sniffed. "She killed Corinne, you know. Ruth did that, not Ken."

He looked at me and I nodded. "That's what I think too. Ruth must have thought Corinne knew about her passing Seleman's research notes over to Dr. Tamaguchi."

"Which is not illegal. Career suicide, maybe, but people ride scandals like that out. The bitch panicked. Poor little Corinne. Ruth poisoned her with Seleman's heart medicine because she thought it would throw suspicion on him, but it just drew attention to Woll Ag. Ruth was such a fool. She should have let me handle things. I could have helped them."

"Duncan--" I circled him uneasily, trying to put the couch between us. "They were using you. Ken Tamaguchi used you because you care about him."

"Shut up! You don't know anything! I don't know what you said that made them arrest Ken, but--"

"I said? Excuse me? I didn't make them arrest him. I'm not with the police, Duncan. That detective is just my friend. But the police know Tamaguchi was involved. Personally, I think Tamaguchi knew everything Ruth was doing. He helped her kill Corinne."

"That isn't true!" Duncan was crying again.

I stopped moving. The couch was firmly between us. Duncan stood next to the end table with the lamp and phone. "Tamaguchi got Ruth to do his dirty work for him. Everybody knew Corinne was eating other people's food. Ruth might know she ate Seleman's burritos, but how would she gain access to Seleman's medicine? All the scientists officed together on the same floor. Ken Tamaguchi had access to Seleman's office, and he cleaned up the burritos. See, Ken and Ruth couldn't know which one Corinne would take, so they poisoned all of them. They didn't care if it was Corinne or Seleman who ate those burritos. And you want to know the worst part? Corinne didn't know anything. She died for no reason. Ken Tamaguchi has been using you, Duncan, just like he used Ruth. He used her and then he killed her."

Duncan's face hardened. "You and your cop friend think you know so much, but you couldn't be more wrong. Ken didn't kill Ruth." He reached into his pocket, pulling out a hunting knife. "I did."

He unfolded it carefully. The blade locked into place with a soft *snick*.

The memory struck me with a blinding flash. I could hear Ellie channeling Ruth's last moments. *"I stole for him. I killed for him."* Him. Not *you*. She hadn't been talking to her lover.

Duncan was between me and the phone. Following my eyes, he picked it up and smashed the receiver to the ground, stomping the bits that broke off. Then he ripped off the wall-mounted phone, hacking away at the cords tethering it.

I backed away, but before I could make a break for the front door, he circled, blocking my exit. He advanced, holding the knife underhanded like a street fighter. I ran for the back bedroom. He would kill me if he could catch me. I was almost to my room when his hand snagged my hair. My hand was on the doorknob. I had the door barely ajar when his weight took me down, knocking the air from my lungs. I was prone on the floor with him on top of me. My arms flailed in a wild panic. I caught him with an elbow and heard him grunt. Then his hands were in my hair again, pulling my head back, exposing my throat.

Billy barked madly. He flung himself against the cracked door and scrabbled at it with his paws.

Duncan's hand was completely tangled in my hair. He slammed my face against the floor. My vision exploded with stars as the bridge of my nose connected with wood. Tears poured from my eyes, obscuring what little vision was left.

He had me down, but I was taller and stronger and I never stopped fighting. He held the knife at an awkward angle. We were mashed up against the right side wall, and Duncan seemed unable to get his arm loose. I slammed him to the right as hard as I could and heard something clatter along the floor. He had lost the knife.

My bucking and twisting again rolled him sideways, and we both grabbed for the knife at the same time. His hand closed on the blade first, but we were now face-to-face. I raked his eyes and face with my nails. He screamed, rolling away as my nails tore through his skin.

I was up and moving, half-crawling, trying to get to my feet. He was right there behind me and grabbed my ankle. I kicked at him as hard as I could.

The bedroom door was flung wide open by an unseen hand. Was this ghostly help? Duncan shrieked and released me. "Get him off me!"

Billy had sunk his teeth into Duncan's leg. Snarling, Billy shook his head like he was savaging his Dingo.

My cellphone rang. I looked around, unable to pinpoint the sound. It was muffled. The couch. It was in the cushions somewhere.

I made it to my feet and flung pillows off the couch. A gleam of silver caught my eye. I grabbed, clicked and screamed into the receiver without checking the number. "He's got a knife. It's Duncan Werner. It's Duncan Werner. He's here!" I prayed it was Fierro.

I had trouble praying before, but at that moment it was easy to beg, to bargain with God for my life and the life of my dog. "Help me! Help me!"

Duncan hacked at Billy with the knife. Blood ran down Billy's side. With a yelp, he let go. Duncan stood over him, panting.

I rushed Duncan from behind. He spun, knife still in hand, and flung me against the wall. His body pressed against me. I hung onto him, unable to let go, trying to pin his arms. The cell lay open on the floor where I had dropped it. I screamed again, hoping it wasn't some telemarketer. In the close quarters, Duncan couldn't get a good stab in. He caught the knife in my sweater, slicing it open. The knife grazed my side. The thin slice burned. He brought his arm back. I head-butted him. He stumbled back, and I brought up my knee as hard as I could. It made solid contact, and he screamed in agony as I drove his nuts up into his throat.

He crumpled, his face white. I drew back my foot and kicked him again. Hard. Duncan curled into a fetal position.

I kicked the knife away, panting. He struggled as if trying to raise himself up. I grabbed Mother's pewter candlestick off the end table and clobbered him with it. I probably hit him more times than was necessary, but the bastard had tried to kill me.

Billy whimpered, a blessed sound. He tried to get to his feet. Equally welcome were the faint sirens in the distance growing closer.

Chapter 23

I sat in the back of the ambulance, wrapped in a blue blanket, my feet dangling, when Fierro pulled up. He screeched his car to a halt near the curb and jumped out, leaving it parked sideways on the street. I shivered and pulled the blanket tighter around me.

"You should go to the hospital," the EMT insisted for the third time. "I've cleaned it and put a butterfly clip on it, but it needs sutures."

The cut to my side was deeper than I'd thought. If Duncan hadn't missed me through the baggy sweater, I could have been dead. The realization had begun to sink in, and I couldn't stop shaking.

"Jesus, Mary and Joseph." Fierro ran his hand through his hair. "Jesus, Mary and Joseph. Is she okay?" he asked the EMT.

"She's in shock. And she needs to go to the hospital to get a cut looked at. It isn't life-threatening, but it needs attention. She's being stubborn."

"She can be that way." He looked at me, his face hard. "I'll take responsibility. I'll see that she gets it looked at."

"Okay." The EMT shrugged. "I'll get a refusal form."

"Tamaguchi was using them both," I said. "He was playing Duncan and Ruth against each other. They both killed for him."

Fierro stepped closer, his face bathed in the flashing red glow of the vehicles. "I'm so sorry." He reached up to touch my hair. I realized his anger wasn't directed at me. His hand shook in a way that had nothing to do with the cold. "I never thought Werner would come here."

I took his hand and pressed it to my cheek. "It's okay. I'm all right."

He closed his eyes, shaking his head. "I should have protected you. I am so sorry. I never warned you about Duncan. I thought he was involved, and I never told you. I should have watched your house."

"Stop," I said. "Look at me." He opened his eyes. "This wasn't your fault."

"Sign here." The EMT shoved a clipboard under my nose. "It says that you refused transport."

I released Fierro's hand to sign the form and hopped off the ambulance. Okay, maybe *hopped off* isn't accurate. Very gingerly, I settled my feet on the pavement.

"I need to check on my dog," I said.

"The dog is okay," the EMT insisted. "I checked him myself before sending him on."

Fierro grinned. "You're a vet too?"

"Hey, that little guy was a hero. He saved your friend here."

"I'll take that into account. Where is Billy?"

"One of the uniforms took him to an emergency clinic over on Spartan," said the EMT.

"He wrote the name down for me," I said. "I want to go there and see Billy for myself."

"I'll drive you," Fierro said. "But only after you get that cut stitched."

"Not to Our Lady. Ethan is working. I don't feel like having that conversation right now."

He grunted in understanding. "Yeah, there's a night clinic over on the east side. I can drive you there."

My knees shook, and for a moment I was lightheaded. He put an arm around my shoulder to stabilize me. "You sure you don't want that ride in the ambulance?"

"Do you have any idea how much that would cost? I don't have insurance."

He nodded. "Point taken."

I leaned my head on his shoulder and let him lead me to his car. "I'm glad it was you."

"Hmm?"

"The phone." I lifted my head up. "I had no idea who it was. I just screamed and hoped it was someone who would send help."

"You scared me half to death with that, I hope you know. I was all the way downtown." He smiled slightly. "I knew North Division would get here quickest. They said you scrambled Werner up good."

I smiled a little myself. "Part of it was luck."

"And part of it was grit too," he said. "Very impressive for a secretary." He gave my shoulder a squeeze and helped me into the passenger seat. I winced at the pain in my ribs as I settled into the bucket seat. The adrenaline had worn off, and I hurt, really hurt. Everywhere. My head, neck, shoulders, sides, legs. My nose was starting to throb. I hoped it wasn't broken.

Fierro sat in the driver's seat.

"I'm gonna need you to sign a complaint on Duncan in the morning. They're booking him for Ruth's murder, but I want him for trying to kill you, as well. And you are gonna have a dandy of a shiner tomorrow. Two of them. Is your nose broken?"

He reached out a finger to touch my nose, but I jerked it away. "Maybe. It hurts. He smashed my face on the floor."

"What the hell is going on here?" Harry's car was in front of the house. He'd leapt out of his seat and left the door hanging open. Standing in the middle of the street, he looked lost.

Fierro leaned his head out his window. "Over here. Your sister is okay."

Harry rushed around to my side. My window sunk down with a hiss. "Portia? What happened? What's going on? There are cops in the house."

"Yeah, um…" I had no idea what to say. I'm such a crappy liar. "Remember I said that there was bad stuff going on at that office I worked at? Well, it was really bad. Homicidally bad," I added. "My boss tried to kill me just now."

"Wow. Ginger doesn't seem so bad anymore."

"It's complicated. It has to do with that girl who was murdered. He killed her, and he thought I was working with the cops and that I knew something."

Violet moved the car out of the street, then she and Harry fussed over me as I struggled to explain. Then Mother and Walter arrived, and things truly became chaotic.

I was forced to get out of the car and explain myself repeatedly. Mother insisted on making a pot of tea once the crime-scene folks allowed us back in the house. I was going to the hospital and she was taking me. We would be going to Our Lady and her future-son-in-law-the-doctor would look at me and that was final, but first we would all have a nice cup of tea since it wasn't an emergency. And then she was buying a mammoth-sized soup bone for Billy.

Fierro tugged my sleeve, and we stepped out onto the back porch. "Looks like you're in good hands now."

"Sorry about Mother. She gets bossy when she's wired up."

"She's a mother. That's her job. How about I go check on Billy for you?"

I threw my arms around his waist and hugged him tightly. It hurt like hell, but I didn't want to let go. He rested his cheek on my hair.

"Call me. He sounds okay, but I want to hear it from you."

He promised and all too soon, the tea was gone and I was in the car with my mother.

* * * *

Mother was still in her salsa costume: a skintight black leotard with vibrant swirls of colored ruffles that draped artfully about the waist. She looked pretty hot for a woman her age. Her hair was a mass of curls, but they were the fat, sexy ones produced by judicious use of hot rollers. I was reminded of how young she had been to become the mother of twins.

"How could you?" she asked. "I warned you not to get involved in this sort of thing. You see what happens when you get so involved? Help them move along, but *never* try to sort out their problems for them."

"You would rather I turn my back and let a killer like that walk around free?"

"Of course not."

"It's something I can do, Mother. I've made different choices from you."

"Have you really?" Her mouth was set in a thin, hard line. "I worry. Receiving your 'gift' seems to have unsettled you. Losing your job and your apartment. Getting a dog. On the bright side, there's your doctor."

"He isn't my doctor."

"Well, not yet. But he will be. I've seen the way he looks at you. This one is a keeper. I realize the last thing you want is advice from your mother, but I like Ethan."

I digested that for a moment. "When did you know Walter was the one?"

She didn't react and I wasn't sure if she'd heard me. "I don't know," she said finally. "He was handsome and charming and...nice. I was at a point in my life where that was enough. He wasn't bothered by my having kids. In fact, he doted on you two. Being with him was comfortable." She sighed. "It's a good thing people pair up when they're young and attractive. I love Walter, but I'm not sure I would pick him out of a crowd now. Lord knows, I've got a few miles on me, as well. But the most wonderful thing about Walter is that he thinks I'm wonderful. If that makes any sense."

I decided it did.

And that Mother probably thought I was thinking about Ethan.

* * * *

The emergency room was just like I remembered: cold linoleum, cracked vinyl chairs, overzealous fluorescent lighting, ghosts roaming the halls. "Look at them all," Mother whispered.

"Shh."

Careful not to acknowledge the hovering spirits, I approached the front desk to check in. It was an imposing U-shaped monstrosity in blue. The harried nurse handed me a clipboard before she even glanced up. When she did, her mouth fell open.

"Oh my God. Aren't you Ethan's girlfriend?" She didn't wait for an answer. Her fingers were already on the intercom button. "Dr. Feller to check-in. Dr. Feller to check-in." She stood. "Are you okay? Of course you aren't. Look at your face."

I hadn't seen it yet, but I was betting from everyone's reactions that I was quite attractive.

"Portia! Oh my God, what happened?" Ethan was justifiably freaked out. "Don't we have an empty spot?" he asked the nurse.

"I think three checked out. We were--"

Oblivious to the dirty looks and gasps from the folks who had probably been waiting for hours, Ethan steered me by my elbow to a cubby and pulled the green curtain around us. Mother winked at me as he snapped it shut.

I tried to explain what had happened without scaring him to death, but it's pretty hard to smooth over something like *my boss tried to kill me.*

He gently probed my side before pronouncing I did indeed need stitches. "You'll heal a lot faster and with less scarring. I don't like Dermabond for something like this, over the ribs. And you'll need an X-ray on your nose." He gently touched it.

"Ow!"

"I don't think it's broken. If it is, nothing seems displaced, which is good. I think it's just soft tissue trauma, but you look like a prize fighter." He shone a light in my eyes to check for concussion. "I can't believe you didn't tell me what was going on. I've worked with some unstable people before, but none of them have ever tried to kill me."

"It's a first for me too. I had no idea things would get so out of control."

"Two people in your office were murdered. How could you not tell me something like that?" He shook his head. "I thought we were honest with one another."

"I barely knew you. We were just starting out. Ow!" The numbing shot stung enough that I might have preferred to get the stitches without it. He left for a moment and returned with a little tray of suturing instruments.

"Maybe you should stay at my place for a little while. What if this guy gets out of jail? Are the police taking this seriously?"

I pictured the look on Fierro's face. "I don't think that will be a problem."

"I'm serious, Portia. You aren't safe."

"I don't need a guardian angel. And I have a mother, thank you."

He stopped and straightened up. "I'm sorry. I'm a little freaked out. This is out of my depth here." He kissed me softly. "I'm glad you're okay."

"It's nice to be worried about. I guess it would be bad if you weren't upset."

"You're going to be very sore. I'll give you a prescription for something a little stronger than ibuprofen if you promise not to borrow the hearse."

I raised two fingers. "Scout's honor. When do you have an evening off?"

He pursed his lips. "Monday?"

"You owe me a date on Monday. I'll give you the opportunity to spoil me."

"How could I say no to that?" He bent down and probed my side. "I'm glad you quit that place."

* * * *

Harry bounced around the kitchen, humming to himself. He rummaged in the back of the fridge, emerging triumphantly with two Cokes he had secreted behind a leftover pot roast. He slammed something in the microwave and punched the buttons.

"What are you doing?" I asked.

"Popcorn." Staccato from the microwave confirmed this. "It's movie night at the Mahaffey house. I've got the original four."

"You mean..."

"*Night of the Living Dead, Invasion of the Body Snatchers, Nosferatu* and *Dog Soldiers*." Harry considered these the finest horror movies ever made, each with its own theme: zombies, aliens, vampires and werewolves.

"I thought Violet didn't like horror movies."

"She doesn't. But Violet is at an art show in Topeka with her friends. It's just you and me tonight. Twin powers activate."

Mother hadn't wanted to go out with Walter, but he had insisted she stop being a helicopter and I had to agree that she was hovering. The sooner I could move out, the better. Living with Harry was becoming more and more appealing, but I was about to disappoint him.

The microwave dinged, and he pulled the bag out by its corner, dropping it and shaking his fingers as the steam burned him.

"That's a lot of popcorn for one person," I commented as he dumped the steaming bag of fluffy kernels in a large stainless steel bowl.

His hand paused with the large shaker of sea salt. "You have a date? I thought Dr. Wonderful was working."

"He is. It isn't a date. I'm going somewhere with Fierro."

He raised both eyebrows. "So you *do* have a date. It's about time you and your cop--"

"It isn't a date, Harry. We're going to church."

He set down the salt shaker. "Are you kidding?"

"No. No, I'm not." I crossed my arms and leaned back against the counter. "We're trying this nondenominational church, and they have a Saturday evening service."

"What's wrong with Mass on Sunday? It would thrill Mother beyond belief if you went with her."

"I haven't been in forever."

"Me, either. So?"

"So it feels funny. But with all I've had in my life lately, I want to give church another try. Fierro and I are trying it out together, like the buddy system."

"I still think it's a date."

"It's not a date. It's church. Church can't be a date."

"Anything can be a date."

"You're so wrong in the head."

Harry followed me out of the kitchen with his popcorn. Billy raised his head and started to get up from his pallet on the couch. I stopped to rub his soft ears. "You had better stay with Harry, Bub. This church is open-minded, but not quite that far." I studied my reflection in the mirror and hoped I had done a credible job hiding the bruising. Maybe it would be dim in there, and no one would notice.

Billy grunted as if he understood and settled back down.

"Just you and me, dog," Harry said.

Billy lowered his head, let out a long sigh and closed his eyes. He snored softly. He looked like Frankendog with his shaved side and stitches running along. We had matching wounds, although mine was a lot smaller.

"Snubbed by the dog," Harry said.

I went to answer the doorbell. Fierro looked good in the new jacket I had insisted he buy, much better than the bulky, heavy jackets that hid his shape, which was a nice one.

"The tailor did a good job." I stepped back to let him in. "It fits you."

He tugged at the sleeves. "It feels good. I like it."

"Next thing is a full suit. You need at least two good ones."

"Hey, Harry." Fierro looked over my shoulder. "How's the hero dog?"

"Sleeping like a baby. How's it hanging, Detective? I take it Portia decided you can't dress yourself." They shook hands and slapped shoulders.

"Aw, she's got pretty good taste."

Harry looked over at me. "That remains to be seen."

My ears burned. "We need to be going. I don't want to be late. I hate walking in after things have started." I eased into my jacket--lifting my arms still hurt with the stitches in my side--scooped up my purse and patted Billy's head one last time. He didn't even pause in his snoring.

"I'm ready if you are." Fierro held out his hand.

Even though I'd get grief from my brother later, I put my hand in his. "Me too."

* * * *

It was late afternoon and I was exhausted from working two funerals back to back. Fortunately the train wasn't crowded. I boarded without too much trouble and sat alone in a car. No demons. No Hephzibah.

I leaned my head back against the seat, closing my eyes. I'd promised to meet Fierro that evening to talk about Starla's situation. We still had her murder to resolve. At least that was the reason we both claimed. I really just wanted to see him.

Someone cleared his throat. "Have you seen my mother?" He twisted his hat.

I had despaired of seeing him again. "Mr. Lester?"

"Yes. Have you seen my mother?"

I smiled. "I know where she is. I can help you get there."

"I would appreciate that. I've been looking for...for quite some time." He frowned. "I've forgotten how long. I've forgotten a good many things."

"It's okay," I told him. "I can help. I'm a Mahaffey. It's what I do."

Meet the Author

Marguerite Butler believes that life is simply better with a little mystery and romance added to it. If it weren't for her pesky day job as a lawyer, she would spend her entire day spicing up life with her stories. Marguerite lives in Texas on a farm where she raises miniature donkeys, poultry, boys and a variety of other critters. When she isn't writing or tending to the critters and children, she is usually curled up somewhere with a book.